P9-CBA-357

The Tea House *on* Mulberry Street

The Tea House *on* Mulberry Street

Sharon Owens

Doubleday Large Print Home Library Edition

G. P. Putnam's Sons
New York

This Large Print Edition, prepared especially for Doubleday Large Print Home Library, contains the complete, unabridged text of the original Publisher's Edition.

G. P. PUTNAM'S SONS
Publishers Since 1838
Published by the Penguin Group
Penguin Group (USA) Inc., 375 Hudson Street, New York, New York 10014, USA • Penguin Group (Canada), 10 Alcorn Avenue, Toronto, Ontario, Canada M4V 3B2 (a division of Pearson Penguin Canada Inc.) • Penguin Books Ltd, 80 Strand, London WC2R 0RL, England • Penguin Ireland, 25 St Stephen's Green, Dublin 2, Ireland (a division of Penguin Books Ltd) • Penguin Group (Australia), 250 Camberwell Road, Camberwell, Victoria 3124, Australia (a division of Pearson Australia Group Pty Ltd) • Penguin Books India Pvt Ltd, 11 Community Centre, Panchsheel Park, New Delhi–110 017, India • Penguin Group (NZ), Cnr Airborne and Rosedale Roads, Albany, Auckland 1310, New Zealand (a division of Pearson New Zealand Ltd) • Penguin Books (South Africa) (Pty) Ltd, 24 Sturdee Avenue, Rosebank, Johannesburg 2196, South Africa • Penguin Books Ltd, Registered Offices:
80 Strand, London WC2R 0RL, England

This Large Print Book carries the Seal of Approval of N.A.V.H.

Published simultaneously in Canada

ISBN 0-7394-5098-0

Printed in the United States of America

For Dermot

ACKNOWLEDGMENTS

Many thanks go to my Irish publisher, Paula Campbell, for giving me this great opportunity; and to the team at Poolbeg, especially Sarah, Brona, Anne, Lynda, Kieran, Georgina, and Claire. A huge thank-you to my editor, Gaye Shortland, for praise and encouragement along the way. A special thank-you to my lovely agents, Ros Edwards and Helenka Fuglewicz, for all their kindness and generosity. Many thanks go to the team at G. P. Putnam's Sons, especially to Carole Baron, and to my editor, Aimee Taub. And finally, thank you to my lovely husband, Dermot, whose idea it was to write a novel in the first place. And to Alice, for all the tea and biscuits. I love you both. To everyone in New York: I wish you peace and happiness.

The Tea House *on* Mulberry Street

• 1 •

The Tea House

Daniel Stanley came hurrying down the stairs from the first-floor flat, and flicked on the lights in the tea house. The room was cold, and he shivered as he crossed the floor of the shop, and pulled open the blinds. The sky was still dark.

It would be another couple of hours, at least, before sunrise. He hurried around the cafe, switching on the small yellow table lamps, and the room was suddenly filled with a warm glow. For a brief moment, the old place looked almost cheerful. The dusty curtains, the faded linoleum, the cracked furniture and the flaking walls were bathed in a golden light.

Daniel peered at himself in a small mirror beside the door. His eyes were large, blue and intelligent-looking, with worry lines settling in around the edges. Well, that was understandable: running a small business was not easy. He was winter-pale, and he needed a haircut. But the fine bone structure he had inherited from his mother—the straight nose and high cheekbones—was still evident while other men's faces had softened and blurred as they filled out into middle age. Yes, even at forty-seven, he was still passable, in a neat and tidy sort of way.

He opened the front door and carried in the day's delivery of milk. He began to switch on the appliances in the kitchen: the toaster, the water heater, the old oven that still worked perfectly although it made a rattling noise when the temperature exceeded 200 degrees. He filled the kettle and switched it on. He looked at his watch. It was half past six. The ancient central heating system rumbled into life then, and Daniel breathed a sigh of relief that it was still working.

While he waited for the kettle to boil, he wandered back to the front window of the shop and surveyed the comings and goings on Mulberry Street.

The city was waking up.

Lorry drivers were already moving along the Lisburn Road with their deliveries. At half past seven, the early commuters would appear. Daniel watched a lorry driver waiting patiently for the green light, tapping his fingers on the dashboard. He seemed to be listening to a song on the radio, too distracted to toot his horn when the car at the front of the line moved off too slowly. Daniel rarely played music in the cafe. He liked the peace of the early morning, and the familiar sounds of the kitchen. The silence helped him to concentrate on his cooking. Today, he would bake a luscious cherry cheesecake and a moist coffee cake with toffee-colored cream piped around the edges.

Across the road, the willowy florist with red hair was arranging a selection of white flowers in the freshly polished bay window of her shop. She handled the stems gently, almost with love, trailing her slender fingers through lush green leaves that were still wet with dew. Her name was Rose. Daniel could not have guessed but she had chosen white flowers that day as a kind of memorial, to mark the end of her short marriage to John. She was single again, and all alone in the city that locals called The Big Smoke. She surveyed the orderly show of ghostly blooms and then, satisfied, filled the kettle to make a cup of tea. Since leaving her husband, she'd been waking up earlier than usual, but the shop had never looked better.

Daniel watched from his cafe her leisurely progress, thinking what an easy job it must be to sell flowers: no lightning hygiene inspections to worry about, and no risk of poisoning the customers either. Red roses for Valentine's Day, fir trees for Christmas, and nothing else to do all year except potter about, arranging steel buckets in the window. Yes, a real soft number. Although the smart, metal containers looked well, he admitted. Rose always put on a good display. They acknowledged each other with a nod, sometimes, when Rose came into the tea house for a sandwich at lunchtime.

Lunchtime! Daniel was awakened from

his daydream of an easy life as a florist, and remembered all the work that had to be done before the first customers of the day arrived. And when there was work to be done, he thought of Penny. It was time to make the first pot of tea of the day. He hurried back to the kitchen.

He flicked open the lid of a little steel teapot and added one tea bag and a tiny deluge of boiling water from the kettle. The water heater gave off a puff of steam at that moment and it startled him a little, as it always did.

"Are you there, Penny?" he called. "Tea's in the pot! Hurry up!"

"I'm up," said his wife, slowly descending the creaking stairs. "What's the rush? We've over an hour, yet, before opening."

She was wearing a long white dress and cardigan, pretty blue shoes, a gold-colored belt with decorative coins on it and big hoop earrings, not to mention full makeup and sparkling butterfly hair clips. That was Penny, always holding things up with her little bit of glamour.

"What do you think?" she said, giving a little twirl. "Do you think the butterflies suit me? They're new."

"Very nice," he said gently. "Not a very practical outfit for working in, of course, but nice, yes."

"We'll have to take down the Christmas decorations, tomorrow," she said. "I'll really miss them." She straightened up some tinsel on the tree.

"The food won't make itself," he reminded her, gravely. "Oven's on."

"We'll get it made in time. Don't we always?"

"I suppose so . . . What kind of muffins do you fancy for today? Blueberry? Chocolate? They're still popular with the office people. For the time being, at least." He was checking the containers on the counter.

"What about banana muffins, for a change? Where's that American flag? I'll stick it in the window and we'll have a coffee-and-muffin promotion."

She found the flag at the back of the storeroom and crossed the shop, yawning, to hang it in place. Daniel told her his baking plans for the day, and Penny wrote it all down in colored chalk on the blackboard and set it out on the footpath. Then she sat down at a small table and gazed out at the few people going past the window at that early hour. She waved at the florist across the road. Rose was dragging a large topiary tree across the floor.

"Rose is up and about, already," she said. "Have you noticed she's been doing that a lot recently? She's changing the window display, I see. It looks nice, don't you think?"

"Mmmm," said Daniel, neither agreeing nor disagreeing. Penny had a hankering for pretty things and he didn't like to encourage her.

She turned away from him. It was a cold Monday morning in January and her back was stiff already, just thinking about the day ahead. Penny Stanley had worked in the tea house since she was a child and could have cut sandwiches and brewed tea in her sleep. She knew the sagging cupboards and the leaking taps in the cafe better than she knew her own body. She had drifted along through thirty-five years of nothing in particular, like a leaf in a stream. Her life had been uneventful, to say the least, and most days she was just grateful it had not been filled with tragedy. There was her parents' car accident, of course. But apart from that, there was nothing at all to write home about. Somehow, she felt ashamed of her ordinary life. There was a resigned stare in her big brown eyes, and her hands were rough and reddened from twenty years of baking bread.

But today, in her humble heart, Penny Stanley felt the stirrings of a revolution. She wanted things to change, and she knew that she was the only one who could change them. It was no use making wishes and waiting for another day. She had done that all her life.

She could not explain it. It might have been a conversation she'd heard on the radio, about the approaching millennium. One woman was spending thousands of pounds on a beach party, which would take place in Australia. She was paying the travel costs for her entire circle of friends and family. Then, there was a man who was taking his wife and children to an isolated cottage, on a remote Scottish island, with enough food and water to see them through a nuclear disaster. Penny did not want to do anything so extreme, but she wanted to do *something.* The millennium was only twelve months away. The earth was a thousand years older, and so was Penny. A thousand years older than she was on her wedding day.

She found an upmarket interiors magazine on a chair and began to turn the pages. Daniel carried a cup of tea and a plain, buttered scone over to her on a tray, and frowned when he saw the magazine. He blamed glossy magazines for most of the unhappiness in the world. They filled people up with dreams of things they could never have.

"Thanks, love," said Penny, and she took a sip of the tea. "Now, here," she said, "is the way a home ought to look! It's a dream house! Look, Daniel, it's a hotel, down south. The Lawson Lodge, they call it."

He peered over her shoulder at the pictures. "That's some inherited mansion full of priceless antiques, Penny. You'll only upset yourself, wanting a house like that."

"There's nothing wrong with dreams. Dreams cost nothing," she said. She put down her cup and rested her pointed chin in her hands. She gazed down at the pictures with longing in her dark brown eyes.

Daniel went back to the kitchen.

"Dreams are what keep you going when real life lets you down," said Penny to herself. Her eyes scanned the photographs, taking it all in.

A stately home on the south coast of Ireland, built in the nineteenth century by an English lord. Nowadays, the lord's descendants had returned to London, where they lived in tiny overpriced flats, and the house was a hotel. Outside: gray stone facade surrounded by ornamental hedges, neatly clipped. Cracked urns on the doorstep, with fresh herbs spilling over the top. Two pedigree dogs with sleek black coats lay on the lawn, which was mown in neat stripes. Inside: rustic kitchen with dozens of copper saucepans hanging from racks above the massive blue stove. Cookery books stacked neatly on a painted Welsh dresser. Pots of homemade jam cooling on the windowsill. Dainty blue gingham curtains at the windows.

And best of all, the huge sitting room, painted a deep dark sinful red. A perfect backdrop for the comfortable white sofas, the ornate white table lamps, the heavy white brocade curtains, the plump white cushions with fringing round the edges. Original oil paintings hung on the red walls—of dreamy landscapes, in gilded frames. And on the occasional tables, there were pretty bowls of potpourri and hand-made chocolates, thick books on modern art, fresh flowers in glass vases. Luxury at every turn.

She sighed and touched the picture gently, as if she could somehow close her eyes and open them again and find herself in that beautiful room, standing by the arched window, gazing out over the topiary to the majestic ocean beyond. She wouldn't even sit on the armchairs, if she were there. She wouldn't lean back on those plump fringed cushions and squash them out of shape. She wouldn't touch anything. She would just look at the paintings and enjoy the perfume of the expensive flowers. Penny loved beautiful things. She felt soothed by beauty, in all its forms.

She brought her empty cup and saucer back to the counter. She laid the magazine reverently on its marked surface.

"Look, Daniel—there's the kind of thing I'd like to do in here. Paint the cafe blood-red. Just look at the effect when the table lamps are switched on. It's so warm and rich."

"Here we go." He sighed, as he polished

the glass stand for the cheesecake. "These walls aren't in good enough condition to be painted. You know that sweetheart."

"Can't we get some people in to fix them? Or just bite the bullet and have a complete renovation? Bigger windows and new furniture. New units in the kitchen? You know we can afford it."

"People like it here, pet," said Daniel firmly. "It's one of the last places in the city that is still family-run and unchanged from the old days. The students from Queen's love it. They say it's 'cool.' Retro-style or something."

"Retro, my foot! They don't have to work in it, and live with it, and see it every day. Anyway, they only come in here because it's cheaper than the nice places."

"We aren't going to waste good money on rip-off builders and fancy designers, Penny. There's no need for any of it. Extravagance is all it is, with so much poverty in the world."

"But it would make me so happy, Daniel! We could have a white sofa, there by the door, and a row of high chairs at the counter . . . I've so many ideas . . ."

"Please, Penny, don't start this again—

not now. We still have to finish the baking. Will you check if the rolls are done? And I'll get on with the cakes." He consulted his watch.

Penny looked at her husband and, for the first time ever, she thought she might stop loving him. She brushed past him, quite roughly, and went into the kitchen where she began to bang the cupboard doors in a small display of rebellion. She ignored the oven and made herself a very thick bacon sandwich with lots of red sauce, and a huge mug of sugary tea to go with it. Daniel might prefer a light breakfast, but Penny had a healthy appetite. She wasn't a robot, she told herself; she would start work when she was good and ready. She sat down on a rickety kitchen chair and enjoyed her breakfast. Daniel sighed, and checked on the bread rolls himself. They were golden-brown and glossy. He slid the tray out of the oven and left them to cool on a wire rack.

Penny and Daniel did not speak to each other again until the coffee cake was ready to go into the oven. And that was only to discuss whether they should open a bag of paprika-flavor crisps or spicy tortilla chips, to go with the sandwiches. Penny watched him expertly spooning cream onto the top of the cheesecake, smoothing the edges with a palette knife. Then, he added the cherry topping, and placed the whole thing on the pretty glass stand with painted mint leaves around the edges. He smiled with pleasure when it was finished. He was very proud of his baking skills. Penny was jealous of the attention her husband lavished on his desserts. She wished he would look at her with the same devotion in his eyes. She quickly made up a batch of banana muffins and bunged them in the oven with casual abandon.

At seven-thirty, Penny unlocked the front door and turned the cardboard sign to OPEN. A smiling postman emptied the letterbox outside the shop, waved to Penny and drove off smartly in his little red van with his cargo of good news, bad news and bills for the citizens of Belfast and the world beyond.

· 2 ·

The Creepy Crawleys

At eight o'clock precisely, two old women came in, peeling off their scarves and gloves and rattling two collection tins. Beatrice and Alice Crawley. Twin sisters and best friends. They laughed and smiled all the time and had numerous friends and interests. The secret of their happiness, they said, was that they were never foolish enough to get married. Daniel did not like it when they said things like that.

They were retired schoolteachers and they had the abrupt manner of all professional educators. They walked everywhere, briskly, linking arms, and had a habit of finishing each other's sentences. Daniel called them the Creepy Crawleys behind their backs.

Beatrice and Alice lived in the small, terraced house at the quiet end of Mulberry Street that had been their childhood home. When they were not engaged in charitable activities, they worked hard at keeping their little house perfect. Starched white lace hung at the windows and the front door was given a fresh coat of dark green paint every summer.

They came into the world together, war babies, born only ten minutes apart. "Identical twin girls," the midwife announced proudly. "Both healthy and strong, thank God."

Right from the start, the neighbors marveled at the girls' honey-colored skin and jet-black hair. "Where did such looks come from?" they wondered, as they chatted on their doorsteps. Mr. and Mrs. Crawley were both pale and fair-haired, with delicate bone structure and eyes the color of forget-menots. Yet, the two girls grew up to be tall and dark-haired, with chocolate-brown eyes. Their mother, Eliza, was a good, Christian woman, who believed in miracles. God had sent two beautiful daughters to her, she said, when she thought that she and her husband would never be able to have a child of their own. And she was not going to query their exotic appearance after God had been so good and generous. By the time the twins were fourteen, they already towered over their devoted parents but, by then, all the fuss about their unusual looks had died down considerably. They passed every exam they ever sat with flying colors and went on to teach in the same school. They were so close to each other, they never felt the need to take on a couple of husbands or move out of the family home when William and Eliza went to their eternal rest.

With no family to fuss over, they spent their days raising money for good causes, shaking their collecting tins on Royal Avenue. They enjoyed setting the world to rights over a cup of tea in Muldoon's Tea Rooms and going on various day-trips and country rambles on a church minibus.

Once a week they went to visit their parents' grave in the city cemetery, and lay fresh flowers there. Their beloved late father, William, was a decorated war hero, and they spoke of him often.

"To think our dear father fought Hitler for the likes of this," Alice would say sadly, as teenage mothers wheeled their fat babies past the window of the cafe. "In our day, girls like that would have been put in an institution. I think there was one round here, actually, until the liberals got it closed down."

"Yes, well. Those places had their faults. I'm not saying they were the perfect answer. But, at the very least, the girls ought to dress more respectably." Beatrice sniffed, observing a cigarette dangling from the glossy lips of one girl who couldn't have been a day older than fifteen. "You'd think they would make some effort to tidy themselves up."

"There are no standards anymore," said Alice. "It all went wrong when people stopped wearing hats and long skirts."

"I can't believe our dear father served his country for such people," Beatrice cried, when she read in the newspaper that a nine-year-old boy was expelled from school for burning down his classroom. "His parents, both unemployed of course, have applied for a grant to employ a private tutor, it says here. Ha! The two of them should be shot at dawn for rearing such a reprobate."

"Yes, indeed," agreed Alice. "Many's the man was shot for far less. And society was all the better for it."

On Sundays, they donned their good gloves and formal hats, and walked serenely along to church, nodding regally to anyone they knew. They sat in the front pew, singing loudly with strong, healthy, smoke-free lungs, and praying hard for the salvation of the world in general, and Belfast in particular. After lunch, they wrote letters of complaint, mostly to their local newsagent, deploring the filthy pornography he sold on the top shelf. And, of course, they had plenty to say about the young people of the city, who were sadly under-represented in the congregation each Sunday.

"Is it any wonder marriage is on the way out?" said Beatrice. "With the young women throwing themselves at this one and that one. And barely a stitch on the whole lot of them. You wouldn't believe some of the things they wear. They've no shame at all. It's a disgrace."

"Indeed," agreed Alice. "And a horrible chip shop on every corner as well, with young men eating chipped potatoes out of a paper bag, on the very street! It shouldn't be allowed! Why, the men have no reason to get wed nowadays: they have both flesh and food in plenty."

The Creepy Crawleys lived comfortably on two good pensions. They had no vices at all, apart from a weakness for new hats and a terrible huge sense of pride: pride that drove them to collect more money for charity than anybody else in the congregation; pride that keep them awake at night, planning their speeches for when they met Her Majesty, the queen; for surely they would meet the queen some day, and be presented with an award, at the very least. A shiny medal in a velvet box. After all their service to the community over the years, it was the very least they could expect.

Alice approached the counter.

"Care to make a donation?" said Alice to Daniel. "Upkeep of the war memorials."

Daniel's face darkened. Anything to do

with charity made him feel uneasy, reared as he was, in poverty. But Penny took a five-pound note from the register, and folded it cheerfully into the tin.

"There you are," she said. "That will start you off today, ladies." She looked at Daniel. It was a look of defiance.

"Good for you, Penny," said a delighted Beatrice. "Lest we forget, and all that."

"God bless our fallen heroes," agreed Alice, and they settled down at their usual table beside the radiator.

Daniel went into the kitchen to ice his coffee cake.

"Tea and toast, is it?" asked Penny, approaching their table with her little notebook.

Daniel frowned as he opened the fridge. He was impatient with the Crawleys now. Because of them he was beginning the day a fiver down. He could hear them deliberate about what to eat. Would it be a sin for them if they had a fried egg and bacon sandwich? How many calories did Penny think would be in a fried egg and bacon sandwich? They just had to make a drama out of every little thing.

Finally, they decided. "Tea and toast, of

course. And could we have some scrambled eggs with that? Oh, let's go mad and have a couple of sausages each, as well. We'd better eat a hearty breakfast this morning. We've a long day collecting ahead of us." They shook their tins in Penny's face then and smiled the easy smiles of the virtuous.

"Scrambled eggs and sausages, tea and toast for two," Penny called, through the hatch.

"Right," said Daniel, and he opened a packet of sausages. The day's business had begun.

A few minutes later Millie Mortimer came into the shop and stood at the counter. She didn't like Daniel, and she wasn't afraid to show it. She always made a point of smoking in the cafe kitchen, even though he had told her on several occasions that it wasn't hygienic.

"Well, Penny, what about ye?" she asked. "I was just out, getting some odds and ends, and here, I says, I'll call in and see me ole mate, Penny."

Daniel sighed. Millie was very common. Her clothes were too tight, her accent was stage-Belfast and the way she inhaled her cigarettes with her mouth open at one side was painful to behold. She was only thirty-six but her fussy perm made her look much older. He didn't know why Penny had bothered to keep up with her all these years.

"Come on in to the kitchen," said Penny. "We can have a wee chat there, in peace."

Millie went straight in, scanning the work counter for tasty snacks. She took off her coat and lit up a cigarette.

"The cut of them two old biddies in there," she said, nodding her head toward the Crawleys. "I thought you had the royalty in, the day!"

She put a chair by the back door and opened it a little, so that she could blow her smoke into the yard. A blast of ice-cold air came rushing in, chasing the warm air out of the kitchen, and Daniel had to bite his lip to stop himself from saying something. The two women had been friends since their school days. Millie was always the one to get the laughter going, but she had a terrible temper as well.

"Thinking of doing the place up, are you?" Millie said, reaching over and taking the interiors magazine from the table. "About time, too, I say." And she made a face at Daniel's back. She licked her thumb and flicked through the pages. "Any particular color in mind, have you?"

"Oh, I'm still thinking," said Penny.

"Nothing like the smell of fresh paint to cheer a body up. Oh, look at this! Lime-green and purple walls in the same room—no, thank you! Here, my Jack is very handy with a hammer and nails, if you're wanting any shelves puttin' up."

Daniel was stirring the eggs carefully. He snorted and muttered something at the idea of big Jack Mortimer hammering and sawing wood in his precious cafe. Then he handed the wooden spoon to Penny and went out to the counter as a group of hungry workmen came in.

"What did your man just say?" asked Millie. "'A waste of money,' no doubt. Oh, what did you ever see in him, Penny?" She kept her voice to a whisper, but she was angry.

Penny smiled as she remembered. "The first time I saw him I thought I would faint, my heart was thumping that much. There was a light shining in his eyes." She reached for some heated plates.

"Oh, Penny, you never change! Lights shining isn't everything! Men aren't just for looking at, you know—they're not ornaments. You could have done a lot better for yourself!"

"We'll never know now, will we?" said Penny, and she went out with the Crawleys' breakfast.

Daniel picked up a list from the counter and said he was going next door to the greengrocer's.

"I was just thinking about that fortune-teller in Donegal," said Penny to Millie as she came back into the kitchen. "That holiday we went on, with the girls from school—what a laugh that was! Six of us in that little chalet by the beach! Remember?" She switched on the kettle.

"How could I forget?" said Millie. "We nearly froze to death. We only brought light clothes with us. I had one coat and six bikinis in my suitcase. It should have been the other way round. And Sionna McAleer got a terrible crush on the boy who took the money for the dodgems. Him with the crew cut and the scar on his neck, remember?"

"Yes—and she claimed she could actually *feel* her heart breaking when he turned her down for a date. Whatever happened to her, I wonder?"

"She married a consultant doctor from North Down. Their house is a listed building in its own grounds."

"She got over her broken heart, then, so," said Penny, as she began to make a pot of tea. "Anyway—remember the fortune-teller? She told me I would meet a tall handsome stranger, in a dark place near water, and that he would have blue eyes, and that he would know my name before I told it to him. I thought that was so romantic—I was only seventeen, after all. And sure, I was no sooner home but I saw Daniel for the first time."

"Now, Penny, don't go over all that ole nonsense again! Your woman probably said things like that to everyone." Millie was the practical sort. "It was the seaside, after all. There was water and strangers all over the place!" She eyed Penny closely. "Would you listen to the fortune-teller if you were there now?"

Penny had settled herself at the table and was pouring tea. "No. Are you mad? I'm thirty-five, Millie. And I don't think meeting my husband in a nightclub near the docks was all that romantic. And he knew my name because it was written on my necklace. And loads of people have blue eyes." She hesitated. "Still . . . she must have seen something. I mean, we're still together, after all this time."

But she wondered about that incident, sometimes. Had she really accepted Daniel's sudden marriage proposal, all those years ago, because of the fortune-teller's fanciful words?

"God help you," said Millie, who believed she had. Penny could have had any man she wanted when she was younger. A beautiful girl, with a good business coming to her, from her father's side of the family. And she had to go and marry the first bucko that came along! "He's obsessed with the business. The way he carries on over those blasted cakes, it's not right. If I had your money, I'd sell up and move to some holiday resort. For good. Put my feet up for a change. Sure what are you killing yourselves for, when you could be living in style, on the continent? Haven't you a right few bob in the bank? I can't fathom it."

"A little apartment in Spain, do you think, Millie?" said Penny as she sipped her tea.

"Oh, aye," said Millie, tossing the butt of her cigarette out into the yard and lighting up another. "Here, me and Jack and the weans could nip over in the summer, and keep you company."

"Well, that sounds very cosy, Millie, and we could do it, I suppose, but I would never leave Muldoon's," said Penny at once. "I was brought up here. Silly, I know. But I can't leave the shop, not ever. I belong here."

Millie rolled her eyes. Those were familiar words. Belfast was divided into the kind of people who couldn't wait to get out of the place, and the people who would never leave the city, no matter what happened. And besides, from the moment she met that stuck-up husband of hers, Penny was like putty in his hands. She'd do nothing unless he gave her permission. Millie decided to change the subject.

"My Jack is putting on a bit of weight, I've noticed. Too many pints and fish suppers. That's the problem in a nutshell, but I couldn't say that to his face. He's very sensitive about his appearance. Any suggestions as to how I could get him to go on a diet without actually mentioning the word 'diet'?"

"Easy," said Penny, after a minute's

thought. "He has to see himself the way you see him. I'll tell you what you should do. Paint your bathroom brilliant white, and hang the biggest mirror in it that you can find. Full-length. Four foot wide, at the very least. And fit a 150-watt bulb into the ceiling light. Then, every time he takes a shower, he won't be able to avoid the sight of himself, in all his natural glory. And when he tells you he's going on a diet, you must act all surprised, and tell him there's no need."

"Penny, you're a genius! I'll do that tomorrow, first thing. You know, they have huge mirrors in them fancy furniture shops on the Dublin Road."

"Lovely, a wee cup of tea," said Daniel, coming through from the shop. "You won't believe this but they've put up the price of lettuce. Fifty-five pence! Not iceberg, mind. Hothouse. There's only about ten leaves on this one here. Daylight robbery. Can you believe it? If I had any room in the yard, I'd grow my own."

Millie didn't doubt it. He set his shopping down on the worktop. The two women looked up at him.

"Did we have any customers while I was

out?" he said, looking at Millie as she reached for a refill.

Millie ignored him and helped herself to a turkey-and-stuffing roll. Penny knew that when Millie had gone, Daniel would ask if she had paid. She hadn't, of course. She never did.

"Nobody's been in," said Penny, setting out another cup for Daniel.

Daniel took his tea through to the shop and drank it sitting at the counter. He began to arrange the freshly baked muffins in a wicker basket. They did look very tempting, nestling there on a fresh, yellow napkin—even though Penny had been too generous with the muffin mix and some had flowed over the sides.

"Few splashes there, I see, on the paper cases," he said, as if to himself.

The two women exchanged knowing glances. Millie tapped the side of her head with the two fingers that held her cigarette. She was convinced that Daniel Stanley was beyond help. A tiny shower of ash drifted down to her shoulder. Men ought to be interested in boxing and football and politics and car engines. All this palaver with pastries was just ridiculous. Penny smiled with grim determination. She was fed up with Daniel herself, but she wouldn't admit that to her best friend.

Millie took a final puff and tossed her cigarette out into the yard.

"I'll head on," she said, reaching for her coat. "I'm going to the hairdresser's. My highlights need doing again. My better half is taking me out for a meal tonight, and I'm a holy show." She pulled on her coat. "Cheerio!" And she was gone.

"Bye!" Penny sighed. Millie's husband might be putting on a bit of weight, but he was very passionate when the lights went out. He might be tattooed and smell of engine oil but he was lacking nothing in the lovemaking department. A real Romeo, that's what Millie said. Sometimes, when they came home from the pub after a good night on the batter, he got down on his knees and sang a love song to her at the top of his voice. Even at two o'clock in the morning. He would sing the song to the very end, increasing the volume substantially if the neighbors hammered on the walls with a shoe. He would kiss the soles of Millie's tiny feet, and work his way slowly up to her laughing lips. Yes, he was a good lover. And they had six noisy children to prove it.

Penny's own husband of seventeen years was more interested in cheesecake than he was in his wife's feet. In all the years they had been together, Daniel had not done . . . anything outrageous in the bedroom. No irate neighbours ever pounded on the walls of the Stanley residence. In the early days, there had been some passionate kissing and dancing close together in smoky night-clubs. But when they came home afterward and made love, it was a brisk and strangely empty experience. Penny wanted to talk to Millie about it but she couldn't. It was impossible to talk about such intimate things to Millie Mortimer or anyone else.

Daniel and Penny had never undressed in the same room. Somehow they had established a pattern of changing their clothes in the bathroom. Penny could not remember how this had happened. If a rugged welder like Jack Mortimer could kiss the stretch marks on Millie's stomach, and even her fluffy permed hair and her tobacco-flavored lips, then what was the matter with Daniel? Penny had a good figure, voluptuous curves and silky-smooth skin. She had pretty lingerie and sexy perfume and perfectly painted toenails. Yet most nights, when Daniel emerged from the bathroom in his striped pajamas, he climbed into bed and settled down with the latest cookery book. They might as well have slept in separate beds.

Penny immersed herself in romance paperbacks and when Daniel was occasionally persuaded to make love to her, she was disappointed with his modest performance. Where was the desperate tearing-off of clothes she read about in her novels? Why did he not hold her to him in the darkness, and declare that if she ever stopped loving him, his life would be without meaning? Why did desire not come to him at unusual times, in unusual places? Millie and Jack had once made love in the sand dunes at Portstewart Strand, within earshot of some Presbyterian day-trippers. Either the paperbacks and Millie Mortimer were telling lies, or there was something wrong with Penny's marriage . . .

What would Millie do if she knew that Daniel had refused to discuss even the possibility of having a child with Penny? He said they had neither the time nor the room for a baby. And that they were far too old for trips to Mothercare and prenatal classes, anyway. If Millie knew that, she would trail Penny up the street to the solicitor's office, and fill out the divorce petition herself. That's what she'd do.

No, it was far too late in the day to ask for help now. Penny's situation was the kind of thing that ended up in the gutter press: *Belfast Couple Make Sandwiches, But Not Babies!*

She would die of shame if anybody knew the kind of life they led above Muldoon's Tea Rooms. And so, she told Millie that they were just too busy to have children.

Penny poured herself another cup of tea and began to make plans.

The main thing was, she was exhausted. She began work in the shop at six-thirty each morning and did not finish until well after nine in the evening. It was far too long a time to spend at work. She rarely left the building, for heaven's sake! Daniel took the daily takings to the bank in the afternoon and managed the money side of things. But Penny knew they had more than enough to hire some staff, and do less work themselves. Penny didn't even have to be in the shop at all, strictly speaking. Daniel could employ a couple of waitresses to replace her. At least they should have a cleaner. Who ever heard of the owner of a business cleaning her own shop? It was embarrassing.

And all the time Daniel spent on the food was beginning to drive Penny crazy. He was—what did they call it? A workaholic. She would suggest to him that they buy some pastries ready-made from a bakery, the way her father used to do, when he was the boss. That way, they could just concentrate on presentation.

And they must consider closing the shop at a reasonable hour each night, never mind the rush for snacks when the soaps were over. But that was going to be a big battle. She would need a lot of courage to even suggest something like that.

The door of the shop opened and a group of untidy schoolchildren came in, spilling bags and hockey sticks on the floor, and forming an untidy queue for filled rolls and shortcake fingers to eat on the way to school. Penny looked at their young faces and wondered if she would ever have a son or a daughter of her own to worry and fuss over. They could all have done with having their uniforms pressed and their hair combed, but they did seem to have healthy appetites, at any rate. Soon, the display case was empty. When they had gone back to school, Penny wiped a tear of longing from her eye and polished all their fingerprints off the glass.

She sliced open more rolls and forked in flakes of canned tuna and generous dabs of homemade mayonnaise, and garnished them with chives. She wiped the tables and washed the dishes. She swept the floor and thought of the beautiful kitchen in the magazine. She dreamed of perfect topiary trees, and dishwashers filled with spotless china, as she filled the sugar bowls, and picked dead flies out of the net curtain on the back door. She dreamed of huge, white sofas and fat, tasselled cushions as she carried the rubbish out to the yard.

·3·

Brenda Brown from Belfast Town

It was nine o'clock in the morning, and the cafe was filling up with customers. Just as the Crawleys were gathering up their money tins and sheets of stickers to go collecting, a disheveled young woman wearing paint-spattered boots came into the shop and ordered a cup of tea. She flicked her black fringe out of her eyes as she handed over the exact amount in payment to Daniel. The Creepy Crawleys often wondered why the young madam bothered to keep the back of her hair so short, if she was going to leave the fringe four inches long and hanging in her face. But the object of their scorn never noticed them glaring at her as she drank her tea and ate her meals in Muldoon's.

"No toast," she said, in reply to Daniel's question.

"Can I tempt you to an Ulster fry? Free-range eggs, you know. It's all the rage. Lovely bit of soda bread, we have to-day . . ."

"No, thank you. Nothing to eat. I'm not hungry."

She was hungry but money was in short supply that morning. Her check from the unemployment office wasn't due until the following day.

Daniel shook his head. With customers like this, he thought, was it any wonder takings were so poor, some days? He shook his head again as she made her way to a seat, and he hoped that the smear of blue paint on the hip of her jeans was dry. He didn't want the chairs marked any more than they were already.

The young woman's name was Brenda

Brown. She was a regular customer in the shop, given that she lived right next door, in a one-bedroom flat. Brenda seemed to prefer her own company. She liked to listen to Radiohead, or Placebo, on her personal stereo. And she never seemed to have a boyfriend. She often sat near the counter, for hours on end, writing long letters on red paper with a gold-ink pen and putting them into red envelopes. The paper and the envelopes were always red, never any other color. Brenda talked to herself, too—that was another strange thing about her.

Brenda was an artist, and consequently penniless. Brenda's mother didn't understand art but she tried to help her destitute daughter. Mrs. Brown was a great fan of car-boot sales and she frequently offered to sell Brenda's collection of paintings for her at such events. The paintings were a bit weird: full of people with blue faces, their too-big eyes weeping and crying. And angry storms and old-fashioned, cracked windows and big blackbirds hovering above bare trees. But still, some people would buy anything. That was the magic of car-boot sales. They attracted the sort of people who might buy weird things. She might be able to shift a few pieces for Brenda.

But Brenda didn't want her great gift to the world to languish on trestle tables in windy carparks. Her paintings were not just something to hang on the wall, she had explained to her mother, countless times. They were not just pictures, something to match the carpet. They were paintings. They were Art. Fine Art. They must be sold in a proper art gallery, to discerning and sensitive people who lived in houses with plain white walls. Anything else would be an insult to her talent. If Brenda was going to sell out, she would start churning out watercolors of pretty Irish cottages and deserted sunny beaches, and be nice and agreeable to everyone, and be done with it.

"I'd think about it, if I were you," said her mother, when she came to visit Brenda in her tiny flat. Brenda's canvases were stacked against the walls in every corner and passageway. There was hardly room to walk about, never mind get busy with the vacuum cleaner. And at twenty-four years of age, she thought, wasn't it time Brenda was earning a decent living? Mrs. Brown herself made far more money, buying and selling bits of old junk, than Brenda ever got for her pictures. To Mrs. Brown's knowledge, Brenda hadn't sold even one painting.

"Money is money, at the end of the day, and this place could do with a good clear-out," said Mrs. Brown, as she tripped over a small canvas, titled *Waiting for My Love*.

Brenda sighed a lot when her mother came to visit, and wondered how her parents, two Elvis fans who had never been anywhere remotely cultural, could have produced a great and talented artist such as herself. And in Belfast, too, of all places. When everyone knew it was Donegal and Dublin that were the cool places to be born. Painfully, unbearably cool. All Celtic wildness and Bord Fáilte landscapes. James Joyce, and all the rest of them, writing poetry in smoky bars that reeked of porter. Would Bono or Enya have done so well, she wondered, if they'd grown up in a small village in County Tyrone that no one had ever heard of? Or if their names had been something terrible like Maisie Hegarty or Francis Magroarty?

Then again, there was Liam Neeson. He was from a town called Ballymena. That wasn't so far from Belfast—well, Brenda had never been there and wasn't exactly sure of where it was on the map. Yet Liam Neeson had managed to achieve worldwide fame as an actor, despite his ordinary name and humble beginnings. (Every rule had one exception.) Brenda made a mental note to go to Ballymena some day and see if there was a Liam Neeson exhibition in the town hall, or a plaque on the wall of his childhood home. Maybe, if she went to Ballymena, and walked the streets that he had walked, some of Liam's good fortune and charisma might rub off on her. She was a superstitious kind of person, full of strange notions.

And so, she persisted with the conviction that it was her boring name and birthplace that were holding her back. Any artist born in a cool place, with an elegant family name, had a head start on the likes of Brenda Brown. Two years it was, since her graduation; two years of painting great works on the subjects of love and loss, and peace and war, and life and death. Mostly death, actually. She spent weeks on every painting, fussing over every detail, mixing hundreds of different shades of blue on her artist's palette. And whole days thinking up poignant titles for them, when they were finished. And not a glimmer of interest from the galleries. Every single gallery in the north had rejected her. There was no justice in the world.

Brenda didn't notice the dabs of oil paint on her clothes anymore, and she whispered softly to herself when she was thinking of her next canvas.

It was a lonely business, being an artist. Other girls her age were only interested in marrying eligible men or having affairs with unsuitable men, going on foreign holidays, buying trendy cars and getting onto the property ladder. They weren't remotely bothered by the kinds of things that Brenda was obsessed with. She spent hours just sitting alone in her flat and thinking about the complexity of the world, and its people. For example: if Vincent van Gogh were alive today, she wondered, would he be doing well on antidepressants and making a fortune? Or, were his paintings only valuable now, because he'd shot himself in the chest, in a cornfield full of crows? Brenda didn't want fame that badly.

Or, if poets and painters were in charge of the world, instead of politicians, would they make a better job of things? Or a worse job? Or was the whole planet simply doomed to stagger between war and famine forever?

Was there a God? And if there was a God, why did He tolerate so much suffering? And why wasn't God a *woman,* anyway?

Strangely, none of Brenda's contemporaries shared her sadness about the weird and self-destructive nature of the human race. Sometimes, people she knew from her college days avoided her in the street. They usually disappeared into the nearest shop when they saw her coming.

Only last week, she saw Emily Shadwick diving into the opticians—Emily, who had perfect eyesight. Brenda knew this but she wasn't really hurt by it. After all, she didn't want to talk to Emily either—about that loser from her workplace, most likely. Emily was making a doormat of herself over him; she was living with him, sleeping with him, paying the rent, waiting on him hand and foot, and he still wouldn't get married. The lazy scoundrel! If Brenda had to listen to the dreary saga of their non-romance one more time, she'd end up chewing blankets in a psychiatric ward. (Poor Emily was delighted if her boyfriend occasionally gave her a bunch of flowers that cost £2.99.) That was the trouble with most girls: no imagination at all. They had wedding dresses on the brain. Brenda was better off on her own.

She had no one like-minded to talk to, so she talked to herself quite a lot. She was fond of a wee nip of gin and tonic and sometimes she looked hungover and haggard when she came into the tea house, counting out loose change in the palm of her hand. Daniel thought Brenda was unpredictable and he kept an eye on the cash register when she was around, but Penny liked her. Brenda seemed to be searching for beauty in this rain-soaked gray city; and Penny could identify with that. Sometimes, when Daniel was not looking, Penny gave Brenda a free sandwich or a second cup of tea, and she smiled at her when she was writing her letters. Penny was the nearest thing Brenda had to a friend.

Penny had often wondered who the recipient of the mysterious red letters might be, but she was too well-mannered to ask directly. Then one day, when she was cleaning the tables, she saw the address and Brenda told her everything. They had quite a long chat about it, over two lattes and a slice of pecan pie. Penny's treat. A wiser woman would have told Brenda to have a titter of wit, or to get real, as they said nowadays. Or, get a life. But Penny was a bit of a dreamer, herself.

Brenda was in love with Nicolas Cage, the actor. She had been writing love letters to him for years, but she hadn't posted any of them. They were simply bits of romantic nonsense: things like wanting to walk through the streets of Paris with him, in the wintertime, kissing him softly amid the swirling snowflakes (they would both wear long black overcoats). Or describing how she wanted to take a black-and-white photograph of him in Père Lachaise cemetery (he would be looking up at the sky, thinking something profound). And afterward they would drink strong coffee in some run-down little bar in the back-streets (hiding from the paparazzi) and hold hands on the table. Stuff like that. She kept the letters in her little flat, under the bed, in a shoebox. There were ninety-two letters in the box now, all stamped and ready to go.

The letters formed part of Brenda's Fine Art degree show in 1997, although by that stage there were only fifty-four of the red envelopes. Brenda had tied them in a bundle with fine wire, and placed them on a cushion made out of razor blades. She called the piece *The Fragile Heart*, and her tutor was very impressed. Brenda got a double first in her degree and lots of praise from the Dean, but unfortunately, no commissions.

Now, sitting in the tea house, her cup of tea within reach, Brenda took a deep breath, flexed her writing hand and began.

January 5, 1999
Dear Nicolas Cage,

I hope this letter finds you well.

I just want you to know that I saw you in Wild at Heart *in the Nicolas Cage Season at Queen's Film Theatre, and it was the most thrilling experience of my life. That snakeskin jacket really suited you, as did smoking two cigarettes at once.*

I've never been abroad but my parents used to own a caravan in Donegal. We used to spend entire summers in it, just looking out at the Atlantic Ocean, while eating cooked ham and tomatoes off a fold-down table. And all the time you were living over there on the other side, in America.

Anyway, I knew, when I saw you in Wild at Heart *that you were just born to become an international star. The way you killed that would-be assassin in the opening scene, with your bare hands. Oh, it was so STYLISH. Normally, I'm a pacifist, you understand? Coming from Belfast, as I do, I feel I should make that clear from the outset. I cannot bear violence of any kind, unless it's very tastefully done, in a film.*

Laura Dern was good, too—driving you across the state line in that old convertible, playing loud rock music on the car stereo; helping you to break parole. Dancing in the desert. Oh, what a film!

My family car was a rust-covered secondhand Vauxhall Cavalier. Mum and Dad and me and my two sisters used to go to Bundoran in it. Listening to rock and roll, all the way there and back again. Elvis, usually. It would have been fantastic in an open-top, with the sun blazing down on us as we sang along to "In the Ghetto" by the King. But the truth is, it was usually overcast. Or raining. We spent most of the time in the Bon Tuck restaurant, in Bundoran town, eating burgers the size of dinner plates. (Word has it, the burgers in Bundoran aren't as big as they used to be.)

I loved Moonstruck, *with you in a tuxedo, and only one hand—going to the opera with Cher. I loved you in the role of the broken-hearted baker. Suffering as you worked. A bit like me. (I'm a painter.) You can roll me in flour anytime you like. (Just my little joke.)*

Please send me a signed photograph. I'm sorry my name is so dull.

I'm writing to you from Muldoon's Tea Rooms on Mulberry Street. It's a peaceful place, and there's a postbox just outside the window, which is handy.

I look forward to your reply. I am a genuine fan.

Yours sincerely,
Brenda Brown

Brenda folded up the letter, and kissed it, and slipped it into a crisp red envelope (25p each from Bradbury Graphics). She wrote on the front, in gold ink: *To Nicolas Cage, Hollywood Actor, Hollywood Hills, Hollywood USA.* She stuck several first-class stamps on the envelope and held it softly against her cheek.

"Ah luv ya, Brenda Brown from Belfast Town," she whispered, in an American accent.

Penny came out of the kitchen just then, with some clean cups and saucers on a tray.

"Writing to him again, are you? If I were you, I'd post that letter right this minute. You're not going to live forever, you know. And neither is he. I saw him in *Hello* last week, and his hairline is receding, for heaven's sake. We'll all be pensioners before anything exciting happens around here."

Brenda was shocked. It was so unlike Penny to be outspoken. She was usually the most docile of creatures. There was something about her today, some bright look in her eyes that disturbed Brenda.

Were her words an omen? Brenda believed in omens.

Suddenly, she bolted from the shop to the postbox outside and thrust the letter into the slot. Then, immediately, she was sorry. She peered into the postbox, but it was too late. The letter was gone, down into the darkness at the bottom. It was now the property of the Post Office.

With knees that had turned to jelly, she tiptoed back inside, and sank into her chair. Her tea was cold. She looked hopefully toward the counter. Penny usually gave her a free refill, but her luck was out today. Penny was back at the sink and there was only Daniel at the counter, with a frown of concentration on his face as he carefully sliced up a big cake with fancy icing on it.

Brenda began to breathe very softly, to calm the panic that was making her heart flutter. And she waited for the postman to come, to make the ten o'clock collection.

·4·

Henry Blackstaff's Dilemma

Henry Blackstaff was the next customer in Muldoon's Tea Rooms that day. He came in just as Brenda was leaving. She did not return his smile. He settled in to his favorite spot by the window and sat down. Daniel was at his side at once. Henry said hello and ordered a full Ulster fry with extra soda bread and a pot of coffee. Daniel was pleased to take down the first decent order of the day. He brought Henry his cutlery and set it down on the table with a showy flourish. An old big-tip gesture from his hotel days at The Imperial.

Henry pulled a copy of the *Guardian* from his jacket pocket. He spread the newspaper on the table, and began to read.

Henry was forty-one and a failed novelist who spent his days sitting behind a large desk in his antique bookshop on Great Victoria Street. He had inherited the shop, his lovely home and a substantial sum of money from his uncle, Bertie Blackstaff. Bertie had made his money building railways in England and when he died without a family of his own, Henry got the lot. He sat in his shop, writing his dreary novels, and selling the occasional book, and living a peaceful life. Then he met Aurora.

She came into his shop one day, hoping to find a first edition of *Jane Eyre,* or a signed copy of anything by Charles Dickens, and found Henry instead. It was love at first sight for both of them. Aurora Blackstaff was an institution in her school. All-Girls of course, and only the brightest students were admitted each September.

English and Drama were her subjects, had been for twenty years, and she was now Deputy Head Teacher. She had dedicated her life to the abolition of regional accents and the promotion of classic English Literature of the Nineteenth Century. In her spare time, Aurora formed a literary appreciation society and called it the Brontë Bunch. The members of the society met at Aurora's house twice a month, when they all squeezed into the sitting room for a cup of tea and a reading.

Aurora wore her long blond hair in a tight bun and swept along the school corridors wearing floral-print dresses. She was forty-five but looked older. Once, she thought she heard the voice of Emily Brontë calling to her when she visited Haworth Parsonage in Yorkshire, with a group of her students, but it might have been only the wind moaning over the moors.

They had no children. Aurora was too busy for that, and Henry's days were filled with dreams of a prestigious publishing deal that never came true. Aurora often commented that Henry was not as tall as he used to be, and Henry assumed that this was due to his disappointment in life in general.

Now Aurora was embarking on her most ambitious plan to date. She was going to have an enormous conservatory built on to the back of the house. She planned to hold the society meetings in it. The Brontë Bunch was growing in popularity. The *Irish News* wrote an article about the society for their culture section, and in the days that followed, a small mountain of letters dropped through Aurora's letterbox. There were twenty people in the society already, and another fifty new applications. Aurora sorted through them carefully. She did not want any social climbers or lonely hearts milling around her Victorian mansion on the Malone Road, or eating her iced cakes and cucumber sandwiches.

Henry Blackstaff did not like the man who came to the house to give them a quotation. He thought that Arnold Smith was oily and brash, and he had a habit of touching things that did not belong to him. Henry remembered that the man had picked up an antique vase and inspected the underside of it, before setting it down again in the wrong place. Henry wanted to ask Arnold Smith to leave the house at once and never come back, but unfortunately Walley Windows and Conservatories of Distinction was the only firm in Belfast that could build the huge conservatory that Aurora wanted. Henry remembered that day in photographic detail. That was the day his whole life changed.

"I don't like that man. He's a greasy little charlatan," said Henry, when Arnold Smith's blue Jaguar went silently down the tarmac driveway. "He'll say anything to get a sale. 'Are you an actress, Mrs. Blackstaff? Your face is so familiar . . . ' He must think we are idiots!"

"He is a colorful character, I'll give you that," said Aurora. "But one must expect a little drama from these trade types."

"When will we know how much they are going to charge for this white elephant? That's what I want to know. I don't see why you couldn't just rent a hall. Or meet in a pub and have a few drinks while you're at it. That's what other people do in these situations. In these clubs."

"Henry, dear, I cannot hold the meetings in some dim and draughty hall or in a smoke-filled public house, with drunken males swearing in the background. The atmosphere would be entirely wrong. It is not simply a book club. It is more than that. It is a society."

"Oh, pardon me! A society, no less."

"Yes, indeed. And a society calls for dignity, Henry dear. A conservatory will be the answer to all our problems. We will have plenty of room to spread out, and you won't have to run away and hide in that little tea house of yours."

"Well, you know I can't stand them all. Especially Mrs. Johnson, trying to look like Queen Victoria with her fingerless gloves and her silly black cloak."

"Stop making such a fuss, Henry. Honestly, you are quite obsessed with Mrs. Johnson and her darling cloak. That garment is a genuine piece of Victoriana, a family heirloom, if you must know. What a fantastic eccentric she is! We might all attend in costume some day. That is an excellent idea, though I say so myself. Now, be a dear, and brew a pot of tea. I want to read over these brochures before dinner."

After dinner, they had a blazing row. That was when Aurora told Henry that most of his beloved garden would have to be removed by the mechanical digger, to make way for the conservatory. He hadn't realized it was going to be so big.

"Mr. Smith assures me," said Aurora, "that his company has years of experience in the safe removal of mature trees. Now, won't that be nice for you? You won't have to worry about the gardening anymore. It's ruining your posture, if you must know."

"But, my greenhouse, Aurora! My little greenhouse! Surely it can stay? It's full of rare specimens—I've all kinds of grafting experiments going on in there—"

"Oh, Henry! You're too much! You can't honestly expect me to read aloud to the society with that decrepit eyesore spoiling the view. Ha, ha! The thought of it!"

"So that's it? It's not even up for discussion? You're just going to throw my prize plants away?"

"A few old bits of half-dead twigs? What do you think? I'm doing you a favor, my darling. And by the way, I thought you might like to grow a mustache; it would look so in-period when you're serving the refreshments."

There was nothing Henry could say to that little speech, without using the kind of language that would make Aurora faint.

* * *

Remembering that moment, Henry shook his head. He couldn't concentrate on his newspaper. Maybe he was a chauvinist, like Aurora said. Maybe it offended him to see his wife make important decisions involving large sums of money.

He looked up as Penny brought him his breakfast. She was carrying the hot plate carefully, with a clean tea towel. It made him feel guilty, to be waited on by this gentle woman. They'd become good friends in recent months. Penny knew all about the Brontë Bunch, and how much Henry resented it.

"Will there be anything else, Henry?" she asked.

He shook his head. "This looks absolutely delicious," he said, to show his appreciation. The cafe itself has seen better days, he thought, but the food is second-to-none. It was worth the long walk from the Malone Road. "It's Aurora," he said, as Penny turned to leave. "Another mad scheme. A very expensive scheme, this time. A conservatory, to be precise. Huge bloody thing.

The whole garden will have to be bulldozed. But she won't listen to me. Oh, no!"

"You're a sweet man. You dote on that woman. I'm very jealous, you know." Penny did not tell Henry what she'd read in a magazine: that buying a conservatory was a sign that a couple needed more space. That perhaps their home was becoming claustrophobic. Daniel maintained that magazine editors made half of the stuff up as they went along. Penny agreed with him, this time. After all, what could possibly be wrong with a lovely conservatory? Penny would love one herself.

Henry was pleased. Penny's comment made him feel like a romantic fool, a rich husband indulging his pretty wife. That was the line he would take. He would pretend he had changed his mind, and he would tell Aurora to go ahead, and buy the best model on the market. No matter what the cost. Then, when faced with actually writing the check, she would hesitate, and worry about spending her life savings. She would announce that the whole project was cancelled and Henry would be gracious and not say "I told you so." And she would adore him again.

He would make it up with Aurora, he decided, and they would laugh at her silly scheme to build a conservatory. Yes, he thought. By this time tomorrow, she would have abandoned the idea. It was an outrageous extravagance, to spend so much money on what was, after all, a hobby. Uncle Bertie's monkey-puzzle, and all the other trees, ripped out on a whim? Surely she wouldn't be able to go through with it?

Feeling much better, he shook salt and pepper onto his breakfast, and began to eat.

·5·

The Secret Life of Sadie Smith

Unknown to Henry Blackstaff, the long-suffering wife of that greasy conservatory salesman, Arnold Smith, had just come into the shop. Her name was Sadie. Head cook in the Smith household. Chief bottle-washer, solitary caretaker of Arnold's bored parents and all-round general martyr.

After making sure there was no one she knew in the place, she removed her headscarf and dark glasses, and made her way to the counter. Sadie Smith was on a diet, but Muldoon's Tea Rooms served the best homemade cheesecake in the city.

Today, they were serving cherry cheese-cake, Sadie's favorite. There it was, behind the glass. Huge, black cherries on the top, dripping glistening sauce down the sides of a pale, yellow base. Sadie willed Penny or Daniel to hurry up and serve her. They were dithering in the kitchen and didn't return to the counter for at least thirty seconds. Sadie was weak with desire by the time she caught their attention. She asked for two slices of cheesecake, fresh cream, two scoops of vanilla ice cream—and a cappuc-cino, chocolate powder on the top. She whispered her order to Daniel, like a spy re-vealing national secrets. As Penny heated up the milk at the coffee-machine, Sadie sat with her back toward the other tables and she waited, with her stomach in a knot of anticipation. When the food came she set upon it like a starving woman. Daniel gave her a wink, the old charmer. He knew what she was up to. Starving women on crash di-ets were very good for business.

Sadie tried not to think of her husband, Arnold. She was breaking her diet, breaking it spectacularly, and Arnold would be very disappointed with her. But Arnold would never find her here. He would not be seen dead in a place like this. Tucked away in a shadowy corner of this forlorn cafe on Mulberry Street, she could eat these sinful foods in secret and get away with it.

Sadie had been living on low-calorie soup and undressed salads for two weeks. She was permanently hungry and very irritable. And she had only managed to lose two miserable pounds. The sheer disappointment she felt, when she stepped on the scales, had driven her here today, in fact. Now, every cell in her body relaxed as the hot creamy coffee caressed her lips. As Arnold used to, she thought sadly. A long, long time ago. Before he became obsessed with conservatories and patio doors and burglarproof locks. Sadie's dainty lips opened and closed quickly. The cherry cheesecake melted on her tongue and filled her hollow self with culinary joy. She closed her eyes with pleasure when she swallowed the last spoonful, and then heaved a sigh of relief. Her sense of physical satisfaction was absolute.

Sadie had been on diets for years, and

every one of them had been a dismal failure. Her bedside locker was filled with books on nutrition. Her attempts at losing weight followed a familiar pattern. First she bought a diet book. She began the new eating plan on a Monday and followed it religiously for about six days. Then, while doing the shopping on Saturday afternoon she gave in to her cravings for bacon sandwiches with tomato sauce, and chocolate éclairs filled with fresh cream. She ate all evening and went to bed on Saturday night feeling disgusted with herself. She threw the scales in the bottom of the bathroom cabinet on Sunday morning and tried not to think about her figure for approximately two months. Then she bought another diet book.

She weighed 168 pounds when she was twenty-one. And she weighed 168 pounds now that she was forty-one. But she was a tiny woman and Arnold called her his Little Toby Jug. Or his Fat Little Turnip. She did not like to think of that. Or of all the years spent counting calories and stirring fresh fruit into plain yogurt. She walked everywhere, rushing around the stores with her shopping bag, but it didn't help at all. Her legs were rounded and white, the bones well-cushioned with soft flesh. She fretted over what to wear on special occasions. She was always looking for something that would hide her short neck, her large ankles, her square back, her wide hips and her dimpled knees.

She looked at her watch. Maurice and Daisy had been on their own for two hours. Arnold's parents lived with them in the bungalow, following a serious operation on Daisy's knee five years earlier. They would be fidgeting for their lunch. With great reluctance, Sadie gathered up her coat and bag and hurried to pay the bill. She dropped her receipt into a wastepaper basket on the way to the door. Arnold's sharp eyes missed nothing. She would buy some flowers on the way home, and say she had gone out to get them for Daisy, to cheer her up following a cold. Her trip to the tea house would be a secret.

Unfortunately for Sadie, Arnold had a guilty little secret of his own.

As she was leaving the shop, Sadie saw her husband's distinctive Jaguar come gliding up Mulberry Street and she shrank back inside the door. She could not bear to be caught coming out of a cafe. He would know instantly that she had eaten rich food. She peeked out from behind the blind. His spotless car approached at a leisurely pace, glittering in the weak, morning sunlight. He was smiling, and patting the knee of a very thin blond woman, and saying something intimate to her. Sadie could tell by the way he raised one eyebrow that he was saying something obscene. He took his eyes off the road then, something he never did when Sadie was in the car, and looked hungrily down the front of the woman's blouse. The woman threw back her head and laughed out loud, showing long, predatory teeth. She reached over to Arnold and straightened his tie and he caught her hand in his greedy fingers and held it to his mouth. As Sadie pressed her round face to the glass in astonishment, Arnold kissed the ring-encrusted hand of his companion as if he were a pantomime prince and she were his Sleeping Beauty. Then, they were turning into Camden Street. And then they were gone.

Sadie stumbled out of Muldoon's and stood in the street, looking after them with her mouth wide open, like a landed fish.

Her husband, Arnold, was a pompous

businessman. He sold over-decorated conservatories to the nouveau riche. He was utterly unremarkable-looking, and a tiny bit overweight himself, but he made up for these shortcomings with his overbearing personality. When Arnold was in the room, no one else could say a word. He had an opinion on everything, and he was always right. It didn't matter if the subject was world politics, or the general decline in the flavor of mass-produced bread, Arnold was always right.

But Sadie loved him. She loved the spirit of determination in Arnold. He never gave up. Unlike Sadie and her failed diets, when Arnold decided he was going to sell a conservatory, he kept on going until he had sold it. He had a knack for assessing people, and he would appeal to their vanity, their weaknesses and vulnerabilities. He convinced them that a conservatory was the answer to all their problems, and he got that all-important signature. He was arrogant, but he was effective.

Sadie forgave his arrogance, and he forgave her disappointing appearance. Their love life was dull and predictable and had produced two sons, now living in Australia. How would she tell them the awful news?

She waited, desolate, for the bus. When it pulled in at the stop, she accidentally spilled all the coins in her purse into the gutter. She couldn't even be bothered to pick them all up. She handed a shiny pound coin to the driver. He punched out a ticket. Sadie didn't say thank you, and neither did the driver. On the way home, she did not allow herself to think about Arnold and his secret love. She did not know what to think. Her brain had turned into a lump of cheese. High-calorie cheese, mature cheddar. She felt foolish and fat and a failure. She got off at her stop, in a daze.

As she trudged up the avenue, the heavens opened, and she was drenched, along with the bouquet of pink carnations she had managed to buy for Daisy. She'd left her umbrella on the tea house doorstep, she realized, as the raindrops stung her eyes and ears. She arrived home dripping wet and in despair.

· 6 ·

The Story of Daniel Stanley

The day passed in a blur of serving and cleaning and washing-up. At seven o'clock, the cafe became quiet, and Penny and Daniel sat down to their supper, in the kitchen. Needless to say, when Penny put her suggestions to Daniel, he was not impressed.

He did not think it was a good idea to employ a cleaner and a couple of waitresses and give Penny some time off. Why would she need time off? There were weeks when the takings were down. And that was the great thing about not having any staff: it kept the overheads to a minimum. He patiently went through the familiar arguments for her.

And then the bombshell: she wanted them to try for a baby before it was too late. He was deeply shocked that she was still harboring the idea at all. He thought she'd forgotten about all that, thought that they were now very cozy running their own business together.

He pointed out to her that it would be impossible to run the tea house and take care of a baby, that they could not afford it. And, by not having children, look at all the trouble they were saving themselves: the sleepless nights, the months of teething, the crawling stage when they might put dropped coins and bits of carpet fluff into their mouths and choke until they had to be thumped on the back . . .

"How do you know all this stuff about babies, if you don't want a child?" Penny wanted to know.

"I heard Millie telling you about it. Her children sound awful. If she turns her back on them for a minute, they've broken something, or hurt themselves."

"They're only small for a short while, Daniel. Then they start to grow up and develop their own personalities."

"That's even worse! You have to find a good school for them. And then they fight in the yard and rip their blazers. And they won't do their homework, and the teenagers are all out of control . . ."

"Oh, Daniel, you're talking total nonsense! You should hear yourself! You sound like the Crawleys. Our child would never be like that. We'd love our child and teach him, or her, how to be a good person."

"There are no guarantees in this life, Penny. How can you be sure you wouldn't change your mind afterward, and want to go back to when it was just you and me and our little shop?"

"Because I just know I'd love our baby, no matter what."

"That's a silly thing to say."

"Not as silly as claiming you'd rather serve tea and toast and cream buns to strangers, than bring a new baby into the world!"

"I thought you loved Muldoon's as much

as I do, Penny! It was your family's after all. You were born into it, and the catering business."

"Daniel, I do love it. And I know you work hard and you're a terrific chef. But I don't want to be here for fifteen hours a day. I'm not getting any younger, and I want a child." Tears sprang to her eyes.

"Don't I have a say in this?"

"Of course you do. But I'll be the one who's going to carry it, and give birth to it, and feed it. I haven't got much time left, Daniel . . ." And she began to sob.

"You're getting very emotional, Penny. Please calm down. All I'm saying is that you might get fed up some day. You might want to run away and get your freedom back."

"Well, why would I do that? Haven't I all the patience in the world?"

"Have you?"

"How do you think I've managed to live with you all these years?" she wept.

"Look, we'll have an early night. Would you like that?"

"Are you going to use birth control?"

He didn't answer. He didn't have to.

"Forget about it, Daniel. I know it's just another chore for you!"

And she flounced out of the cafe and went up the stairs to the flat, to run herself a hot bath. She would take a bottle of chilled wine into the bathroom with her, and a crystal glass to drink it from, and a new paperback as well. She would stay in there all evening and let Daniel serve the last customers and tidy up on his own, if he liked the catering business so bloody much.

"Honestly," she told the bathroom mirror, "I can't believe it! Now, he's trying to convince me I don't want a child, when a child is all I've ever really wanted. I didn't even tell him I think it's time we spent our savings on a proper home with a garden. I'm beginning to think Millie is right about that man! He's not dealing with a full deck."

She arranged her glass of wine and a thick novel on a chair beside the bath, and stepped gently into the hot water, with ten inches of bubbles on the top of it. But she did not read that evening. She just stared at the ceiling, and sipped her wine and made her plans until the water went cold.

Daniel sulked in the kitchen for a long time. He knew he'd said the wrong thing to

Penny. As he had so many times before. When he had locked up the tea house for the night, he sat at one of the tables and contemplated his life, and the journey that had brought him to this crisis. For he sensed that it was a crisis. Penny had talked of starting a family for years, but he had always managed to convince her it was better to wait awhile: until they had more savings in the bank, until the political situation was more stable, until they could train up a new person to take over Penny's duties. But now he knew that the time for avoiding the issue had run out.

Yes, it was a strange situation, and it had been a strange sort of life, too.

The great reluctance of Daniel Stanley to part with his cash was legendary throughout the catering trade. In all the years he had worked as a chef in the Imperial Hotel in Belfast, he had never been known to buy a round of drinks, not even on special occasions.

Once, the waiters glued a five-pound note to the floor, and laughed until their sides were sore as they watched Daniel trying to get it off. Their laughter faded, however, as he steamed it off with a kettle, dried it on the radiator and put it carefully in his pocket. They knew then he was mad. But the staff of the hotel, all born and reared in the city, were familiar with madness of one sort or another, and after a while they accepted Daniel and his thrifty ways.

Once a year, the staff hired a bus and went to the seaside. Usually, they made for Newcastle, with its spectacular view of the Mourne Mountains. They loved its gaudy amusement arcades, with the joyous sound of coins clattering loudly into pay-out slots. The jukebox played lively tunes that floated out to sea, over the heads of the happy crowds. The puppet fortune-teller in her little glass box always predicted good things.

John Anderson, the head waiter, was responsible for booking the coach and collecting the money for the fares, and keeping the appointed driver sober, so that he could drive them safely home again. Everyone looked forward to the trip, and they sang songs all the way there and back again. It was easily the best day of the year.

The party of twenty spent the day drinking pints of ale in the ancient bars that lined the promenade, and filling the fruit-machines with their wages. They ate fish and chips liberally doused with salt and vinegar; and every year wondered why a fish supper always tasted better with the smell of the sea in the nostrils. They consumed dozens of whipped ice creams and clouds of pink candy floss, and they bought glass trinkets and bars of sticky, seaside rock to take home to their families.

To end the day, the men held a race along the shore, and the last one to finish was borne down to the water's edge, and heaved into the glittering waves, fully dressed, with much cheering and shouting from the women.

Daniel Stanley had never been on holiday in his life. Every year, John Anderson asked Daniel if he would be reserving his seat on the bus, and every year Daniel said no, thank you, he had other plans. He never revealed what these other plans might be. He told them nothing about himself or his background. He was a man of few words. But Daniel's background was about to catch up with him. It was 1981, then. Daniel was twenty-nine, and a man of mystery to all who knew him.

He never told his colleagues, for example, that his beautiful mother, Teresa, had abandoned him in 1956. Daniel was four at the time, an only child, his father long gone to America. Teresa was two weeks married, and six months pregnant, when her new husband took the boat to the New World. Teresa cried for three months, and then Daniel was born. Afterward, she put away the wedding pictures and got on with things. There was plenty of work in the city in those days. All the young people were emigrating to warmer, gentler places. She got a job serving drinks in a city-center tavern and moved to a small house on Magnolia Street, where the rents were lower than average. Half of the street had been destroyed in the war, and it was still waiting to be rebuilt. Soon she had another lover. And then another. Most of her companions were charming, and they were all good-looking, but none of them wanted to settle down with a married woman and her little boy. One by one, they made their excuses not to see her anymore.

Daniel saw his mother for the last time on a sunny day in June 1956. He was out playing soldiers with his friends in the sun-baked rubble of the ruined houses. Daniel always had to be Hitler because he was the smallest boy on the street. The bigger lads chased him up and down the road, throwing chestnut hand grenades at his bony back.

Teresa called him inside and gave him a big slice of cake with jam and cream.

"Be a good boy," she told him. "Keep yourself clean and tidy, and work hard, and I'll be back for you in a little while."

Then she took him over to the house of the lady who looked after him when she was at work, and kissed him good-bye. But she did not go to work. Teresa left a note at home on the table, saying that she had to go away for a little while. She took nothing with her when she left, except her red lipstick and a pair of new shoes.

A neighbor called in at lunchtime to borrow some tea leaves, and discovered the note on the kitchen table. Within minutes, a small crowd had gathered outside the front door, where they stood whispering and waiting for information. The children were told to be quiet and stop playing their war games. The authorities were alerted. Mrs. Stanley was known to have several gentlemen friends but none of them came forward in response to appeals for information.

A priest was called to the house—the Parish Priest himself, Father Ignatius Mulcahy. He said he would pray that Teresa would regret her decision and return to her young son. He would put a notice in the parish magazine, he said. He patted Daniel on the head, and sighed, and gave him a shilling. There was nothing else he could do. These lone mothers, he thought, sadly. They all went a bit funny in the end, without a firm husband to guide them. He must preach more sermons on the importance of marriage.

A young policeman with eager, green eyes searched the house from top to bottom for clues, and found a final demand for rent on the mantelpiece, and eleven other unpaid bills in a cake tin on the dresser. It was assumed that Teresa Stanley was overwhelmed by debt, and the balance of her mind disturbed. A crime was not suspected. The little house was re-let to a couple from Portadown, who were not superstitious about moving into a house of sadness. The street was subdued for several months, but eventually Teresa Stanley was forgotten.

But Daniel did not forget. He kept the silver shilling given to him by Father Mulcahy, and he knew that his beautiful mother would be back when she was finished with her adventure. She was not like other mothers. She wore red lipstick, she was beautiful, she sang songs from the movies out loud in the house, and she did not bother with baking bread and housework.

Great efforts were made by several charities in New York to trace the father of the unfortunate boy who sat quietly in his Aunt Kathleen's parlor, on the Carlisle Circus in the north of the city. Months went by. But the father of the young child proved impossible to find in such a huge city, and eventually custody was awarded to Kathleen. Although Kathleen and Teresa were sisters, they were as different as two sisters could be. While Teresa was beautiful, wild and romantic, a daydreamer and a flirt, Kathleen was plain and practical. A no-nonsense sort of woman. A hard ticket. That's what they called her.

"Look after the pennies," she used to say to young Daniel, at least ten times a day.

"And the pounds will look after themselves," he used to answer quietly, just as she had taught him. It was the only thing they said to each other. The only closeness they shared.

Kathleen wasted nothing, not even the string from parcels, or the smallest piece of soap. She was single, and worked in a cigarette factory. She was not used to children, and did not speak to Daniel very often, except to say, when he asked for a bicycle or a bag of toffees, that it was a hard station to be lumbered with Teresa's child. Kathleen did not waste her hard-earned money on fresh flowers for the parlor and tortoiseshell combs for her thick, brown hair. She did not hanker after shop-bought cakes and slices of cooked ham. She did not buy toys for her miserable nephew, either. Such extravagance, she used to say, was the finish of poor Teresa.

Daniel became thin and withdrawn, and he grew up with the dusty smell of the charity shops on his clothes and the shame of poverty in his heart. He thought of his mother often, and prayed that someday she would come waltzing up the street to take him home, and buy him treats, and spoil him. But his prayers remained unanswered.

When he was a teenager, his aunt got him

a place in the technical school, to study for a career in the catering trade. He slaved for many long hours in various eateries throughout the city, having learned the lesson early on that the only sure way to success was through hard work, and plenty of it. By the time he was twenty-four, he was a chef in one of the best hotels in the city, and well-respected by everyone who knew him. When his aunt died suddenly, leaving her home and a small fortune to the Catholic church, Daniel had already closed his heart to the world. He buried his aunt without the distraction of flowers or a headstone. It was what she would have wanted.

He moved into rented rooms and busied himself with his career. His dedication to the job earned him promotion and a modest pay increase. However, no matter how many extra shifts he worked, and no matter how hard he saved, he never seemed to have enough money in the bank. He began to economize. He gave up his tiny flat on Eglantine Avenue, and rented an unheated room in the student quarter. The Holy Lands, as the area was known, was not quite as pretty as Eglantine Avenue. The students who lived there didn't bother themselves with keeping curtains neat or gardens trimmed. He missed the two-story houses and the chestnut trees and the bay windows of Eglantine, but he reminded himself that such things were not as important as financial security. He walked everywhere, refusing to take the bus, even on freezing winter mornings. On his rare days off, he read library books, and went strolling around the Botanic Gardens, sometimes sitting in the Palmhouse to keep warm. He gave up cigarettes, newspapers, fish suppers, and anything at all that was not essential. He hurried to the bank each Friday to deposit his wages, and he hid his account book under a loose floorboard in his room. He did not bother with women. Women were unpredictable creatures with expensive tastes, and were known to disappear suddenly on sunny days.

One day, when he was hunting through the storeroom for some peppercorns, he came across a crate of supplies for the hotel beauty parlor. There, packed carefully in the wooden container, were sweet-smelling potions and lotions of luxury quality. Almost without thinking, he reached into the crate and took out a bar of soap and a bottle of shampoo.

He smuggled them out of the building that night, with his heart pounding as he said good night to the doorman. They were only little things for his own personal use, he told himself. A little perk of the job, as it were. To make up for the low wages and long hours that were the scourge of all hotel workers. It gave him a good feeling, a rare feeling of power in his otherwise humdrum existence.

As the weeks went by, Daniel kept his eyes open for more opportunities to help himself to hotel property. Cupboards left unlocked, deliveries not yet counted. He took bundles of paper towels and a tin of shoe polish from the caretaker's cupboard. He took handfuls of tea bags, packets of chocolate biscuits and individually wrapped portions of cheddar cheese from the staffroom tea-bar. When the barman's back was turned, he took wings of cooked chicken and bottles of orange lemonade, hidden under a tea towel. From the bedrooms, he took a luxury bath towel, some fitted sheets and a kettle.

He was caught up in the excitement of it

all. It was so easy to do and the hotel was so busy that no one noticed him slipping along the corridors. Once, he walked through the crowded lobby with a cut-glass rose-bowl balanced on his head, underneath his crisp new chef's hat. Even when he stole a travel clock belonging to Mrs. Constance Delargy, one of the guests, and the police were called in, his pockets were not searched. He was above suspicion of any kind.

He began to gain confidence in his thieving ability, and rarely left work without some little item on his person. Within six months, his room was piled high with supplies, and then he hit on the idea of selling them on to the public. He travelled to outdoor markets all over the north, selling bits and pieces out of a suitcase. He was sure that no one would recognize him, as long as he stayed out of Belfast. The money came rolling in. At last, his bank balance began to look healthy.

Daniel's crime spree seemed perfect in every way. An everlasting supply of hotel stock and wealthy guests to prey upon; and his market customers were all too eager to pick up some good bargains, even if they were of dubious origin. But it could not last forever. As Kathleen once said: all good things come to an end. It was on the occasion of his thirtieth birthday when he lost all self-control and lifted a mediocre watercolor of Portstewart Strand straight off the wall of the conference room. He took it home wrapped in his cashmere coat (bought secondhand from Oxfam).

The owner of the hotel, a Mr. Ivor Tweedy, noticed the disappearance of the painting at once, and instructed the staff to look out for light-fingered guests or possibly even one of their own. A security guard was hired to stand in the lobby, and all the remaining paintings were fixed to the walls. Mr. Tweedy laughed with his guests and smiled broadly at everyone he met, but he was a man who despised theft of any kind, on any scale, and he was watching.

Daniel's career in the hotel-catering business came to an abrupt end two months later, when he was finally seen selling canned fruit, linen tablecloths and assorted crockery at a market in the neighboring seaside town of Bangor. It was a dull Monday morning in September and the sharp-eyed witness was John Anderson, the head waiter, himself.

John Anderson did a double-take when he saw Daniel handing over two tins of pineapple slices to a woman in a green coat. The woman held out some coins and Daniel checked the amount and then dropped the coins into his pocket. At first John thought his eyes were deceiving him, but there could be no mistake. Daniel Stanley, it certainly was, with his jet-black hair combed straight back off his tanned forehead. Watching from across the crowded harbor, John realized his old friend and colleague was a thief.

The head waiter ordered a double whiskey in The Anchor Bar while he pondered the situation. It was very hard to betray a fellow worker. Very hard, indeed. Maybe the poor fellow was in some sort of financial trouble, and the wages at the hotel were criminally low. He might be in debt to a bookmaker, a pawnbroker or even a loan-shark. On the other hand, if the hotel was losing money, all their jobs were at risk. John Anderson smoked a couple of cigarettes, and ate a shepherd's pie. Then, with a heavy heart, he telephoned the owner of the hotel from the pay phone on the bar counter.

Mr. Tweedy's face flushed crimson with rage when he took the phone call, a roast beef and mustard sandwich suspended halfway to his open mouth. He ordered Daniel's locker to be forced open by the hotel handyman, and it was found to contain forty tins of Canadian salmon, twenty teaspoons, one hundred bars of lavender-scented soap and a silver-plated gravy boat. An investigation was launched, and the accounts were examined. It was concluded that Daniel Stanley had been stealing from the hotel for more than a year. The information buzzed through the building with feverish excitement. The female staff were nearly hysterical when they heard that Daniel Stanley was nothing more than a common criminal. They rushed home after work to tell their families all about it. Mrs. Doherty, from the laundry room, said that she always thought there was something fishy about the head chef. Nobody's that perfect, she said wisely.

Mr. Tweedy had to sit at the bar and drink four brandy and ports to steady his nerves. His right eyelid twitched violently when he thought of the lovely painting of Portstewart Strand and Constance Delargy's little clock, and God only knew how many tins of the best Canadian salmon—all whisked away from under his large, purple nose by a man he would have trusted with his life.

When Daniel reported for work that evening, they were waiting for him in the staff room. Mr. Ivor Tweedy expressed his grave disappointment in his best chef, and dismissed him with immediate effect, and without references. It was all he could do not to punch Daniel Stanley square in the face, he said, but he was a religious man who did not believe in violence. He informed Daniel that he would not involve the police, in order to avoid a scandal, the Delargys being old friends of his. However, he would personally see to it that no other hotel in the country would give Daniel an interview. He knew all the hoteliers in Ulster, he shouted, and he would make sure that Daniel was not given alternative employment, not even in a back-street chip shop!

The humiliated Daniel was swiftly escorted from the building by two sniggering doormen, one of whom whipped off his white chef's hat, and closed the door in his face. He stood forlorn in the cement yard, beside the bins and the empty beer kegs. It began to drizzle softly. For the second time in his life, Daniel Stanley was alone in the world.

For days afterward, he sat brooding in his rented room on Palestine Street. Without references, he could not get another job. He had considerable savings, but nowhere near enough to set up in business on his own. Thank goodness he had had the presence of mind to tell Mr. Tweedy that he had gambled all his ill-gotten gains on the horses! At least he got away without returning the money. He studied his big blue eyes in the peeling mirror, and thought again of his lovely mother, Teresa—a beautiful woman who dreamed that her face would surely bring her good fortune.

Well, life had not been kind to Teresa. If it had, she would surely have come back for him. But there was more money about the city these days. Maybe there was a wealthy widow-woman or divorcée out there, who would be willing to share her earthly possessions with a charming companion?

And so, Daniel Stanley got himself done up in a new suit, an investment from Dodds

& Sons of Chichester Street, and made his way to a fancy nightclub in the city center, not far from the river. They were advertising a New Romantic night, whatever that was. Daniel thought it might attract revellers from the more select neighborhoods of Malone and Cultra. His hand trembled as he handed over the five pounds entrance fee to a teenage doorman with two earrings in his left ear. He made his way to the bar and ordered a soft drink with ice and a slice of lemon. He leaned one elbow on the counter, struck a pose that he thought suggested worldly sophistication, and he waited. A spider on his web. Waiting for a juicy bluebottle.

Penny Muldoon was that bluebottle. She was waiting near the bar for her best friend, Millie, to arrive. She fell for Daniel the moment she laid eyes on him. She was wearing a new pair of shoes that crushed her toes together, but when she spied the mysterious stranger in the brilliant white shirt, the pain in her feet melted away. She felt as if her two legs were filled with fizzy lemonade and her heart began to batter like a whole regiment of drums. She thought the man at the bar had a look of Bryan Ferry about him, gazing into the middle distance with his ice-blue eyes. And he doesn't even drink pints, she thought, as he sipped his tall soft drink in a genteel way. A refined-looking, sober man. A rare enough sight in Belfast. And no sign of a girlfriend, either. Or a wedding ring. Bingo!

Penny walked straight up to Daniel. He noticed a golden necklace glinting against her white throat. It read: PENNY.

"Excuse me," she said. "Are you waiting for anyone?"

Daniel looked at her necklace, which was catching the light.

"Penny," he said. "Is that your name?"

"Yes," she replied, forgetting the necklace, and thinking of the gypsy's words.

"That's a lovely name," he said.

"Thank you. What's yours?" She sat up on a high stool, beside him.

He was rigid with embarrassment, but he managed to stay calm. Some waiters from The Imperial Hotel had just come in and were standing near the bar, and he knew they were watching him. The woman was very young, about seventeen. He did not think she was rich enough or lonely enough to be of any use to him, but he put on his brightest smile, for the benefit of the watching waiters. He liked her name. It was a suitable name for the wife of a thrifty man like himself. The lights dimmed and the glitterball began to twirl. The music became louder. Daniel offered to buy the young lady a drink. It was either that, or he would have to ask her to dance. He had never danced in his life, and he was not about to start now, with his ex-colleagues looking on. Penny ruffled her hair and smiled and asked for champagne.

"Thank you, I just love champagne," she said. "Although I must warn you, the bubbles make me quite giddy. I haven't seen you around here before. Are you new in town?"

"No," he replied. "I was born and reared in the city. I just don't go out socializing much, that's all. I'm not much of a dancer, I'm afraid."

They began to talk. By the time Millie came hurrying into the nightclub half an hour later, Penny was already in love.

The waiters, watching keenly, were amazed to see Daniel Stanley in a nightclub, all dressed up in a fancy suit. Brand-new, by the look of it. Shiny shoes, fashionable haircut. A white shirt, open at the neck to reveal a golden chest, tanned by several months selling stolen goods in the open air. And talking casually to a pretty girl half his age. "It just goes to show you," they said. "You never know what is round the corner."

There used to be talk in the hotel that Daniel Stanley was not interested in women at all. That he might have leanings in the other direction. Why else would a man of acceptable appearance stay well away from the women, when other, plainer men spent all their waking hours in pursuit of the fairer sex?

"Isn't life just full of surprises?" they said. "On the rob, for ages, he was. And got away with it, too. Old man Tweedy was too proud to go to the Peelers. No prison sentence for Daniel Stanley. Oh, no! And here he is, large as life, out romancing a real dish. Barely out of school, by the look of her. Lucky old dog!"

Daniel and Penny went to sit at a tiny, marble table, and the conversation moved up a gear. Millie had to sit with some other girls she knew, and watch helplessly while Penny flirted and batted her eyelashes at the older man. Millie was dying to meet Daniel, and ask him a few searching questions. Belfast was a small city, in many ways, and it made sense to know what you were dealing with from the start. It wouldn't take long to find out everything there was to know about this new man. Where he went to school; where he worked; if he had any money, jealous ex-wives, or dependent children. Or a criminal background, maybe? Some men forgot to mention certain details to new lovers. But Penny did not wave her friend over to the table once that night. She had met the man of her teenage fantasies and she was not going to let him get away. She would not be able to seduce him with Millie looking on. Penny sat up straight and squared her shoulders, in order to make the most of a small bust, and she twirled her hair round her fingers and made plenty of eye contact.

Daniel leaned over to hear what Penny was saying, and nodded a lot, and went to the bar for more drinks at regular intervals. Millie and the waiters watched, fascinated by the age-old courtship ritual taking place before them.

Penny did most of the talking while Daniel kept his eye on the door, looking out for a better proposition. Penny was telling him she had once met a film star in a chip shop in Blackpool. The man was so drunk, she said, that he could not get the money out of his pocket to pay for his supper, so the owner of the chippy let him have the meal for nothing. Daniel was not interested but he smiled. He was thinking that perhaps he ought to join a golf club, or enroll in a night class at Queen's University. Where did the rich go to pass the time these days, he wondered.

Penny told him she did not usually approach strange men, but that she felt there was something special about him. Something dignified and old-fashioned. He was not interested, but he smiled. She told him that she was an only child, the daughter of elderly parents. And that she helped them to run the family business, a tea house on Mulberry Street. Muldoon's Tea Rooms, it was called. Now he was interested. He knew the place. It was only a couple of streets away from his own humble bed-sit. A small, little place, it was. But well-placed in the middle of the student quarter; completely surrounded by young people away from home for the first time. Middle-class, most of them; they probably couldn't even butter their own bread. Likely, the cafe was a proper gold mine. Daniel smiled his brightest smile and Penny's heart turned over.

The DJ played a record that Penny loved. "Spend How Ballay," he thought she said, the name of the band. But it was Spandau Ballet, with a Belfast accent, he later learned. Some people had made their way onto the dance floor and were beginning to make strange jerking movements, their arms raised in the air, as if playing invisible drums. Daniel thought one of the men on the dance floor was wearing eyeliner, but he couldn't be sure. And he counted twelve buckles on each of his black suede boots. What a carry-on, thought Daniel, in the middle of dear old Belfast! Well, it hadn't harmed the man's chances with the women: he was dancing with a real stunner in a velvet dress. Daniel watched them for a few seconds. The girl wore lots of silver bracelets on her bare white arms. They reflected the flashing lights on the ceiling. The dance did not look too difficult, Daniel thought, as he studied the bohemian couple.

His young companion was tapping her

feet and nodding her head in time to the music. He asked her to dance. They stood up. Penny was tall and so was he. They looked well together as he led her out onto the floor. They stayed there for half an hour, and when the slow set began, Daniel slipped his arms round Penny's back and her arms went round his neck in a gentle movement that was both tender and erotically charged. They were pressed close together like lovers, swaying together like professional dancers. Daniel whispered something into Penny's ear and she laid her cheek against his shoulder and closed her eyes. The waiters were dumb with jealousy, and Millie knew she would have to find a new friend to trail round the pubs and clubs of The Big Smoke.

They married quietly. It was New Year's Eve, 1982. Daniel was approaching thirty-one and Penny was just eighteen. There were only twenty guests at the wedding, all from Penny's family circle. Daniel's Aunt Kathleen was dead and gone, hopefully to better things. He had no other relatives. He kept his mother's disappearance and his recent dismissal a secret. He told Penny that his late mother was called Kathleen, but that he did not go to visit her grave often as it upset him too much. He told her that his boss thought the world of him, and had given him as much time off for the wedding as he wanted. He invited none of his old friends from The Imperial. He said that he would not invite a coachload of guests, when Penny's father was paying for the whole thing. And he had so many friends, it would be hard to narrow it down. And what was the point, anyway? He was so in love with Penny, he would not care if they were all alone in the church. Penny was enchanted. He gave his bride a lovely painting of Portstewart Strand as a wedding present.

It rained all day. They drove in a convoy to a crumbling hotel in Portrush, on the north coast, for the reception. The small group posed for a photograph on the promenade, where a sudden gust of wind blew Penny's hat over the railings and into the sea. The silk flowers on the brim turned a dark color in the freezing water. The hat bobbed up and down for a minute and then sank quietly beneath the waves, like a wreath at a burial-at-sea. If she had been there, Brenda Brown would have pronounced it a bad omen, but, as Penny's wedding hat was going to its watery grave, Brenda, aged seven, was coloring in the patterns on her mother's new wallpaper with a packet of permanent markers.

The dining room in Portrush was draughty, but the small party put on a good show of merriment. They had homemade vegetable soup and soft bread rolls with butter curls, and then stuffed breast of chicken and creamed potatoes. The waitresses served baby carrots and cauliflower florets from stainless steel dishes, scraping the spoons loudly against the metal containers. Daniel let his eyes wander over the silver candlesticks, but he kept his hands under the table. Tiny bowls of sherry trifle and cream were served for dessert. The wedding cake, with its pretty silver horseshoe decorations, was cut, and the teas and coffees were poured from scalding pots.

The speeches were short. Penny's father coughed to hide the falter in his voice as he told the guests how much joy Penny, a surprise late baby, had brought to their lives. He said that he hoped that Penny and Daniel would be as happy all their lives as they looked on this day.

He then announced his intention to retire from the catering trade and give his beloved tea house to the happy couple as a wedding gift. There was a little flat above the shop, he said, which would suffice for living quarters until they bought a house of their own. Everyone clapped and cheered, and stood to drink a toast to the handsome groom and his blushing bride. Daniel put his arm round Penny and kissed her warmly. Penny's father signalled to the band that it was time to begin the music and the dancing, and everyone stood and raised their glasses.

Daniel and Penny were jostled onto the floor and they began an unsteady waltz. Penny closed her eyes and was completely happy. Only months before, a fortune-teller in Bundoran had told her she would marry young. And here she was, swept off her feet by this gorgeous man. A mature man of thirty, she thought. Not an awkward boy her own age, trying to get the clothes off her on the first date, and not even looking at her face.

She was delirious with happiness. She could barely wait for the honeymoon to begin. Her bridesmaid, Millie, had warned Penny that it might be a good thing to wait awhile, and get to know Daniel better before tying the knot. He was too good to be true, that's what Millie said. But Penny knew that poor Millie was sick with jealousy. Millie's latest boyfriend, Jack, worked in the shipyard and had a face that literally frightened small children.

Daniel was delighted with himself. He had hoped to be offered a position in the family business, and now he was being handed the whole thing *on a plate.* (Pardon the pun, he thought.) His ship had come in at last. He wondered if his father was still alive; maybe sitting on a rocking chair, on a porch somewhere in America, eating corn bread. He thought of Teresa, and he knew she would be proud of him. She would have enjoyed this party, everyone dancing so close to the sea. And he thought of his Aunt Kathleen, stern-faced and silent, still looking after heavenly pennies, high above him in the darkening sky.

• 7 •

A Lady in a Velvet Hat

The night that Penny brought up the unfortunate subject of trying for a baby, Daniel slept in the spare room. He tossed and turned on the stiff mattress all night. He briefly considered giving in to Penny's desire to reduce her working hours. But that would mean hiring new staff. And if Penny had more time off, she would only spend it looking at baby clothes in the shops, and begging him to give her a child. And if they had a new baby, what then? She would want a new house to live in. A proper house with its own front door, and a garden with a swing. And maybe another baby to keep the first one company? That was the problem with women, they were always having ideas. They would be bankrupt in less than five years. He couldn't support a family home and extra staff out of selling tea and sandwiches, no matter how hard he worked.

The next morning he brought Penny a cup of tea in bed and told her he would think about what she had said, hoping to buy himself some time.

"In the meantime," he added, "we'd best go on as usual. Right, I'll start the baking and you tidy up the cafe. I noticed the floor could do with a wash."

"Listen to me, Daniel," she said, slowly, settling back on the pillows. "I'm not cleaning the cafe today, or ever again."

"What?"

"Not ever. Do you hear me?"

"Have you gone mad?"

"I'm worn out and that's the truth. Either a cleaner does it, or you can do it yourself. It's up to you."

"But I do all the baking!"

"I'm working eight hours a day from now on, and not a minute more. It's my cafe, too, you know! I'm entitled to some say in the running of it."

"Is that so? Well, what are you going to contribute to the business, exactly?" he asked.

"I'm going to start work at nine o'clock, and serve the customers and make the soup for lunch. Now, let me get back to sleep, or there'll be ructions in this flat. If you want the floors done, you'd better shake a leg. I'll not detain you any further." And she finished her tea, lay down again and pulled the duvet up to her nose.

Daniel stood there, for a moment, completely speechless. The old Penny had gone away in the night, it seemed, and the new Penny was not afraid of standing up to him anymore. It was already a quarter to seven, and there was nothing in the oven, a pile of dishes from last night to wash, the whole place to clean . . .

"Have you gone on strike?" he asked.

"Yes, I bloody have."

"But you can't, Penny. It's your own shop . . ."

"Aha!"

"This doesn't make any sense—"

"And another thing, you can sleep in the spare room from now on. There's no point in you lying in here, reading cookery books half the night, keeping me awake!"

Daniel went out and closed the door quietly, as if someone had died in the house. Penny waited for him to explode; to shout at her, strike her, even. She imagined a passionate struggle on the stairs as he tried to drag her down to clean the cafe, an erotic tangle of limbs in the dark hallway. But he went downstairs quietly and started the baking on his own. She listened for the early-morning sounds of the equipment starting up, the milk bottles being brought in. She could hardly believe what she had done.

When she heard the lonesome scrape of the mop bucket in the yard, she almost ran down the stairs to help him, but then she thought of Jack and Millie Mortimer. If someone had told her, on her wedding day, that she would ever be jealous of the love life of that pair, she'd have laughed until her face ached. No, she was going to get her own way or die in the attempt. She closed her eyes. Her whole life had taken on a fragile quality. Every moment was stretched and full of tension.

But even though she was a nervous wreck, she knew she would not change her mind. Daniel was not used to her doing things on her own initiative, that was all. He would get used to it, he would have to, she fumed. She would say how tired she was, over and over, every time he asked her to do anything. He would have to leave his precious cakes and roll up his sleeves and do the donkey-work himself. She was not giving in this time. She would make life so difficult for him, he would be a broken man in a couple of months. All she had to do was stay calm, and keep gently pushing her husband round to her way of thinking. Gradually, very gradually. That was the way to do it. The balance of power was shifting, slowly but surely, to Penny's side.

That afternoon, a wealthy-looking woman came into the cafe and approached Penny to ask if a magazine had been handed in. An interiors magazine, it was, with a picture of an antique armoire on the front, she explained, with real worry in her big gray eyes. Penny was startled by the woman's beauty, and only half-listened to the details of her question. Her makeup was perfectly applied, smoky eye shadow tapering into a neat point beneath exquisitely waxed eyebrows. Penny noticed little things like that, and she knew it was the expensive makeup that came in fancy packaging, from big department stores. The waft of designer perfume was almost overpowering. Some feminine instinct in Penny made her glance around the cafe to make sure Daniel was not in the room.

The woman was dressed in layers of plum velvet: a floor-length coat with beading on the hem, a large, floppy hat and an embroidered scarf.

"So, did you find it, I wonder?"

Penny had, of course, but she didn't want to give it back.

It was very precious to her, the woman explained, that particular edition. It was the only copy she had of the first magazine she had edited single-handedly. Ten years old, it was. Penny hadn't even noticed the date on the cover.

"Is that a fact?" she said. She wanted to

keep the luxurious magazine. "I can't say I've found an old magazine."

"Oh, it doesn't look out-of-date. That's because the rooms featured have a timeless beauty," said the woman, tucking a stray strand of hair behind one of her small, perfect ears. "Oh, it must be here! A nice-looking man served me. Maybe he has it? Maybe I should speak to him?"

Well, Penny wasn't having that.

"Wait a minute." Penny made a half-hearted show of looking under the counter. "Oh, here it is . . ." She reluctantly handed it over. She knew when she was beaten.

"Oh, thank you so much! I'm always losing things," said the woman, and she ordered a cup of herbal tea.

Penny watched her from the kitchen, wondering if Daniel had found her attractive. He hadn't mentioned anything about her.

Very well-dressed, she was. Much wealthier-looking than the regular clientele in Muldoon's. And she had a strange accent that was a mixture of Belfast and New York. Well, she was in the publishing business, after all, thought Penny. Jet-setting around the globe, living here and there, staying in fabulous hotels like the one with the red sitting room. She wondered what the woman was doing in her back-street cafe. Hopefully not writing a feature on Belfast eateries.

Penny and Daniel did not speak to each other for a week. When they did communicate, it was only to confirm orders in the shop.

Daniel slaved for a month, doing most of the work himself. Then, he gave in and hired a cleaner in the middle of February. She was called Mary Little, but she told him her friends called her Mary Soap. She came in every day at one o'clock and had the whole place spotless in less than an hour. Penny was amazed by her efficiency and the way she mopped the floor with strong, rhythmic strokes, never going over the same bit twice. And it looked much cleaner than it ever did when Penny cleaned it. The tiredness began to leave Penny's face and she began to smile again, and look forward to Mary arriving each day. She paid Mary out of the cash register, and tried not to notice the hurt in her husband's eyes.

Mary knew that something was not right with the Stanley marriage, but she was not in the counseling business. She was only paid to clean the shop, and that's what she did. She knew the stories that went about the hotel trade, about Daniel Stanley and his peculiar ways. They said he was reared by a mad aunt who wore the same coat for fifty years; and that he wasn't the full shilling himself.

But Mary wasn't the sort of woman to carry gossip.

· 8 ·

Brenda Has an Exhibition

Brenda Brown was in great spirits. Her pale face was shining with hope when she came into Muldoon's at five o'clock, for a cheese-and-pickle toasted sandwich, tortilla chips and a large cola with ice and lemon. She wrote a letter with her gold pen as she ate.

February 28, 1999
Dear Nicolas Cage,
Did you get my last letter?

I'm still waiting on a signed photo. I have a little silver frame, all ready for it.

Did I tell you? I'm a painter, and I'm holding an exhibition of my most recent paintings in a local gallery. Myself and a few other graduates have rented the gallery between us, for a fortnight, and we are each exhibiting five pieces. There were endless discussions about who would hang what, where. Everybody wanted the big wall opposite the window. Tom Reilly-Dunseith got it, in the end. He said he had to have that space, as the light coming in from the outside was an essential part of his sculptural forms. Pretentious old fish, that he is. Basically, he makes big question marks out of car exhausts.

The rest of them are in the gallery now, fussing and fretting with their cans of white emulsion. There was a hole in the stretch of wall that I got, but I patched it up with masking tape and paint.

I enclose a postcard of one of my paintings, called Waiting for the Cortège. *It's about the funeral of a teenage boy who died during a riot. Tom Reilly-*

Dunseith said it was, and I quote: "Boring, unimaginative and passé."

I told him he was only welding pieces of junk together, and trying to pass it off as modern art, because he can't actually draw very well. In fact, he failed his life drawing unit in second year, but I wouldn't embarrass him by telling people that.

Do you like the painting? You see, the crowd is full of pretty girls who fancied him. (The dead boy.) It's about all the things he could have done, and experienced, if he'd lived in another time and place. It's a comment on the futility of violence.

I'm thinking of changing my name to something more mysterious than Brenda Brown. Something Irish that reminds a person of old money and a pioneering spirit.

Maybe Aoife Fitzgerald-Conway?

Maybe Geraldine Murphy-Maguire.

Maybe I'm being daft.

We'll be having a few jars later, at my place, before the off—I mean, we'll be having a few drinks at my apartment, before the exhibition begins.

I'll probably wear my black trouser suit and white shirt, as usual, and slick my hair back with gel. Androgynous and timeless. Lots of dark eye shadow, nothing on the lips. I'm not the sexy type. But I have a kind of spiritual beauty, I like to think. Something above and beyond the merely physical. (I hope.)

Anyway, must dash. Wish me luck.

Yours sincerely,

Brenda Brown

PS. I am a genuine fan. Please send me a signed photo.

Brenda savored every bite of her toasted sandwich and tortilla chips. She decided to spend some of her meager budget on a bottle of gin, some tonic water and a bag of ice cubes at the store, before going home to change into her good suit. She would need a couple of drinks to steady her nerves before the show.

She made a mental note to hide the gin before the other artists turned up. Penniless, the lot of them. They would have all the gin down their throats in a heartbeat. Some cheap lager, she would buy, to offer round. They weren't real friends, Brenda reasoned. They were just gathering at her flat because it was close to the gallery. In fact, she would have to hide her paints, her spare canvases, her Radiohead CD and even her jar of good coffee, before they arrived. Some of those art graduates were so desperate for money, they would steal the eye out of your head. Except for Tom Reilly-Dunseith, of course: he couldn't make enough of his sculptures to meet demand, even though he was charging eight hundred pounds for the useless piles of junk. It was only because of his fancy name that people were interested in him, Brenda thought, bitterly.

And then she remembered that Emily Shadwick had also been invited. Brenda wondered how she could avoid being dragged into any discussion of Emily's love life. She decided to turn the music up really loud, and pretend that she had wax in her ears. She didn't want Emily to bring her mood down just before a show.

Some local journalists had been invited, and they might want a quote or two from the artists. Brenda rehearsed what she would say to them, and she decided not to smile if anyone was taking pictures.

She looked out at the old red postbox that would take her letter on the first stage of its journey to America. She smiled at Penny, and waved the letter in the air, and Penny nodded and gave her a thumbs-up.

• 9 •

Aurora Signs on the Dotted Line

Henry Blackstaff was at home. He stood at the kitchen window, waiting for the kettle to boil. His cunning plan to outsmart Aurora had backfired spectacularly. When he told her that she could have the conservatory, if that was what she really wanted, Aurora wept with joy. She telephoned all the members of the society to share the good news, and even ran in her bare feet to tell the neighbors.

Arnold Smith was all over the house with his electronic measuring-device and planning applications were submitted with frightening speed.

Soon, Henry's beloved garden would be no more. Uncle Bertie's monkey-puzzle would have to go to make room for the foundations. So would Henry's makeshift greenhouse. Aurora had chosen the most expensive model in the range: hardwood frame as high as the house, stained-glass windows, under-floor heating and wrought-iron roof supports. Arnold Smith's flashy pen totted it all up as he panted with breathless greed.

The telephone rang in the hall. Henry answered it.

"It's for you," he called. "Someone called David Cropper, from the BBC."

Aurora was ecstatic all evening. David Cropper turned out to be a producer, who had read about Aurora in a newspaper, and was thinking of making a television documentary about the Brontë Bunch. Aurora told him that she was having a Victorian conservatory built, in which to hold the meetings. The members of the society were going to dress up in period costume and listen to Aurora as she read aloud from famous works of fiction. The producer said he would call back in a few weeks to see how the building was going, and that the whole project sounded fascinating. Henry sighed. If there was even a chance that his wife was going to be on television, there would be no reasoning with her. She seemed to have forgotten her contempt for all things modern.

The next morning, at nine o'clock on the dot, Arnold Smith stood on the doorstep of the Blackstaff residence, with his greedy face only millimeters away from the brass door knocker. In his hand he held the quotation for the conservatory. The amount was outrageous. Six figures, his biggest ever sale. Even Head Office were phoning him about it. He would have to use every last one of his salesman tricks to secure the contract. He hoped the husband was out. Mr. Blackstaff did not appear to share his wife's enthusiasm for the project. But Arnold Smith was lucky that day. Aurora answered the door and ushered him into the sitting room. She barely glanced at the figure before signing a check for the deposit with an old-fashioned fountain pen. Then, she guided him back to the front door, without offering him a cup of tea.

"Now, you will use reclaimed bricks, won't you?" she said. "That is of paramount importance. The entire structure must look as if it has been there since the day the house was built. And don't forget to leave enough room on the left-hand side for my bookcases. I just adore the smell of old books. So romantic! A breaking heart on every page! Unrequited love: the cruel sword plunged through the soul of Everyman. That's how I met my husband, you know."

What? Dotty old bat, thought Arnold Smith.

"You have exquisite taste," he purred, as Aurora closed the door in his face. He made a mental note to clear the check before he ordered the materials. Maybe the woman was a lunatic.

When Henry came back with the morning paper, he and Aurora had another row.

"How *much*? You must be joking! We could buy a second home in France for less! I can't believe you went ahead without me. You should have booked that room in the museum, as I suggested. That's where most of your friends belong."

"Well, that's just typical! You know your trouble, Henry? You've sat in that shop, gathering dust, for too long. When was the last time you even sold a book?"

"What has that got to do with anything? It's my shop, and I'll run it my way."

"You inherited that shop, and you'd have closed down years ago without Bertie's money to keep you going." She was breathless with fury. "I'm using my own savings for this. Why can't you be happy for me? It will not cost you a farthing."

"It's costing me my garden, isn't it? What am I supposed to do now on my days off? And that's another thing: you've only got savings because I pay for everything in this marriage. Every last cup of overpriced tea those stuck-up fools pour down their necks was paid for by me."

"Well, I'm sorry you begrudge my friends some light refreshment. They are very cultured people, if you would only get to know them. Don't you see what an opportunity this is for me?"

"No, I don't, if you want the truth."

"I'm going to be on television, for heaven's sake! Maybe more than once. Maybe they'll make a series. And they're bound to make me head teacher at school."

"Pie in the sky. Dreams."

"Well, at least I've got a dream! You have no imagination. That's why no one ever wants to publish your damn novels, you ridiculous *little* man!"

"That was cruel, Aurora. I don't know what's come over *you.* You know how much I love that monkey-puzzle. Uncle Bertie planted that tree himself."

"And I don't know what's come over you! Making such a production out of a few old trees. When I met you, I thought you were different from other men, sitting there amid your lovely books. Not like the typical male with his endless talk of football matches. You were from another era. You were my Mr. Rochester. My hero." She held out her arms to him, in a heartbroken kind of way.

"And you were my Jane Eyre," he said, fondly. "My pale fragile governess. But now, with this conservatory business—"

"Now, I see you're just like the rest, trying to stop me from making something of my-self." She went to the window and looked out at the site where the great conservatory would eventually stand.

"I don't want to hold you back. I just want to save my garden. Couldn't you make the conservatory smaller, so that the monkey-puzzle won't have to come out?"

"No, I can't. There has to be enough room for sixty chairs, two thousand books and a small area for performing," she said firmly. "Mr. Smith has made the calculations and I have given them approval."

"I could stop this, you know. The property is joint-owned. I could go to court and have it stopped."

"Well, well, well! So. The gloves are off. Let me tell you, Henry Blackstaff, that you have left it too late to discover that you have a spine! The masterful husband routine simply will not work. I won't let you stop me. I'll chop that tree down myself, if I have to."

"I could tell all your precious friends that your real name is Gertie Leech, and that you changed it by deed poll in 1974. And that your father was a cross-dressing poker-addict, with a criminal record for fraud. That would have the freeloading snobs scuttling out of my home, all right. They'd all get stuck in the French windows!"

"If you do that, I swear by almighty God that you'll be joining your Uncle Bertie in the next world a lot sooner than you think! I'm sure there are plenty of monkey-puzzle trees in paradise!" And with that, she swept up the stairs and into the master bedroom, slamming the door so hard that the banisters shook.

Henry sat down on a spoon-back chair, feeling suddenly weak. Aurora was furious with him. She would not forgive him for weeks. And why should she? He had just threatened his own wife with the loss of what she valued more than anything: her reputation. He really was becoming a textbook villain. He should have given the project his blessing at the start. It was going to happen anyway.

The worst thing of all was that Uncle Bertie's tree would have to be pulled up by the roots. Arnold Smith seemed to think that was the safest way to remove it. It was like uprooting Bertie himself. It was a terrible betrayal of his dead benefactor.

"I have chosen to read from *Wuthering Heights*," announced Aurora, a couple of days later.

Henry was not listening. He knew Aurora

was not talking to him. She was trying out her reading voice.

She ignored Henry completely. "Penned by Miss Emily Brontë. Published in 1847." A pause. *"On that bleak hilltop the earth was hard with a black frost, and the air made me shiver through every limb . . ."*

Dear God, thought Henry, and he went to put on his coat. He would go to Muldoon's and console himself with a portion of steak and kidney pie.

·10·

An Encounter in the Europa Hotel

Clare Fitzgerald was back in Belfast again. She sat in the bar of the Europa Hotel and ordered another drink. White wine was her favourite tipple, and the hotel had a good selection of half bottles. She must ask to see the menu in a minute. She was hungry after her day's work. Although very few people would believe her, it was very tiring work, selecting locations for photo shoots and making phone calls all day long. On the table beside her was a stack of glossy magazines to study for style and content, and a pretty handbag by Lulu Guinness. What else would a woman of culture be seen with?

She noticed a nearly handsome businessman looking in her direction with hope in his eyes and she turned away, not wanting to encourage him. He was well-dressed and seemed pleasant enough, and it wouldn't have been the first time she had spent the evening in the company of a pleasant stranger. But tonight she was not in the mood for company. She looked over at him. He was waving at her. Damn it.

This second trip to Belfast had been a mistake. She had been foolish to think it would not affect her like this. It was just the same when she came over to visit her aunt in early January, although she hadn't had as much time to brood then because she was travelling with her parents. Before that, she hadn't been to Belfast for years and years, but it was as if she had never left. She was a lost teenager again, caught in a sudden fit of melancholy. Going to Muldoon's and reliving old memories that she should have left behind two decades ago, along with her youth, had only made her feel worse.

Stop this at once, she told herself. Everything will be okay when I go back to America. It's just this stupid town that makes me feel this way. I am flying home to New York first thing in the morning, and then I'll be fine.

The hopeful businessman sent the barman over with a bottle of the most expensive wine in the hotel, and she nodded her thanks politely. Her time in the publishing business had taught her never to be rude to anyone until she found out who they were. She poured some and took a tiny sip. It was a superb vintage. For a second, she considered asking him to join her. There was no harm in having a conversation with the man. He did seem rather charming. Maybe they could enjoy dinner together?

But it was no good. Her mood was too bleak. He would want to know all about her job, and about New York, and then she would have the delicate task of letting him know she didn't want to spend the night with him. It would be like a military operation getting through the meal without offending him. She looked over in his direction. He was still watching, waiting for a signal from her. She would have to return the bottle to him, and thank him, and say she was suffering from a headache, or something like that. But even that seemed too much trouble, the way she was feeling.

Suddenly, she stood up and collected her things, left the bar and went quickly into the lobby. The expensive wine was left behind on the table, as forlorn as the face of the rejected male in the bar. She pressed the button to call the lift. She would just have to order some food to be sent to her room. She didn't want the man to follow her into the dining room. She could see the disappointment on his face as the lift doors closed. Sometimes it was a nuisance being so attractive.

She was beautiful, she knew. There was no point in denying it. She had huge gray eyes and a little tiny mouth. Even without the makeup, men stared after her in the street. But when she covered her eyelids with sparkly, silver eye shadow, and painted her lips with deep-red lip gloss, she was so beautiful it was impossible for men not to desire her. She was a 1925 Tamara de Lempicka self-portrait, *Tamara in the Green Bugatti*, come to life. With her perfectly cut bob and her vintage velvet clothes, she was the envy of every woman she had ever known. Another woman could wear the same clothes and the same makeup, but they never managed to achieve the same effect. It was not easy to be friends with someone so beautiful. In fact, no woman was ever friends with Clare Fitzgerald for long. They just couldn't bear it when men looked only at her. It was Clare they wanted. Always Clare.

Clare tried dressing down, but that wasn't her style. She hated jeans and tracksuits and scruffy trainers. She loved her embroidered scarves, her long fringed coats, and her expensive creams and perfumes. She had crates full of silver bangles and glass rings and amber necklaces in her light-filled apartment in New York. Reluctantly, guiltily, she kept those frivolous things and said good-bye to female companionship.

Her detached, otherworldly air earned her huge credibility in the New York publishing community. In a city where every other person had talent to spare, personality counted for a lot. After only five years in the business, she was the editor-in-chief of a high-quality magazine dedicated to upmarket and artistic interiors. Antique four-posters in New England mansions, collections of valuable paintings in million-pound apartments in London. Paris lofts full of movie memorabilia and artists' easels; unmade beds with white sheets in fishing villages in Cornwall—with headboards made out of driftwood. That's what got Clare Fitzgerald interested.

Celebrities and millionaires were falling over themselves to get their lavish homes featured in her magazine, but if Clare didn't think they were special enough, they didn't get in. The vulgar mansions favored by pop stars and glamour models were not even considered. Clare Fitzgerald had the kind of taste that money alone just couldn't buy.

She sat in her cozy office in New York selecting the locations for shoots, and sending her assistants out for deli and wine and cappuccinos, and sometimes dreaming of her lost love, Peter. Peter was the only man she had ever loved. They had spent one night together, in a tiny flat on Mulberry

Street in Belfast. She had only known him for nineteen hours altogether.

She was a student then and the flat was the first home she had created for herself. A tiny little cupboard of a place, barely twenty feet square, but it was better than having to share a house with other students and the legendary squalor they lived in. Even as a teenager, Clare wanted to live in a nice place. The day she moved in, she cleaned the flat from top to bottom, and decorated it with colourful throws and cushions, free postcards from an art gallery, three house-plants, two lamps donated by her mother, a small bunch of flowers and two cheap rugs. She bought a new mattress for the bed and threw the old one in a skip. She hung Indian scarves and strings of glass beads on the Victorian headboard. She felt very grown up, buying her groceries at the supermarket, remembering to buy carpet cleaner and bleach, as well as soap and shampoo and toothpaste. She wasn't a typical student.

The flat was next door to a cafe called Muldoon's Tea Rooms. That was the best thing about the flat. If she had a lot of work to do, she could buy coffee and a salad roll on the way home from college, and be sitting at her desk a minute later, enjoying her supper. She could smell the aroma of coffee coming through the walls as she lay in bed in the early morning, listening to the rain hammering down on the skylight above her.

Peter was pale and quietly spoken, but very intense. She liked that. He had a fringe of black hair hanging in his eyes and he had to flick it to one side to see her. He wore a T-shirt with the name of a pop group on it: Human League. She liked the group, too. That's how they met. Through music. At a nightclub near the docks. Clare saw him looking at her, and she smiled at him, and after a while he came over to talk to her. That's how it began. That's how easy it was.

She asked him if he liked the band and they both laughed because he was wearing the T-shirt and two badges as well.

One song in particular, she loved: "Don't You Want Me?" She blushed sometimes because she could still remember the name of the song. Even now. (It was just a simple pop tune but at the time she thought it was fabulous.) He said he knew it well, and it was very good.

They danced together when the floor began to fill up, and when the night was over, he offered to walk her home. Twenty minutes could be a long walk when you were on your own, in the dark, Clare thought. She said yes. It was cold and windy. He held her hand.

She was only nineteen. He was older than Clare at twenty-two, just coming to the end of his own student days. She asked him what he was studying. He told her, English. Did he think he would go into teaching, she wanted to know? Or journalism? He said he hadn't a clue—he'd only come from Fermanagh to Belfast to study because there were no jobs at home. Likely, he would end up going slowly insane in the Civil Service, like many other Arts graduates before him.

She asked him if he had ever been beaten up because of his effeminate hairstyle, and black eyeliner. He admitted he had been chased three times, by football fans. It didn't seem to bother him. He could run a lot faster than they could, he explained. That was the great advantage of being thin: he didn't have a lot of weight to carry.

By the time they reached Mulberry Street, she knew quite a lot about him. He was the eldest child in the family. He had six sisters. His mother was a nurse who went to mass every day. His father was a mechanic who liked to restore vintage cars in his spare time. They were a close, happy family. He had a guitar, but couldn't play it very well. He liked chocolate biscuits.

She had the key to her flat in her pocket. She turned it over and over in her hand. Her other hand was tingling, where he was touching it. She decided to invite him in.

She didn't know what was going to happen when they went up the little stairs and switched on the light. Would he kiss her? Those were the days when men didn't automatically assume they would be invited into the bedroom on the first date. (The good old days, she thought. Would they ever come back?) She offered to make coffee. They stood in the middle of the sitting room. The air around them was charged with anticipation. She could hardly breathe with nervous energy. He commented on the decor, and said it was very artistic, and that he would very much like a cup of tea.

They talked for a while, about pop music mostly, and about other harmless things. When Clare got up from the little sofa to make toast on the 1950's grill, he followed her into the kitchen. She'd thought that with all those sisters, he would be spoiled in the house, but he told her he was very domesticated. He kept an eye on the bread while she hunted through the cupboards for some powdered milk. When the toast was buttered, she noticed he had grilled it on one side only, so that the bread was soft underneath. She hadn't made toast that way before, so she tried it, and it was very nice, and she grilled her toast on one side forever afterward.

He looked at her lips as if he wanted to kiss her, but he didn't. His restraint made Clare weak with desire. She told herself, he must feel something for her or he wouldn't have walked her home. But the moment was too precious to spoil it with an awkward attempt to embrace him. They listened to music for a while, sitting on the little sofa, eating toast. Neither of them spoke. Clare willed herself to touch his face and kiss him, but she couldn't move. At four o'clock in the morning, she knew it was time for him to leave, but she didn't want him going out alone into the empty streets. He looked very vulnerable with his thin coat and his even thinner face.

"Stay with me," she said, suddenly, before she became too shy. "I mean, just stay with me for a little while longer."

"I'd like that," he said, softly.

They went into the bedroom. He sat gently down on the bed.

"I'll just take my boots off, if that's okay." It took him several minutes to get them off because there were twelve buckles on each one. "Come here," he said. "It's cold." He held out his hand and she sat down beside him. When he looked into her eyes, as they lay down on top of the bedclothes, she almost believed that she was obsessed with him already. He had some tapes in his trouser pocket. There was a small stereo on a chair beside the bed. He found one that Clare liked and put it into the stereo, pressed the repeat button, and then pulled one of Clare's throws over them both. The room was absolutely freezing. Their breath came out in visible gasps of white smoke.

"Can I kiss you?" he asked. His lips were hot and strong. His kisses were long, lingering and gentle. They were perfect kisses. Clare had no sexual experience and hadn't a clue what to do. She thought of telling him this, but he seemed to know already. He made no attempt to seduce her.

They curled up under the throw together, kissing for a long time. He held her in his arms and told her that he was in love with her. She didn't believe him. Later, he made more tea in the tiny kitchen and carried the tray very carefully to the bedroom because he had filled the cups to the brim. They sat up in bed, drinking it, listening to the cassette, and Clare congratulated herself on having powdered milk in the cupboard. It began to rain heavily then, and he switched off the music and they lay in each other's arms listening to it drumming on the window. The streetlight coming through the glass made a pattern on their faces. He told her he loved her for a second time. They slept for a short while when the rain stopped.

At seven o'clock in the morning he told her he would always love her and, this time, she believed him. They lay in each other's arms and slept until well after lunchtime.

Nothing she had felt since had even come close to the ecstasy of that night, the feeling of closeness they had shared. They might have been the last two people alive on the planet. Nothing else, and no one else mattered. Most of the time, she was able to push it to the back of her mind. But, if she wanted to, she could conjure up a photographic image of his face, and everything else that had happened on the night she decided, on a whim, to go to a disco.

When they finally emerged from the flat at four in the afternoon, they went to Muldoon's for something to eat. Peter wrote his address and telephone number on the cassette sleeve of the tape they had listened to, and gave it to her, and asked her formally to be his girlfriend. She said yes. She put the cassette in her little beaded handbag. She promised to call him the next day. He kissed her gently at the bus stop and waved to her as she set off for home, to visit her parents for the weekend.

As the blue Ulsterbus wound its way through the city streets, on its way to Saintfield, Clare lay back on the seat and closed her eyes with pleasure. She was so happy she wanted to tell the bus driver that she had met the man she would marry and love for the rest of her life. She should have invited Peter to come home with her and meet her parents, she thought suddenly. She missed him so much already, it was like an ache in her heart. She worried that he would get knocked down by a car, or hurt somehow, if they were apart for any length of time.

The brick came through the side window of the bus like a bomb. The noise it made was fantastic. BOOM! And then the peculiar sound of safety glass shattering into a thousand pieces. The floor of the bus was covered with it. Like giant grains of sugar, they caught the light, and sparkled. Clare thought the glass was very pretty and then she realized she was crying.

Her hair was wet. There was blood on her cheek. She knew then she'd been hit on the side of the head, and she felt dizzy. The driver skidded to a halt, but started up the engine again when he saw a small group of angry young men running toward the vehicle. Everything seemed to be happening very slowly and quietly.

"Keep going, mate," shouted an elderly passenger. "They're gonna wreck the bus!"

The other passengers were calm. They were used to small acts of sudden violence. They knew they would be given a chance to get off, before the bus was set on fire and used to block the road. Even in what the police called "a riot-situation," there were set ways of doing things. Clare's whole body was trembling. Then, she felt the first wave of pain, and she put her hand up to cover the gash above her right ear. Two women came across to her and one of them supported her while the other one held a tissue to her wound.

The women swore at the tearaway teenagers through the empty window frame.

"Ye wee bastards! Away home 'til your ma's!" A shower of smaller stones struck the sides of the vehicle, before it sped up and left the mob behind.

At the bus depot, she was given scalding hot tea in a paper cup, but could not hold her hands steady to drink it.

The police came. Had Clare seen anything?

She couldn't remember.

Anything at all?

"Just the cubes of broken glass, sparkling on the floor of the bus," she whispered. "Like giant grains of sugar. Like big, glass beads . . ."

The shock jolted through her. Her handbag! Oh, God, where was her handbag? Her little beaded handbag with Peter's address inside . . . Could someone please look for it on the bus? Please? But she was told the bus had been checked over already. No bag had been found. Were they sure? Yes, there was nothing.

The disappointment she felt was like a bereavement.

Clare was taken by ambulance to hospital where her distraught parents sat up all night, making plans. Their daughter was not seriously hurt, but she could have been. The city was like a wounded animal, they said: it could turn on a person and bite them without warning. They had been thinking of moving away from the city for some time. This near-tragedy was the push they needed to make a new start. They would move to Cornwall in England, and run a small guest house. It had been a dream of theirs for a long time.

When Clare left hospital two days later, the moving-house arrangements were well under way. Her parents did not ask her if she would prefer to stay in Belfast and continue with her studies. When Clare hinted that she might want to do this, her mother complained of chest pains. The family home was already up for sale.

Clare telephoned the university and left a message for Peter, but she heard nothing back. She decided the person who took the call must have forgotten to write down the message, or maybe the office staff were always getting pestered by lovesick young people, and just didn't bother taking messages anymore.

Three days later, she waited outside his classroom for an hour, but she did not see him. Shyly, she approached some of the students and asked if they knew a boy called Peter Prendergast. She was directed toward a girl with long plaits in her hair. The girl was sitting on the floor, under a notice board. She said she knew Peter and could pass on a message. Yes, she would be seeing him soon, probably that very evening. Hugely relieved, Clare gave her a note in a sealed envelope. And the girl gave her Peter's address, but said she was unsure of his phone number.

Full of hope, Clare went home to wait. If they still felt the same way about each other when they met, she would stay in Belfast. They might even move in together.

But when Clare had left the building, the girl opened the envelope, read the note carefully and then threw it in the bin. She had hopes of Peter Prendergast herself, and she wasn't going to go around delivering notes for a snob from the art college. She was delighted with herself for giving Clare Fitzgerald the wrong address for Peter, a dump of a place she had lived in years ago.

Clare hung around the flat for days. Then, fearing the girl had not delivered the note, she wrote to Peter at the university. But still there was no response.

She was bewildered. Hadn't he said he loved her? Three times? She was grief-stricken when the second week came and went and there was no contact.

A buyer was found for the house, and the contents were sent on to a rented cottage in Cornwall. Clare began to think that she had imagined the depth of the connection between Peter and herself. The shock of the riot had undermined her confidence. Her dreams of true love were marred now; by broken windows and buses full of swearing women, and policemen looking at her with pity in their eyes. She wondered about the girl with the long, plaited hair and her relationship to Peter. Why had the other students directed her so unhesitatingly to that girl? Was she his girlfriend?

Was it true, what her friends thought? That Peter was only spinning her a line, hoping to seduce her that night? And that he'd probably decided not to get involved with her now, when he knew that she wasn't the sort of girl to date casually, and then drop. None of them had ever met a boy who said he was in love with them on the first night. Or who kissed them all night, under a warm blanket, and did not try anything on. It sounded very weird.

Clare packed up her things in the tiny flat on Mulberry Street, all the time listening for a knock at the door.

Peter couldn't understand why Clare hadn't phoned him. He walked past her flat several times, hoping to catch her coming out. He was ashamed of himself for declaring his love so strongly, on the night of the disco. Why had he done that? It was an adolescent way to carry on. She must think he was very immature, or half-mad. As the days went by, he felt less and less confident. She might think he was unstable, or insincere. Twice, he did knock on the door, but Clare was not home. He stopped going to his lectures for a while, unable to concentrate. He thought of leaving a letter in the communal postbox of the flats but, without knowing what impression she had of him, he didn't know what to write. If he could see her face, then he would know what to say. Eventually, however, he left a carefully worded note with the old man who owned the tea house, a Mr. Muldoon.

When there was no response even then, he was so desperate he sat on the doorstep of the flats, determined not to move until he saw Clare.

But, by that time, Clare was living in England, and trying to get over him. When he did discover that she had moved away, he was in despair. Obviously, he had meant nothing to her.

Peter nearly failed all his final exams because of the hangovers he gave himself, drowning his sorrows in the student union bar.

But Clare didn't know any of that. Peter

was the one she wanted, and she had lost him. That was all she knew for certain. She turned down nine proposals of marriage, over the years. At thirty-six, she was still single. It was lonely being such a perfectionist.

•11•

Sadie Sponge and the Bitter Lemons

Sadie Smith sat in her modern kitchen in the Belfast suburb of Carryduff and flicked through the local paper in a half-hearted kind of way. There was nothing interesting in it at all. There was a tedious squabble over funding for a new bypass, and an article lamenting the cost of vandalism to the city bus company. Some self-important council officials were pictured looking delighted with themselves beside a new flower bed. There was a sign sticking out of the flower bed that announced that it was sponsored by a fast-food chain. Sadie snorted her contempt. What were people paying rates to the council for, she wondered. To finance junkets abroad, most likely.

"Parasites in pinstripes," she said to the smiling faces in the newspaper, and she jabbed them all with her finger. "That's what you are." Sadie knew a lot about parasites in pinstripes. She was married to one.

Her mother-in-law came into the kitchen and plucked at the dead flowers on the windowsill. "Carnations," she said, unimpressed. "I prefer roses. White roses with long stems, and plenty of greenery."

"I'll remember that in the future," said Sadie. "Just in case Arnold increases the housekeeping money."

"What are you fixing for the tea?" asked the old woman. "Maurice fancied a nice bit of fish, fried in butter. If you hurry, you could still make it to the fishmonger's."

"Fish, it is, then," said Sadie. "I think I have some cod steaks in the freezer. Excuse me."

She rushed out to the chest-freezer in the

garage and closed the kitchen door behind her, so she wouldn't hear Daisy saying Maurice hated frozen fish.

When Arnold pulled up outside the house in his navy-blue Jaguar, he was in a terrific mood. He had just sold another conservatory. That brought his tally so far this year to twelve. His commission would be fantastic. Head Office were very pleased with his performance figures, and were going to present him with an award at the next Christmas party. Aurora Blackstaff's order had put him streets ahead of the other salesmen. That demented, snobby old trout with her tatty, dusty books! He smiled at his reflection in the rearview mirror and ran his fingers through his hair. He would take Patricia away on a trip, to celebrate the sale. He had been planning a little break for some time, a couple of days away from Sadie and his parents.

Sadie Sponge and the Bitter Lemons. That's what Patricia called them. Patricia was good at nicknames. She was very good at lots of things, most of them wicked. She was a clever lady in many ways—not for nothing was she the manager of a gift shop in the city center. (Arnold had met her when a disgruntled ex-employee smashed the window of the shop with a brick, and his company had been contracted to replace it.)

They would fly to Paris together, and make love in a tiny hotel near the Seine. There would be muslin curtains billowing in the night air, and the smell of fresh coffee floating up from the street cafes below. Patricia would wear something black and see-through with lots of straps. Afterward, they would order room service and Patricia would pour him coffee and bring it to him in the bed, her small breasts bare and bouncing. He loosened his collar at the thought of it.

Best of all, they would be far away from his grumbling parents and his dull little turnip-shaped wife.

"You old rogue," he told his reflection, "you've still got the magic touch." He collected his newspaper and the briefcase from the backseat of the car and hurried up the path to the house.

Sadie was in a mood. He could tell at once, the way she was banging the kitchen drawers. Sadie was always in a mood these days. Arnold blamed her burgeoning waistline. It must be awful to be such a tub of lard, he thought sadly. How can she bear to look in the mirror?

She did not turn to greet him when he came down the hall. Maurice was complaining about the fish and refusing to eat his supper. Sadie was opening a can of soup, mashing potatoes and buttering bread, all at the same time. Arnold kissed his mother on the cheek. Daisy asked him to move some old flowers away from the windowsill, as they were spoiling her view of the garden.

Sadie closed her eyes and inhaled deeply. Then, she smacked the plates down on the table, and rushed out of the kitchen.

"Aren't you going to have something?" called Arnold, after her.

"No! I'm not hungry," she shouted back.

"That makes a change," said Arnold to his parents, and they all laughed, co-conspirators. "The old girl must be losing her appetite."

"I bet the owner of Cadbury's chocolate factory is getting worried," said Daisy.

"Ho, ho! You better not let Sadie hear you," said Arnold, "or you could find yourself without a cook!"

"Ha!" snapped Maurice. "Cook, you say? Frozen fish! Your mother never let convenience food into the house. Oh, I can still smell the lovely things she used to make for me! Shepherd's pie and apple charlotte and roast chicken! Rhubarb jam and wheaten bread! Jam and bread, she made herself. It would make your mouth water just to think of it. That's what she gave me to eat. That's why I've lived to such a great age."

"Yes, indeed," said Arnold sadly, thinking of his father's money.

"You'll never see fifty, son, eating this rubbish," said Maurice, bitterly.

Arnold was going to tell them about his great sale that day, but then he changed his mind. He might have to reveal how much money he had made. His parents had been dropping heavy hints about wanting to go away on a trip, while they were "still above ground." But the thought of being cooped up in a hotel with the two of them, and Sadie, was just too awful. He would retreat to his study after supper and plan the magical weekend in Paris with Patricia. Maybe book a couple of tickets to see a sexy show in the Moulin Rouge? Wasn't that the sheer beauty of being a manager? All those boring old conferences to attend . . .

Sadie closed the bedroom door and sat down on the bed, shaking. She did not trust herself to sit at the table with Arnold tonight. She could not bear to look at him eating the fish and mashed potatoes as if nothing had happened. As if his lips had not kissed the hand of another woman, as if he had not patted her knee and whispered intimate things in her ear, as if . . . She might ruin everything by getting up on the table and screaming until her face turned blue. She might grab the heavy potato saucepan and swing it out through the double-glazing. Vertical blinds, potatoes, glass and all, lying on the lawn. That would stop them sniggering. She closed her eyes. What with Maurice and his fresh fish, and Daisy and her white roses, and Arnold with his laughing blonde, it was hard to stay calm. And she must stay calm. She would have to find out what Arnold was up to.

Her natural instinct would be to ignore Arnold's romantic adventures. Maybe he was having an affair, maybe he wasn't.

Whatever he was up to, he couldn't leave Sadie. No way. Sadie took excellent care of Arnold, his clothes, his parents and his home. She did a thousand little things for him every week. Without her, he would not be such a smooth operator. He'd never find a woman to replace her. Still, just to be on the safe side, she'd like some more information.

She would go back to Muldoon's in the morning, and have a good think. In the meantime, she fished a bag of salty pretzels out of her bottom drawer and tore it open. She might be cracking up with rage and humiliation, but she wasn't going to start missing meals over it . . .

•12•

A Strange Marriage

Penny was doing the ironing. She told Daniel she was taking the afternoon off to potter round the flat. She was feeling very restless and couldn't stand still behind the counter. Pressing the crumpled clothes with a hot iron helped her to relax. She lifted the jacket of Daniel's striped pajamas out of the basket, and spread it over the board. Penny wished Daniel would throw his old pajamas in the dustbin and sleep with his chest bare. He had lovely shoulders, she thought wistfully.

"Oh, Daniel," she said, out loud, although she was alone in the flat. "Did you know that on our fifth wedding anniversary I offered myself to a twenty-year-old plumber with a bleach-blond mohawk and tartan bondage trousers?" And she almost wept with embarrassment when she remembered how he ran out the kitchen door, when the phone ringing distracted them.

Her arm wobbled and she had to set the iron down. She went to the mirror above the electric fire and looked at her thirty-five-year-old face.

Why did I do that? she thought. I stood too close to him when he was filling out the receipt. My cleavage was practically in his face. God forgive me, but he was gorgeous. His skin was flawless. I sometimes can see why men have affairs. In the presence of such beauty, it's impossible to resist.

She touched the skin on her throat. It was still smooth. It was not too late to find desperate passion of that kind. Was it?

I even had a line ready for when it was over . . . I thought to myself, I will tell him he is sweet, and that I will never forget him. I gave him that meaningful look, the look they use in old black-and-white films, where you know they're going to make love. Eye contact, no blinking, no talking. He was terrified! Is that what's wrong with me? Am I too melodramatic?

When the spell, that day, was broken by the shrill ringing of the telephone, Penny had rushed out to the counter to answer it. It was a neighbor of her parents, phoning to say they had been involved in a car accident—could she meet him at the Royal Victoria hospital? Mr. and Mrs. Muldoon were both seriously injured, but he couldn't tell her that on the phone.

Speechless with worry, and guilt and lust, Penny nodded that she would call a taxi straightaway. When she went back to the kitchen, the back door was open and the plumber was gone. (He left his bill on the counter.)

Penny spent the next twelve months scuttling between the shop and her parents' home. Until they died within three months of each other, a year later, Penny didn't have a single day off.

She was too busy grieving for her parents

to worry about herself, for a few years after that.

Daniel was almost glad of the distraction the accident caused. He knew Penny expected more of him, but he wasn't sure how to provide it. He knew he was a disappointment to his wife, but he could not change. It was too late. At night, his dreams were filled with images of his mother, Teresa, laughing, her lips red and perfect. Then, shock. A priest. Telling him his mother had gone away and nobody knew where she was and then giving him a shilling. Then, his miserable Aunt Kathleen. She didn't want him. She gave him stale bread to eat.

Often he woke up in a cold sweat and lay awake all night. Even when Penny begged him to talk to her, he shook his head and walked away. She asked him what he was saving all their money for. He could not tell her. He didn't know himself. He knew only what his Aunt Kathleen had told him when he was a little boy: that extravagance was the ruination of Teresa.

Now, neglecting her ironing, Penny wandered over to the sideboard, lifted the silver-framed photograph of the two of them on the wedding day and held it up close to her face. Big happy smiles on the faces of the two of them. Daniel, relaxed and quite handsome; he was very tanned at the time of the wedding. Penny's own skin was glowing with happiness. There was her beautiful hat with the big flowers on it—moments before it blew into the sea. And there was Millie, smoking her cigarette, just about to walk out-of-shot, in the background of the picture. She was wearing a pink bridesmaid dress that clashed with her hair. Did Penny and Daniel get married too soon, like Millie said?

"Did I ever know you, Daniel?" she said aloud, sadly.

·13·

Dear Nicolas, It's Brenda Here

March 19, 1999
Dear Nicolas Cage,
It's Brenda here. Brenda Brown from Belfast Town.

I just thought I would tell you how our little exhibition went. It went well enough. There was lots of free wine, and we all got rather smashed, and so did one of the sculptures by Tom Reilly-Dunseith. He went berserk, but a couple of us had a good giggle when he wasn't looking. It looked better broken than it did before. He sold everything in the show anyway, even the broken one. I didn't sell anything. I blame my boring name.

Still, it wasn't all a waste of time. I got a nice letter from an art gallery in Galway. They have offered to display some of my paintings, and maybe even stage a solo show, and I'm going to travel down there and meet the owners. I'd like a few days away from The Big Smoke, just now, because my parents are splitting up.

They decided it would be a good time to tell us, halfway through Sunday lunch at their house, that they are getting divorced. There's not even a good reason. They're just bored with each other. That's the nineties for you. Boredom has suddenly become unacceptable. They've been bored with each other for twenty years, from what I can see, but nobody said a word about it until now.

I really think I will change my name, now. What do you think of Emily Fitzwilliam-Morris, Anne Connolly-Smith or Mary Montague-Skye?

Please send me a signed picture.
I am a genuine fan.
Yours sincerely,
Brenda Brown

Brenda posted her letter as soon as the gold ink on the envelope was dry. It was the third letter she had posted to Nicolas Cage. She imagined him opening her letters while eating breakfast beside a turquoise swimming pool in LA. He was bound to notice her letters first, before all the others in his pile of mail. The pretty red envelopes would stand out in the mountain of fan mail he must receive every day. He might be wearing dark glasses and a brightly patterned shirt. Unbuttoned. Did Americans eat marmalade with their toast, she wondered. Or toast, even? No. Probably pancakes and syrup. Yes, that was it. Pancakes and syrup on a white plate beside the red letters with gold ink on the front. It was a pleasing image. She might put something like that in the background of her next painting.

·14·

Three Mugs

Rose Thompson sat down with a sigh, in the back room of the flower shop. There was a stack of mail to be answered and several bills to be paid. On the positive side, there was lots of flower arranging to be done. There were ten identical, formal bouquets to be made up for the conference room of a luxurious hotel, and the stock for the coming months to be ordered from the wholesalers. On top of that, she had to go back to the house she had shared with her husband, John, for four years, to collect her things. Her remaining dresses and shoes, an overgrown cheese plant, a wooden giraffe ornament from Africa and thirty-one books on flower arranging. It wasn't much to show for four years in the city.

She would go after work. It was cowardly of her to have avoided it for three months now. She would clear out the back of the delivery van at lunchtime, to make room for her stuff. Hopefully, John would be out. He was a very attractive man, and she didn't want to complicate things with a good-bye kiss that might lead to something more. They were not compatible, and that was the end of it. It was not a good idea to stay married to a man just because you fancied him like mad.

She switched on the kettle and reached for the first letter in the pile. Today would be the day she tidied up a few loose ends.

At six o'clock, she closed the shop and put on her cardigan. It was only a ten-minute drive to the house. It was a bright evening, and she was feeling pleased with herself after all her industry that day. She might have a meal in Muldoon's when she was finished with the clear-out. She almost enjoyed the journey and soon she was driving down the familiar Edwardian terrace toward her marital home. She was disappointed to see that he had let the garden go. She had only been gone twelve weeks, and already there were weeds establishing themselves in the cracks of the tiled path. The tiny lawn badly needed a trim. There were two crisp-packets in the hedge. And the plants in the hanging baskets above the door were dead. They were dried up and yellowed, the baskets twirling round and round in the breeze. John had forgotten to water them, she fumed. After she had gone to such trouble to find plants that only needed to be watered once a week. Any thoughts of a good-bye kiss evaporated. The man had no regard for the garden at all. She opened the front door with a sigh, stepped in and closed the door quietly behind her.

The house was a mess. Pizza boxes on the coffee table, newspapers on the floor. Cups and plates on the mantelpiece. The cheese plant hung neglected and limp in its corner.

There was a sudden movement in the kitchen. Rose swung round. There was an attractive young woman standing there, wearing one of John's shirts, and nothing else. Actually, she wasn't a woman. More like a girl of twenty. Peroxide white bob and tanned legs. Toenails painted baby pink. Blue eyelashes like spiders from another planet. She appeared to be waiting for the kettle to boil.

"You must be Rose," said the young woman.

"Yes," said Rose. "I'm sorry. I don't know who you are."

"I'm Cindy. John didn't say you'd be coming today."

"I didn't tell him. I just decided to turn up, unannounced."

"Oh. Well, he's upstairs. I'll call him."

"No, don't bother. I'll go—"

"Someone to see you, Johnny!" the girl called out. "It's Rose!" Bit of a hippy, she thought, and she did up a few more buttons on her shirt.

"Oh my God!" A man's voice. There was a scramble in the front bedroom and Rose's shamefaced husband came hurrying down the stairs and into the sitting room, wearing only his trousers. He handed a dressing gown to Cindy and she slipped it on quickly. He stood beside Cindy. They looked like a proper couple, somehow. More than John and Rose had ever looked. Rose thought she was going to cry with jealousy and embarrassment and grief. Now she could see why he hadn't had enough time to water the flowers in the hanging baskets.

"Rose," he said, "I wasn't expecting you. You look nice." He folded his arms. It wasn't much of a speech, after his dramatic entrance. He made a face at Cindy and nodded to her to leave the room and go upstairs. But Cindy wasn't keen to leave the two of them alone. She smiled at him and pretended not to understand.

"Well, John," said Rose. "I must say, I'm sorry for barging in like this. I didn't know you had company . . ."

"Rose, this is Cindy, my new assistant. And Cindy, this is Rose. My wife. My ex-wife. Ah, this is a little embarrassing, ladies."

Cindy smiled at Rose, without blinking her blue eyelashes once, and Rose smiled back at Cindy, through gritted teeth. John grinned at the two women. An awkward silence descended. The three of them stood there, as if they were waiting to go into the theater, or catch a bus. Rose wondered if she had remembered to take off yesterday's mascara. (She hadn't.) Or if her lilac toenail polish was chipped. (It was.) She also wondered how John could have replaced her so quickly. He was truly modern, after all. Keep moving forward, that was his motto. No time for nostalgia and memories in his busy life. She knew then that she would have to collect her things that day. She didn't want to come back here, ever again.

"Well," she said, coolly. "I'll just gather up some odds and ends, and be out of here, as soon as I can. You two just carry on with whatever you were doing when I interrupted you."

"Now, Rose, there's no need to be like that," began John. "You left me, after all! I never wanted you to leave." Cindy's smile didn't waver, but she looked slightly deflated.

"You wanted me to sell burglar alarms and computers, John."

"You could have said no. You didn't have to move out, for God's sake."

"You know I'm a florist. That I love flowers."

"Yes, indeed I do." More than you loved me, he thought.

"What do you mean by that?" said Rose, picking up on the tone rather than the sense.

"Nothing." Cindy never disagreed with him the way Rose did. Cindy thought he was great.

"Would you like a cup of coffee?" asked Cindy, trying to keep things civilized.

"No, thank you. But don't let me stop you having one . . ." She went up the stairs in a daze, while Cindy withdrew to the kitchen, satisfied there would be no emotional making-up scenes that day.

As John and his new assistant perched on the sofa, sipping their coffee, Rose went up and down the stairs like a whirlwind, flinging books and sandals into carrier bags, and deliberately not looking at the bed, which was in total disarray. There was a pair of pink, fluffy handcuffs dangling from the headboard. Rose's last remaining feelings of love for John finally withered up and died like the hanging baskets at the front door. Within minutes she was ready to leave. The wilting cheese plant was rescued and placed carefully in the back of the van.

"There's the key," she said. "I don't expect I'll be needing it anymore." She pressed it firmly into his outstretched hand.

He nodded his thanks.

"Well, John, I'll say this for you. You don't let the grass grow under your feet. So to speak. It's just a pity you weren't so energetic in the garden."

"Oh, sorry. I've been too busy, what with one thing and another. I've been training Cindy up, you see . . ."

Cindy blushed when he said that. Rose noticed the way her husband's dark chest hair curled into little circles. She still found him highly desirable, but she knew she had made the right decision. He was the sort of person who lived only for the moment. He would never be a gardener.

It was time: the good-bye–moment had arrived. John stood up. So did Cindy. John wanted to hug Rose but he couldn't. He had the key and the mug in his hands, and a possessive assistant standing beside him.

Cindy spoke first. "I'll be upstairs," she said to John. "Ah . . . nice to meet you, Rose."

"I'll just have that, if you don't mind," said Rose, whipping the china mug from the young girl's hand. "That mug was a wedding present from my sister."

"So it was," said John. "You may as well have this one, too. It's a matching pair." He swallowed the last of his coffee and handed his mug to her. It was still warm. They both watched the back of Cindy's perfect legs going up the narrow staircase.

"Good-bye, Rose," John said. "I'll miss you."

Rose held the two mugs to her chest and, without saying another word, walked out into the evening sunshine without looking back. She clambered into the van and placed the two mugs on the passenger seat. She tried not to see the irony of the situation as she pulled out from the curb.

"There are three mugs in this vehicle," she said softly.

The front door of the little house was closed again, with John no doubt on his way to join Cindy in the bedroom.

On the way back to her temporary home, Rose waited for the tears to fall, but nothing happened. She felt numb. In a way, it was a good thing to have any silly notions of a reunion crushed like this. It was time to move on. She thought of Connemara and her childhood home. That was what she really missed, if she was honest. She needed to be back there, so her soul could start to heal itself.

He's a buck-eejit, she thought sadly. But a very handsome buck-eejit.

·15·

Sadie Has a Plan

Sadie Smith was good at hiding things. She had packets of chocolate buttons hidden all over the house, for sweet-toothed emergencies. Early one morning, before anyone else in the house was awake, she got up and put on her pink satin dressing gown. She lifted Arnold's car keys off the hall table and dropped them into a jug on top of the dresser. Then, she went into her tidy kitchen and put some milk on to boil. Sadie loved coffee made with milk. She hummed a marching tune as she placed the breakfast dishes on the table.

When it was time for Arnold to leave the house, he discovered his keys were missing. Sadie expressed surprise and joined in the hunt, searching down the back of the sofa with great enthusiasm. After half an hour, they gave up. He had to use a spare set of keys to go to work.

"Don't worry, I'll find them when I'm dusting," she said cheerfully, as she waved him off. "They won't have gone far."

When she had washed the breakfast dishes and settled her parents-in-law in front of the radio in the sitting room, she crept down the hall with Arnold's keys in her dressing gown pocket. She opened the study door and went inside. Just like her husband, it was neat and tidy, and self-important. There was an elegant desk, a comfortable leather chair and hunting prints on the dark green walls. Arnold didn't need this silly study. It was just an excuse to get away from them all when they were watching television in the evening. She realized suddenly that he spent hardly any time with her, or the parents he claimed to love so much.

Sadie tried the desk drawer. It was locked. Examining the bunch of keys, she found a small bronze one and tried it in the lock. It worked.

There were holiday brochures for Paris inside.

"Mmmm," said Sadie. "Very nice."

Underneath the brochures was a photograph of Arnold at a double-glazing exhibition in England. Beside him was the mystery blonde. She was a spiky creature, thought Sadie, as she peered at the picture. Feathery blond highlights and pointy red fingernails. Stiletto heels and long false eyelashes. Her tanned legs were so thin, Sadie wondered how they could even hold her up. She was fleshless and bloodless, like a vampire.

Sadie's face flushed as red as the nails of the hateful cuckoo in the picture. Turning the picture over, she read the back. It said: *Arnold and Patricia, Essex, 1998.* She had to find out if they just worked together, or if her cocky little husband had managed to find himself a stick-thin lover.

Later that morning, Sadie went shopping. She had to buy a new cardigan for Maurice, and collect a prescription for Daisy. On a sudden impulse, she went to Muldoon's Tea Rooms. She would ask if they'd found the umbrella she had left on the doorstep, on the dreadful day of the discovery. There were a few empty seats near the window, but Sadie went over to the table in the corner where she had eaten the cherry cheesecake. She needed somewhere private to think, she told herself. She needed peace to make her plans without Maurice and Daisy distracting her every five minutes. She ordered the chicken special with extra chips, and for pudding the chocolate fudge cake, with extra cream. For once in her life, she did not count the calories. She could feel whole layers of fat melting away with suppressed rage.

On the way home, she called into the locksmith's shop on Fountain Street and had another set of Arnold's keys made.

Sadie had a plan.

"I'll get you, you overdressed, overbearing, oversexed little creep," she said, as she marched, burping, to the bus stop.

Beatrice and Alice Crawley were planning to call in to Muldoon's. They were eager to tell

Penny about the important letter they had received from City Hall.

At last, at long last, their charity work was going to be publicly acknowledged! The Mayor of Belfast was hosting a formal lunch in the City Hall for all those people who had collected large sums of money for the maintenance of war memorials across Europe. A small gathering of select individuals would be served a five-course meal in the banqueting suite. Afterward, several important guests would each make a speech.

When the speeches were over, there was to be an exhibition of wartime photographs in the foyer of City Hall, and they were invited to submit some pictures of their father, Sergeant William Crawley, of the Pioneer Corps.

There would be some VIP guests there, but no exact details could be given at this stage. The letter said: *Arrangements are ongoing.*

Reporters would be covering the event. Beatrice and Alice might end up in the papers. They would definitely be on the teatime news. Frank Mitchell, one of the presenters with Ulster Television, would be there to interview them. They were giddy with speculation as to the identity of the mystery guests.

"Do you think the queen might be coming?" whispered Alice.

"Oh! Maybe that's why they didn't say who it was. For security reasons." Beatrice had her hands over her mouth. Both women looked at their reflections in the antique mirror above the fireplace. Then, they hurried up the stairs as fast as their old campaign legs would allow them and began to try on hat after hat after hat.

·16·

Something Good Happens to Henry

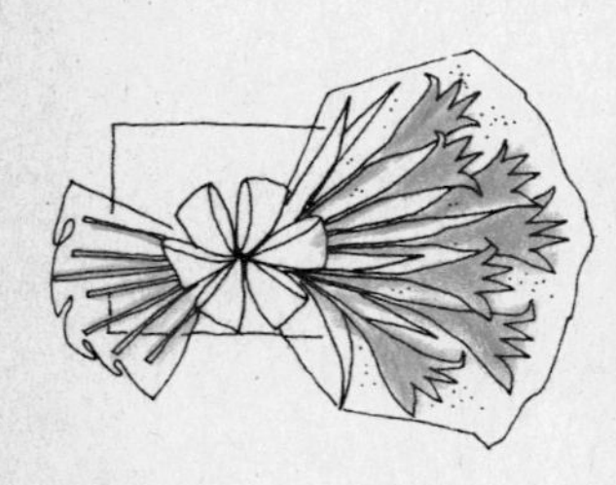

Henry left the house, with a folded newspaper clutched in his hand. He walked aimlessly along the Malone Road and the Lisburn Road. Out of habit, he crossed into Mulberry Street, and ended up outside Muldoon's Tea Rooms. He often came here when he was feeling lonely. He went in. Penny was behind the counter.

"What can I get you, Henry? You look like

you need cheering up. I can recommend the custard slices, and the chicken special."

Henry smiled at her, but ordered only coffee and a sandwich. He stared out of the window, wondering what to do. I suppose I can live with this, he thought. If it makes Aurora happy, I suppose I can live with it.

"What would you say if your husband wanted to spend his life savings on home improvements?" said Henry to Penny, when she brought his order.

"I'd kneel down on the floor and kiss his feet," said Penny. "And I'm not exaggerating."

"Goodness me," said Henry. He'd always thought Penny was not aware of how shabby the interior of Muldoon's was. He knew now he would get no sympathy from Penny where home improvements were concerned.

"How's the building work coming along?" asked Penny.

"It's starting any day now," he said. "Just a few formalities."

"Don't worry," said Penny. "Something good will come of it."

Henry stirred his coffee and looked out of

the window. A graceful woman with long red hair came out of the florist's shop across the road and lifted some flowers from one of the containers. As she straightened up, the sun caught her copper-colored hair and it shone like fire. It was not the first time Henry had noticed her but today, somehow, was different. The woman's face was pale and very beautiful, and she had thin white ankles. She was wearing a red dress with an Indian-style print on it, a black sweater and red ankle boots to match her skirt. The sight of her, with her white face and ankles, and her red dress, and the bunch of lilies in her arms, made Henry feel suddenly young and old at the same time. He felt intense desire.

The woman went back inside the shop. Henry continued to stare at the empty doorway. He had a daydream in which he was kissing her, not lustfully, but gently. Tenderly. Holding her delicate face in his manly hands. He did not kiss Aurora very often. He hadn't tried to for ages. He was afraid she might give him marks out of ten for effort. It was hard to compete with fictitious heroes riding wild stallions across the moors of Yorkshire, through horizontal rain and biting winds.

"Was that all, Henry?"

Henry realized that Penny was still standing there.

"I think I will have that custard slice, after all," he said, smiling up at her.

"I knew you'd cheer up, eventually," she said.

Henry went across to the flower shop when he had finished his sandwich. He told himself he wanted to buy Aurora some premium lilies, to show her he was sorry for the fuss he'd made about the conservatory. But the truth was, he wanted to see that beautiful woman with the red hair again. His heart began to beat faster as he went into the cool, dark interior of the shop.

There she was. She was picking up leaves and petals from the floor of the shop. She looked up at him with narrow green eyes. Her face was covered with hundreds of pink freckles. She was much younger than he was. Early thirties?

She smiled and said hello.

* * *

Aurora loved the lilies. Even though she made a little joke about lilies being associated with death and funerals. But anyway, she did love them. And the perfume was magnificent. She forgave Henry at once. Arnold Smith was informed that the work could begin without delay, the moment planning permission was granted. The diggers moved in and Henry's greenhouse was taken away in a skip, with the sweet-smelling herbs and rare flowers still inside it, wobbling frantically in their pots. On the day that his uncle's tree was wrenched out of the soil, Henry felt a pain in his heart and had to leave the house and go for a walk. On his return, he received three more rejection letters from various publishers in the post.

The building work took over their lives. There were burst pipes, power failures and arguments with the neighbors about the noise and the dust. Aurora took time off work to keep an eye on things. Henry was spending more time than ever in his bookshop and eating most of his meals in Muldoon's. Aurora hardly noticed if he was there or not, as she sat in the half-built conservatory, considering applications to join the Brontë Bunch and fussing over her costume for the BBC documentary: a black dress with a hoop and petticoats and a white lace bonnet.

David Cropper phoned again and invited Aurora and Henry out to dinner. He was very excited about the filming, which had been given the go-ahead from a senior director in the BBC. A late-night slot on BBC2 was cleared for the documentary, he told her. Aurora accepted at once but didn't invite Henry. He wasn't interested in the project, she told herself. He would only be suffering in silence at the table. Or worse, telling Mr. Cropper exactly what he thought of the Brontë Bunch. And so, she told Henry she was dining out with a group of filmmakers from the BBC. All terribly boring, and no need for Henry to be there. Well, she didn't want to make her husband jealous, when there was no reason for him to be.

But, when David Cropper rang the doorbell at Aurora's house, and she met him for the first time, she changed her mind. He was absolutely gorgeous, and Aurora was sorry that she had worn her hair in a tight knot and a matronly jacket with a high collar. She was as tongue-tied as a silly schoolgirl, making hopeless quips about the weather. However, he seemed delighted with her. They went down the steps together, arm in arm, and he opened the door of his car for her and closed it gently when she was safely settled in the passenger seat.

He took her to a lovely restaurant on Linenhall Street, and they had a delicious meal of lobster and dressed salad, and two bottles of white wine. Aurora was very impressed with the oil paintings on the walls, and the polite and discreet service of the waiting staff, and she was even more impressed with David's sleepy brown eyes and his impeccable suit. His black hair was flecked with gray, but somehow he looked well-educated and upper-class, not old at all. As the perfectly chilled wine did its magic work, Aurora and David became quite flirtatious. He was able to finish off any quotation she began. It was very exciting.

Aurora was thrilled when some other television people came into the restaurant, and David stood up to introduce her to them, and there was lots of hand-shaking and air-kissing. The new arrivals eventually sat at another table, but they sent over a couple of drinks for David and his companion, and Aurora felt that she was now part of a select (and small) group of Belfast intellectuals. Halfway through the evening, she felt like she had known him, always.

She had been more than a little tipsy, she told herself later, when she remembered some of her dramatics at the restaurant table. Halfway through her chocolate pudding, she had told him how close she felt to Emily Brontë, and how she thought Emily had spoken to her in the parsonage at Haworth. It was a kind of vocation, her desire to spread a love of literature. She must carry on the great work that Emily had begun. David listened to the tale without blinking or looking away once. In fact, at one point, he laid his elegant hand on Aurora's arm and gave it a little squeeze.

She apologized afterward, of course, when the effect of the wine began to wear off. But he told her he was delighted with her. "Enchanted" was the right word, really, he added. He could feel a certain chemistry between them, he said, as he ordered two Irish coffees. They were on the same wavelength. Together, he told Aurora, they would show the rest of the world that there was more to Belfast than people thought. More than bombs and protests and flags and hysteria.

Keep talking, you handsome devil, she thought. But she only smiled demurely at him and picked a small box of matches off the counter, with the logo of the restaurant on it, when they were leaving. To keep as a memento.

During the drive home, with David appearing sober as a judge, he explained how the film would be made. He must be a man accustomed to business dinners, Aurora thought, as she struggled to stay awake. She had an overwhelming urge to lie down somewhere, but she wasn't sure if it was the wine, or David Cropper's brown eyes, that was the reason for it. Budgets and schedules were discussed. Aurora thought she saw a twinkle in his eyes when she described the yards and yards of white cotton that would be required to make the petticoat for her costume, and she became shy, and changed the subject.

Too soon, they were back at the house. When Aurora stepped out of David's rather shabby little car, she stood on the pavement, watching him until he drove round the corner and out of sight. He was very attractive, she thought, and for a moment she fancied that he might find her attractive, too. But then she laughed at herself. She was far too old for a love affair. It was just the excitement of the television program that was making her feel light-headed.

She went inside the house, picking her way past Henry's collection of flowerpots. Really, there were too many of them on the doorstep. It was hard to get past when the flowers were in full bloom. She would say something to him about it when the shock of losing his garden wore off.

Henry was lying on the sofa, sipping a glass of red wine and reading a seed catalogue. Aurora was irritated by the sight of him, in his crumpled slacks and an old jumper. He might have tidied up the house a little. He might have done the vacuuming, for heaven's sake.

"There's not much call for catalogues anymore," she said, suddenly, before she could stop herself.

"I suppose not. But I like looking at the pictures. Did you enjoy the meal?" There wasn't a trace of jealousy or suspicion in his gentle voice. "You were gone hours. Where did they take you?"

"Christies Brasserie—it was fabulous," she told him. "Lovely sauce on the lobster. I've no idea what it was. And they have the place decorated so nicely. I can't think why we haven't been there before, ourselves." She was amazed at how easy it was to tell lies to Henry. Concentrate on minor details, that was the secret of being a good liar. "Did you manage to fix something for yourself?"

"I went to Muldoon's for fish and chips," he said. "I didn't bother to cook just for myself. I had a banana split as well."

"You'd want to be careful, Henry. You're going to get fat," said Aurora, thinking of David Cropper's very flat stomach and the silver buckle on his black leather belt. And then she hurried up the stairs to run a hot bubble bath for herself, anxious to get away from Henry—partly because she was feeling a bit dizzy with all the wine she had drunk and partly because she was feeling very guilty for being so unkind to him.

She was secretly delighted when Miss Wilkinson announced her retirement a few days later, and Aurora was appointed as school principal. The first person she called from the staffroom with the good news was David. He congratulated her warmly and arranged to take her out again, to celebrate.

•17•

Clare and Brenda Have Dinner

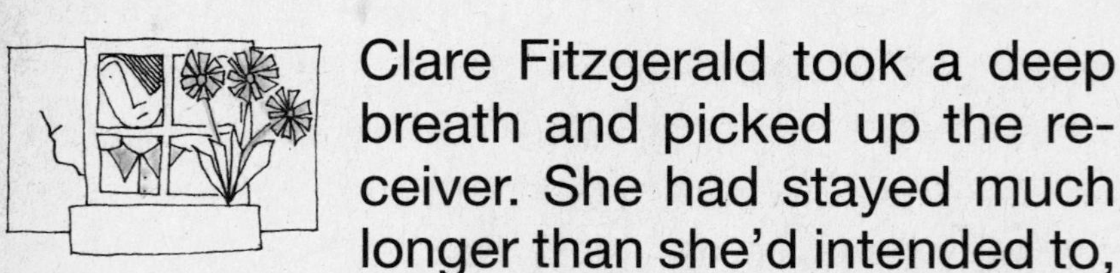

Clare Fitzgerald took a deep breath and picked up the receiver. She had stayed much longer than she'd intended to, on this third trip to Belfast, visiting old friends and relatives, and just walking around the shops taking in the atmosphere. She couldn't shake off the feeling that there was unfinished business to attend to—maybe she was hoping to bump into her long-lost love, Peter Prendergast.

The Waterfront Hall was impressive, as were those city-slicker apartments across the river. Who'd have thought stubborn old Belfast would have something so modern? And there were some decent restaurants, too; like that very minimalist place, on the Malone Road. It was a pity she hadn't the time to write a feature on it. But now, it was time to go home.

She sat on the bed in her hotel room and dialed the long number carefully. She began placing her tubes of vanilla-scented hand-cream and her pretty glass bottles of perfume in the suitcase, as she waited for the call to be answered.

"Hello, the editor's desk, can I help you?"

"Hello, is that you, Mike? Hi. How are you?"

"Clare! I'm good. You?"

"Yes, everything's fine here."

"Are you missing us, at all?"

"Yes, I think I'm finally ready to come home. Did you get the films in the post?"

"Sure did."

"The pictures, how did they come out? What did you think? Lovely old house, wasn't it? Original fireplaces and everything."

"Oh, yeah, real nice."

"They had a really gorgeous rose garden, actually, and a crumbling old summerhouse with ivy all over it. I might even put a shot from that film on the cover."

"You want me to go ahead with that?"

"Mmmm . . . yes, that one with the pink roses over the door of the summerhouse. And I thought, white lettering laid over the dark ivy on the left-hand side? Yes. Go ahead with the design, will you?"

"Okay. So, what's the deal? How are you?"

"How am I? To tell the truth, when you first suggested a feature on Belfast, I thought you were mad, but it was good. I've had a bit of a wander down memory lane."

"That's what I figured. Meet anyone interesting?"

"Me and a few school chums had a great night out at the weekend."

"Clubbing?"

"At my age? In Belfast! No, we went to a quiet little restaurant."

"Any cute guys there?"

"No, I didn't meet anyone. Do you never give up? I've told you a million times, I like being single."

"Yeah, right!"

"Yes, I do."

"Whatever. You sound tired."

"Yes, I'm a little tired. I'm glad I'll be home tomorrow. Doing the tourist-thing does drain my energy."

"What flight are you on? I'll send a car to pick you up."

"I'll be in JFK about seven PM. Your time."

"So, what are you doing, the last night in your hometown?"

"Tonight? I'll just have dinner sent to my room."

"Come on!"

"No, really it's easier that way. Trust me. I've been doing that most nights. I'll go to bed early this evening, and I'll see you tomorrow."

"Okay."

"No problems there with you? Did you manage to get a fruit-picking ladder for the French linen shoot?"

"Yeah, I did. And it wasn't easy."

"Good. Good-bye, then."

"Bye, Clare."

She hung up. Mike was the best personal assistant in the business. He took care of the office when she was away and he did things the way Clare wanted them to be done. Not like some assistants who could make themselves very comfortable, indeed, in the boss's chair.

Clare knew she could send the photographer on assignments, on his own, to get the pictures. He was very good, but she just felt better when she was there, too. She was good at spotting the little details that gave the magazine its character. That old summerhouse in the garden of the mansion in Stranmillas, for example. Would he have thought of taking some romantic pictures of it? With the evening light falling on the creeper, and the door just a little bit open so that you could see the wicker chairs inside, it would make the most romantic cover ever. There was a real feeling of longing in those empty chairs. What lovers had sat there, over the years?

Stop it, she told herself. Stop daydreaming. That was all such a long time ago. And it was probably nothing, anyway. It probably meant nothing to him. He was just being nice to me because I was an innocent teenager. He wouldn't know me now if he met me on the street. Oh, I'm such a drama queen . . .

But it was no good. She was going to have to go there again, for a last look. One last look at her old flat and Muldoon's, and that would be the end of it.

She put on her blue coat, and a navy felt hat that came right down to her eyes, and she left the hotel. She walked slowly along Shaftesbury Square, stopping to look in the window of a new art gallery, and then along the Lisburn Road, and turned eventually, into Mulberry Street.

The cafe was open. The owner's hadn't changed it one bit in all this time. Not even the sign. It was a strange little place, really. It was like a magical shop in a children's book; ordinary-looking from the outside but magical within. Or was her imagination just running wild again?

The moon and stars were visible in the sky. It was getting dark. The overhead lamps in the tea house made a bright pool of light on the pavement, criss-crossed by the shadows of the people inside. There were quite a few customers sitting at the tables at that moment. In fact, she couldn't see one empty table, and she didn't want to have to share with anyone. That would mean another long chat about America. She wanted to be alone with her memories. She would not go in yet.

She walked on a few steps and stood looking up at the window of the tiny flat where she had spent that night with Peter, all those years ago. Such a small little window. The very sight of it made her shiver. There were dandelions growing on the sill, she noticed.

A pale face appeared at the dark window, with a black fringe hanging over one eye. Clare froze with the shock of it. The short black hair and the prominent cheekbones were the same. She was shaking and her hands went up to her mouth. But of course it wasn't Peter. He would be forty by now. She must be going mad. Then, the apparition looked right at her and she realized suddenly the pale face was that of a young woman. And she looked almost as shocked as Clare was herself. Clare hurried away down the street but seconds later she heard the sound of a door opening, and Brenda Brown was calling after her.

"Are you all right? Is something wrong?"

"No. Not at all. I thought you were someone else. I'm sorry if I startled you."

"That's okay. I thought you were going to

collapse or something. That's all. But I've lived here for years. Are you sure you have the right address?"

"Oh, yes. But the person I knew never lived here. I did. You just look like—them, a little bit, that's all." Clare was reluctant to tell Brenda that she had spent the night with a man she had only known for a few hours, twenty years earlier. Or that she had mistaken Brenda for a boy. "I'm sorry," she said again, and turned to leave.

"Please, don't go! Not yet. Have a cup of tea, at least. Would you like to come in and sit down for a minute? You look very shaken. I'm Brenda Brown, by the way. I'm an artist."

"Clare Fitzgerald. Pleased to meet you." They shook hands.

Clare knew she shouldn't go in. It was asking for trouble. She wasn't sure she could handle the emotional minefield of seeing her old home. But she went up the stairs like a robot and entered the first-floor flat without saying a word. Brenda hovered behind her as she went into the sitting room.

"My God," said Clare, "it's just the same. The same carpet, the same table, the same sofa. The furniture hasn't even been moved. There's nothing different at all."

"Yes, well, the landlord is a total Scrooge. I daresay it is the same."

"You're an artist, you say?" Clare was standing in the middle of the room. She was looking at the paintings stacked around the walls. Her curiosity was aroused in spite of the upsetting circumstances.

"Yes."

"What do you paint?"

"Oh. Things. Sad things." Now that Brenda finally had an interested audience, she couldn't think of one profound thing to say. "Just ordinary people. Disappointed people."

"Do you sell them?"

"Yes and no. They're for sale, but nobody ever buys them."

"Can I look?"

"Feel free," said Brenda, handing Clare a list of the titles.

Clare read the list aloud. "*Waiting for Silence, The End of the Day, A Belfast Mother, A Shankill Kitchen, Waiting for the Priest, Waiting for Dawn* . . ."

"Mmmm," said Brenda. "There's a lot of waiting, isn't there?"

Clare looked at the paintings for a little while. She thought they were good. A little over-the-top. But good. A lot of potential, if the subject matter was less intense.

"Can I see the bedroom?" asked Clare suddenly. For a moment, Brenda thought she was talking about a painting called *The Bedroom*. She was puzzled. Had she a painting somewhere, called that? Then she realized that this strange woman wanted to see her actual bedroom. Brenda was worried. This glamorous stranger might well be mentally ill, asking to see someone's private rooms. But something in the older woman's face was calm and reassuring.

"It's in there," she said, indicating an open door in the hall.

"I know where it is," said Clare, and she went in as Brenda hovered in the doorway. It was the same bed: a cheap, wrought-iron Victorian bed with part of the flower design missing. Faded floral wallpaper. A kitchen chair instead of a locker. Only the carpet was different. Plain gray. (That was Brenda's doing. She had ruined the old one by dropping a tube of oil paint on it. Months, it took her, to save up for that new carpet.)

"The carpet in this room used to be as

awful as the wallpaper," Clare said. A fat tear rolled down her cheek.

Brenda looked away while Clare dried her eyes. Would this emotional woman buy a painting, she wondered. She could do with the money but she didn't like to ask.

"So? You say, you used to live here?"

"Yes," said Clare. "I was a student here, ages and ages ago. I lived here in this very flat for a year or so."

"Survived here, you mean," said Brenda. "It's like Siberia, in the winter."

"Still no central heating? It shouldn't be allowed in this day and age. I still have a spare key, actually. At home, somewhere."

"Locks have been changed a few times," said Brenda, "judging by the state of the door." She hesitated, looking at Clare. "Who did you think I was?"

"Well, I just thought you were an old friend of mine."

"What was her name?"

"That's the funny thing . . . it was a boy, actually, with the same hairstyle. I mean, I couldn't really see your face behind the fringe. You don't look like a boy at all, of course."

"Old boyfriend, was it?"

"Yes and no, to borrow your phrase. I didn't know him that long but I was hoping it would lead to something special. Just an instinct I had."

"Yes. I know what you mean. Sometimes, you just know."

"Seeing anyone special yourself?" Clare thought she had better say something normal to lighten the strained atmosphere.

"Yes. I am." Brenda wondered why she had said that.

"Are you in love with him? I'm sorry, you don't have to answer that. I'm terrible for asking. I'm a hopeless romantic."

"It's okay. Well, yes, I am in love, but it's not easy for us. He doesn't live in Belfast."

"Where does he live?"

"He lives in America."

"Wow. So do I. What part?"

"Los Angeles."

"I'm based in New York. What's his name?"

Brenda thought of telling the truth, but then she decided to bend it a little. She thought of the film, *Moonstruck.*

"He's called Nic. He's a—a baker. He bakes bread. It's a family business.

"Really?" said Clare. "How fascinating.

Listen, speaking of bread, I'm starving. Why don't we go next door and get something to eat. My treat. And you can tell me all about it."

Brenda hadn't eaten all day and was already reaching for her jacket. The two women went down the stairs. Clare's hand shook a little as she switched off the light. She took a last look around the shabby hall and pulled the weather-beaten door closed behind them.

"So tell me about this boyfriend," said Clare, as they settled down at a free table in Muldoon's.

"Well, he's Italian-American. Very handsome. Even though he's only got one hand. He could give up work but it's a family business. The Italians are funny like that—about work, you know? Very strong ethic. He loves opera music, and he looks pretty fabulous in a tuxedo." Brenda didn't know why she was telling such outrageous lies, but she had started now, and she couldn't stop. Maybe she wanted to be an entertaining dinner companion to this elegant woman who had taken such an interest in her work.

"Just order whatever you like," said Clare. "You need feeding up, I can see. You students are terrible at taking care of yourselves. And I know how much it costs to be an artist. I was at the art college, myself, you know. For a while."

"Here in Belfast? Really? When?"

"Too long ago. 1982. I did fine art, too."

"Are you a working artist now?"

"No. I work in publishing—interiors," Clare responded as a pretty woman in a pink wool dress came to take their order.

Penny smiled at Brenda but didn't address her by name. Penny was a professional person, as well as being very polite. Interiors? Ah, yes, that was where she had seen this woman before—she had spoken to Penny some months before, looking for that fancy magazine.

"Chicken in sun-dried tomato sauce and garlic wedges. Selection of bread and butter. Pot of tea. Coffee cake and whiskey ice cream," said Brenda quickly, scanning down the menu. Then she looked at Clare. "Is that too much?"

"Not at all," said Clare, kindly. Really, it wasn't polite to order dessert without being invited to, but the young girl looked so hungry. "I'll have the same, I think," she said to a smiling Penny. Penny hurried into the kitchen to tell Daniel that Brenda Brown had found herself a rich friend. A magazine editor, no less. Maybe she was on the road to fame and fortune at last.

"So, tell me why you don't pick up sticks and follow this young man of yours to America?" said Clare, as they waited for the food to arrive. "Seems such a waste, to be apart, if you care about him so much."

"Well," said Brenda, "it's partly because his mother doesn't want him to be with me. She wants him to marry a nice Italian girl, to help him in the bakery. And partly because of my career. I want to establish myself here, as an artist. It's very important to me that my work is understood in my hometown.

"I see. Your boyfriend must be very understanding. To wait for you, I mean."

"Yes. He is. What was the name of the fella you knew, when you lived in the flat?"

"Peter."

"Peter what? I might have heard of him."

"Prendergast."

"No, don't know any Prendergasts. Sorry. Where did you meet?"

"At a disco. We liked the same sort of music. I was crazy about music when I was younger. My favorite group was Human League—"

"I know them. They're still together, still giving concerts."

"Yes, I know. I've seen them many times. And the three of them still look absolutely fantastic! I really admire them."

Brenda studied her new acquaintance. She wore far too much makeup. Red lipstick. Red lip liner—corners on the top lip instead of soft curves. Dyed black hair. Severe bob hairstyle. That velvet coat was a bit pretentious. All those bangles jangling on her wrists. Four rings on each hand. It was a bit much, in all fairness. Still, she was a generous person; she was paying for the meal, after all. And she was very easy to talk to.

"Do you still like 80s music?" asked Brenda.

"Oh, yes, I'm afraid I do. I love it."

"All those wacky hairdos?" smiled Brenda.

"Well, I had a little penchant for men with unusual hairstyles back then."

"Oh, yeah, that's right." And she touched her fringe. "So. Tell me about your job. How do you pick the houses for your magazine?"

"I look for details that are special, unique, uplifting. Inspiring."

Brenda had a sudden feeling that her own paintings were too depressing. Was that why she never sold anything? Should she try using a bit more color?

Clare seemed to know what Brenda was thinking. "You know what?" she said, thoughtfully. "I think I'd like to buy one of your paintings, before I leave tomorrow. Do you think I could come round very early in the morning and choose one before I go to the airport?"

"I'd be delighted," said Brenda, happily. And her joy was doubled when Penny arrived with the food, and Brenda noticed at once that Penny had given them much larger helpings than Daniel would have done.

"Have you got your eye on anything in particular?" said Brenda, as she reached for the salt and pepper shakers.

"Well, yes. There was one. A small square painting. *Waiting for My Love*, I think you said it was called."

"That's a self-portrait. Of me. I'll reserve it for you."

"It's very good. I like it very much."

·18·

Clare Confides in Penny

Penny was stacking cups on the counter early the following morning when Clare came in carrying an expensive-looking handbag and a brown-paper-wrapped package. Penny recognized her as the magazine editor. She had paid for a hefty meal for Brenda Brown and herself the night before, and several cups of coffee as well, the two of them had been engrossed in conversation for well over two hours. Penny wondered how they knew each other.

"Excuse me," said the woman. "My name is Clare Fitzgerald. I wonder if you could help me?"

"I'll certainly try," said Penny.

"I'm trying to find someone. You'll think I'm quite mad, but I'm trying to find a man I knew, in Belfast, about seventeen years ago."

"Well, what's his name?"

"Peter Prendergast."

"Oh, dear, I'm afraid I don't know any Prendergasts. And he lives around here, does he? I know the district well, I might be able to put you in touch with somebody else who might know him."

Clare smiled sadly. She wondered if she was losing her sanity, asking this brightly dressed waitress if she knew some man from the distant past. But the cafe was empty and the woman behind the counter looked very sympathetic. She decided to press on.

"I don't know anything else about him, actually. But I sat with him in this very cafe, you see . . . and I suppose I was hoping against hope he might sometimes come back here . . . We sat there, by the window, and talked for a couple of hours. I fell in love with him. Hopelessly. The way you do when you're young."

Both women laughed nervously.

"He wrote his address and telephone number on a cassette, and I put it in my handbag. Anyway, I lost the bag. There was a riot and I left it on a bus. I'm always losing things."

"Oh, dear," said Penny sympathetically, "but—forgive me for asking but—did you not give him your details?"

"Well, I didn't have a telephone in my flat, in those days. He knew where I lived, though. It was right next door from here, you see. He couldn't have forgotten the address."

(Ah, so she had lived in Brenda's flat!)

"But he didn't call. I searched for him at his university and left messages. I got an address for him from this girl, and I wrote. But I heard nothing. Then, my dad decided to move to England and soon we left. Cornwall, it was." She paused, and sighed. "I eventually moved to London to study. Then, when I got my degree, I went to America. I work in publishing now. Interiors. Storage is my thing. A place for everything, and everything in its place. Useful for a person like me! But, about Peter . . . you might think it was just a crush, but I never forgot him. And I thought . . ."

"And you thought it couldn't do any harm to look him up," said Penny quickly. "I understand. Tell me, did you not think of putting an ad in the *Belfast Telegraph*?"

"Oh, I'm not sure . . . that seems a bit extreme . . . he might not appreciate that . . . I mean, who knows what his circumstances are . . ."

"Yes, I know what you mean," said Penny. "Look, if you have no objections, I'll put a wee note in the window, and if anyone asks, I'll pass on the message. Will that do?"

"Thank you," said Clare. "You're very kind." She gave Penny her business card, with the name of the publishing house on it.

"That's okay. It's no problem. I know what it's like to be in love with someone you can't reach," said Penny, sadly.

Penny poured a cup of coffee for the lady in the velvet coat. "On the house," she said.

Clare Fitzgerald took it and went to sit near the window. Penny saw her touch the table with the palm of her hand, as if connecting with the long-ago encounter. They would have sat on the same chairs, at the same table. Peter and her. Nothing ever changed in Muldoon's. Penny was moved by the gesture and filled with sudden longing herself. The ache to hold a man, and feel wanted, and feel desire, had never been stronger.

And then, suddenly, Penny remembered something. A vague recollection of a letter, an image of a handwritten name.

She took Clare's business card and hurried to look in a drawer in the kitchen. There was one particular drawer that they hardly ever used; it was full of nails and thread, string and screwdrivers, paper bags, old receipts and business cards. Penny pulled the handle, but it wouldn't budge. She peered in and saw a piece of cardboard or something wedged down the side. In a sudden burst of temper, she grabbed the handle with both hands and pulled with all her strength. The cardboard tore, the drawer came right out of the dresser, and its entire contents scattered across the kitchen floor.

"This blasted kitchen!" she hissed. "Nothing works the way it should!" Bending down to retrieve the junk of years, she spied a faded envelope among the debris. There it was! It said, on the front: *To Clare Fitzgerald*.

Penny gasped out loud. She had probably seen it in the drawer dozens of times over the years but this was the first time the name meant anything to her. She hurried back to the front of the cafe with it. Clare was still sitting at the window.

"It's extraordinary but—I just found this, in a drawer," said Penny, breathless. "I wonder, could it be for you?"

Clare took the envelope and held it in both hands. Her breathing almost stopped. Penny went back behind the counter and tried not to stare.

Clare opened the envelope and read the note with tears in her eyes.

Dear Clare,

I feel a bit silly doing this, but I haven't heard from you and I'm anxious. I've called at the flat a few times, but there was no answer. You might have thought I made a fool of myself that night, when I said I loved you, but I meant it. If you still want to see me again, please get in touch. As I might have to move out of

my student house soon, here's my parents' address. I really miss you.
Love,
Peter

She turned the note over, and read the address on the back. Then she rushed to the counter and asked Penny to call a taxi right away. Penny was so excited herself, that she had to dial the number three times before she reached the taxi depot.

Clare went back to the table and sat, sipping her coffee to take her mind off the tangled mass of nerves that her body had become. She thought of Peter, and then tried not to think of him. She kept the painting she had bought on her lap, afraid to set it down, even on the table, in case she lost it. *Waiting for My Love*. A small canvas. Clare would be able to take it on the plane with her, as hand luggage. Only three hundred pounds. A bargain at twice that price. Clare wanted to pay more, but Brenda wouldn't hear of it. Socialist principles, she'd said.

Clare peeled off the brown wrapping paper and studied the self-portrait of Brenda Brown. With those deep shades of blue, and the vigorous brushwork, it could have been the face of a man or a woman. It could almost be a portrait of Peter. She would have it framed as soon as she got home, and hang it in her office in New York.

Her heart seemed to be fluttering in her throat. She concentrated on Brenda Brown.

Brenda was a funny little creature. She was living in that awful dump next door, until her boyfriend in America found a place for the two of them in L.A. and broke the news to his old-fashioned mother that he was going to marry an Irish girl. Poor Brenda, taking on a traditional Italian momma! Good luck to her. Usually, these holiday romances faded away with the suntan.

And she wasn't a bad painter, either. Maybe she would have more luck with her career when she moved to America. Coming from Belfast, she would have some novelty value. Brenda had refused to believe her when Clare said that, although she assured her it was true. Sometimes, an artist just had to move away to a new place to be taken seriously. Nobody wanted to listen to a know-it-all from their own town.

Clare had taken one of Brenda's brochures and a nice snapshot of her and said that she might put a little note about her in the arts section of her magazine. She gave Brenda her business card, as well as the check for the painting.

Clare had achieved a lot, on this trip, in one way or another. She had enough photographs of the gentleman's residence in Stranmillas to fill an eight-page spread. She had the gorgeous pictures of the summerhouse, and one of them was definitely going on the front cover. She had met a Belfast artist and bought a beautiful painting. She had a small piece for the arts section, too. Whatever happened now; whether this note would lead her back to Peter or not, it had been a worthwhile trip.

All the same, she hoped it would help her to find Peter. She hoped with all her heart. When the cab pulled up outside the window of the tea house, and beeped its horn, Clare's heart contracted to the size of a walnut, with sheer desperation. She drank the remains of her coffee, gave Penny a huge hug, and went out to the taxi, hugging the portrait of Peter to her chest.

•19•

The Crawleys Go Shopping

Beatrice had been reading over and over the important-looking invitation from the City Hall in Belfast. In fact, Alice warned her that it was becoming a little bit grubby round the edges. Just to be on the safe side, they placed it in a pretty gold frame and set it on the mantelpiece.

"In light of the good work that you have both done for worthy causes, over the years," read Beatrice, *"the Lord Mayor in-*

vites you to join him for a formal lunch, followed by the official opening of our Wartime Memorabilia Exhibition. Please note: formal dress. RSVP." The 26th of September was the date of the lunch. Of course, they had replied the same day they received the invitation. Beatrice turned triumphantly to Alice. "I knew something like this would happen some day! All our good work rewarded at last!"

"I still can't believe it," whispered Alice. "We *must* find out if there are going to be any royal guests. Though I suppose they wouldn't say yet because of security reasons. There must be somebody on the council we could ask. Isn't Mrs. Cunningham from church something to do with bins and sewage?"

"Never mind that," said Beatrice. "She might not know either. Why would they tell Mrs. Cunningham, and not us? But what are we going to wear? Where are we going to find two perfect hats?"

"Don't panic," said Alice. "There's plenty of time."

Beatrice was doubtful. "The time will go quicker than you think. And there's so much to be done!"

They gave details of their father's regiment and military service, his many medals and heroic achievements and a selection of faded photographs to the organizing committee. There was one picture of Sergeant Crawley standing at the gates of Belsen concentration camp that the committee found very moving. They decided to have the picture enlarged and given pride of place in the exhibition. There was also a picture of them standing with their father in a war cemetery in France on Remembrance Day, 1973, five months before he died. It was their most treasured possession, but after the committee promised faithfully to take good care of it, they agreed to lend it to the exhibition.

Their acceptance of the invitation to the formal luncheon was confirmed and they booked special appointments at the local hair salon. Beatrice went on a diet, and Alice read all the vulgar celebrity magazines in the newsagent's from cover to cover. She was soon familiar with every well-known face in the Western world, and who they were married to, and what charities they supported. It was all very interesting, but she would never admit that to her sister, who read very intellectual poetry in the evenings.

"I don't want to come face-to-face with a VIP and not even know who they are," she said firmly, when she lifted a stack of magazines from her shopping bag and Beatrice raised her eyebrows in disapproval.

They continued to agonize about their outfits. They did not want to let Belfast down. They must look well on the big day, no matter who the guest of honor was. There would be photographers present and a camera crew from both of the local television stations. They might even appear on the national news. If there was nothing else of interest that day.

Of course, they did not want to outshine the VIP guests either. That would not be in good taste. They had a lengthy discussion about it and decided that they must assume the queen herself would be there. They must not, under any circumstances, appear underdressed. Or overdressed. The queen was known to wear dowdy colors from time to time. She was a conservative dresser by nature.

If they wore red, white and blue, they would appear embarrassingly over-patriotic. They didn't want to look like two left-overs from the Twelfth of July. Black was too somber. Black was for funerals. Royal blue was too *Margaret Thatcher.* White and cream were too bridal. Green was too Irish. Pink was too common, purple too regal. Alice worried that a busy pattern might give the queen a headache. Beatrice dismissed tweed as too provincial.

The days slipped by and still they had not chosen. They would have to find matching coats, hats and shoes, as well as dresses, handbags and accessories.

"Brooches!" cried Alice. "We must have brooches. The queen always wears a brooch high up on one shoulder."

"We can't afford to buy good jewelry," fretted Beatrice. "And I, for one, am not wearing paste to a royal luncheon! What if one of the stones falls out and we don't notice?"

The guest of honor had not been officially revealed yet, but there was a rumor going round the Crawleys' church that someone had overheard a local councilor telling his wife that the queen was definitely going to be there. It was a matter of life or death that they look fabulous on the most important day of their lives.

In desperation, they caught the train to Dublin. They had never been to Dublin before, but all the Belfast boutiques were full of sequins and embroidery and feathers. Who bought these ridiculous garments and where they wore them, was a mystery to the sensible Crawleys. There was nothing suitable for an occasion as grand and solemn as a Wartime Exhibition combined with a Formal Lunch and a Royal Visit.

They finally found exactly what they were looking for in Brown Thomas. The assistants were very kind and cheerful, and the sisters were amazed that nobody mentioned the partition of Ireland once. They paid for the biscuit-colored items, and crept out of the elegant store feeling like a couple of traitors. Beatrice transferred her purchases into empty HARRODS bags, just before the train pulled into Belfast. It was already dark as they hurried along Mulberry Street to their own little house.

"Tell no one where we bought these things," said Beatrice, as she paraded before the hall mirror. She studied the beige woolen dress and matching coat, and the brown hat and shoes. "Do you think I look like a shortcake finger that's been dipped in chocolate at both ends? Tell me the truth."

"You are the epitome of elegance," said Alice, laughing. She tried on her own finery: an oatmeal-colored jacket and long skirt, with blue sandals and a dainty hat with cornflowers on the rim. They had cream leather handbags with little gold clasps. "We look like royalty ourselves," continued Alice. "We could be mistaken for the crowned heads of Europe in these clothes. Nobody knows what the European royals look like anyway. We have only to get two brooches now, and we're ready. Do you know how to make a curtsy properly?"

"Well, of course I do," said Beatrice. "The trick is to get as low down as you can without actually falling over to the one side." And she promptly attempted one and fell in a heap.

"Now, when are we holding our tea party, and what kind of food will we serve?" asked Alice, when the two sisters sat down on the sofa with their bedtime mugs of Ovaltine.

"What tea party?" Beatrice was confused and still a little shaken after her tumble.

"Well, you don't think we are going to rub

shoulders with royalty without telling anyone, do you? We must invite the Reverend Pickford, and everyone in the choir. And we must get some of those biscuits that Prince Charles makes in his own kitchen."

"I'm going to bed, Alice dear," sighed Beatrice. "We'll talk about this in the morning."

·20·

Richard Allen Comes to Call

A handsome man came into the tea house a few days later and walked confidently to the counter. This rundown cafe wasn't his usual type of haunt but he was doing a spot of business in the area—yet another batch of young families moving out and selling their terraced homes to the developers. The demand for student bed-sits had sent house prices sky-high.

"Hiya! A coffee, please. Mocha, if you

have it." Richard Allen put his briefcase on the counter. His aftershave smelled very expensive and his sparkling, hazel eyes were full of mischief.

"Take a seat," said Penny, brightly. "I'll bring it right over." She was still on a high from the good news she had received that morning. Clare Fitzgerald had telephoned from America to say that when she turned up at the address on the back of the note, Peter's mother herself had answered the door. They didn't have long to talk because Clare's plane was due to take off in a couple of hours, but yes, Peter was still alive and well. And single.

"And would you believe it?" laughed Clare. "She told me he was living in America, too! In Boston, to be precise. All these years and I never knew!"

Clare had asked Mrs. Prendergast for his contact details and was delighted to be given both his home number and address, and his work details as well. Of all things, he was a detective!

She called him from the airport in Belfast. She couldn't wait to consider if he would be asleep, or anything. (He was.) She was afraid to leave things until she got home to

New York, just in case something else happened, to keep them apart. In case he met an attractive girl that very day and fell in love with her instead. Peter answered the phone on the second ring, and Clare wept into the phone like a lunatic.

"You won't believe this, Peter," she said, "but I just got your note today. I knew the lady in the cafe would be able to help me, and I'm so sorry we missed each other, before . . ."

"What?" said Peter. "Who is this?"

"It's Clare," she wept. "Clare Fitzgerald, from Mulberry Street."

This fantastic result had Penny riding high on a wave of emotion. Of course, another way of looking at things was that her absentminded father had forgotten to pass on the note, and so had kept the couple apart for all those years. But Clare seemed to have forgiven the Muldoon family for this terrible crime. She'd told Penny that they'd arranged to meet very soon, and that she was sure everything was going to pick up where it had left off.

Penny prayed for their happiness as she worked in the cafe. She had decided that Daniel would not be allowed to return to their bed until he had changed his ways for good. Tough love, that's what it was called, on the daytime television shows that Millie loved.

She watched Richard Allen slip off his designer jacket to reveal broad shoulders and a trim waistline, and she felt a long-dead tingling feeling in her heart. A hammering and a shortness of breath: the hallmarks of desire. She looked in through the hatch. Daniel was filling pastry shells with fresh cream and strawberries, lost in concentration, as usual.

Oh, I'm going to flirt with this new guy, she thought. *I am!*

Penny poured the coffee into one of the fancy chrome cups they didn't use very often, as they had to be hand-polished after use, and put two complimentary biscuits on the saucer. She pulled a tendril of curly hair from behind her right ear and let it dangle over her face. Then, she straightened herself up and glided over to Richard Allen's table. He was checking details in his notebook and did not look up.

"One mocha! Will there be anything else?" she said in a breezy voice.

"Ah, no. That's lovely, thanks," he replied.

"I haven't much time. I'm seeing a buyer in ten minutes."

"A buyer? Are you an estate agent?"

"Yes. For my sins. Are you thinking of selling? Let me give you my card . . ." He took a crisp, white business card from his breast pocket.

"Richard Allen. Thank you. I might just give you a call."

"Please do. I'll give you a good look-over!" he said.

I wouldn't say no, thought Penny.

"Well, I'm not thinking of selling the shop, as such. But, I am tinkering with the idea of buying a house in the area. Penny Stanley, is the name. But you can call me Penny."

"Well, I'm your man, Penny. Give me a call when you're ready to roll!"

"I'll do that, Mr. Allen. Thank you very much."

"Please, call me Richard."

Penny went back to the counter and dusted the shelves with renewed vigor. Daniel heard her humming a happy tune, and he was pleased. She must be in better spirits today, he thought.

•21•

Brenda's Priceless Melons of Delight

June 19, 1999
Dear Nicolas Cage,

I hope this letter finds you well.

I had a spot of good luck the other day. I sold one of my paintings! Hooray!

I'm in Muldoon's Tea Rooms, having a lovely meal as a reward. Scampi and chips. I mean, French fries. The person who bought the painting was a very cultured lady who happened to be passing by my flat. I mean, apartment. She's Belfast-born, but lives in America, like yourself.

I think the sale was a good omen because I got a letter this morning from the gallery in Galway that I went to visit. They want to stage a solo show for me. My first solo show. It opens in December, in the Blue Donkey Gallery. Which is kind of weird because most of my paintings are blue. I mean, the color blue. Not the jazz blue.

I am going to paint day and night and pour my heart and soul into every piece. I have sixty canvases already and they want me to do three really big ones for the window. I'm going to bring the whole lot down in a hired van and let them decide what to show.

It's so exciting, I've been on a high all day.

The small painting I've sent you is called The End of an Era. *It's about a factory closing down. It is one of my personal favorites. I hope you like it. It is to thank you for all the pleasure your films have given to me. (*Wild at Heart *is still my favorite, though.)*

Fond regards.
Yours sincerely,
Brenda Brown

PS. Please send me a signed photo.
I am a genuine fan.

Brenda read through her letter to Nicolas. It was quite short, and lighthearted in approach. That was good, because she wasn't feeling lighthearted at all. In fact, Brenda was feeling more than a little unstable, in recent days. She felt that her time as an artist was coming to an end. The credit card debts were getting very high; she could barely pay her bills last month. If the show in Galway was a flop, she would have to face up to her financial problems and get some sort of a job.

The people from the employment office were contacting her, all the time, with details of various vacancies. They told her that unless she accepted something soon, they would have to withdraw her benefit and rent checks. They must have been instructed to get tough with the long-term unemployed. Up until recently, they had seemed quite tolerant and even friendly. Seven job interviews they had arranged for her; and seven times Brenda had made a total mess of things. And it wasn't deliberate, either. She just couldn't stop herself from telling prospective employers what she thought of their businesses. It didn't help that she always had a few gin and tonics beforehand. But that was only to steady her nerves. The very idea of going to an interview in a sober state was unthinkable.

She told the people at the chemist's that she thought most of the beauty products on sale were simply little plastic pots of overpriced gunge. And that she wasn't a good enough liar to convince desperate old wrinkly women to buy them. And also, that she wouldn't be able to discuss any product of a sexual nature with the customers.

She told the butcher that his blood-spattered chopping block was upsetting her. And would he ever consider turning the place into a vegetarian soup parlor? She'd be happy to work there, if only it was a vegetarian soup parlor. They had such places in the U.S., she explained helpfully, and they were very popular with all sections of the community. Everybody loved soup: Catholics and Protestants, and everyone.

She told the civil servants at the local government headquarters that she didn't believe in democracy, and she wore a T-shirt with an anticapitalist slogan on it. She tried to explain her theories to them: how she thought that intellectuals should be in charge of the country. (Not career politicians in designer suits.) Jobs and the environment were the fundamental issues of the modern age, not flags and trivial religious squabbles. But the interviewing panel said they were only looking for temporary filing clerks and, unfortunately, they didn't have the time to discuss global politics with Brenda Brown or anybody else.

Brenda said that was the whole problem of the world in a nutshell: everybody was only interested in their own little empire, and they couldn't see The Big Picture. That planet Earth was just a fragile, little blue ball; spinning toward who-knows-what?

On her way out of the interview room, she reminded them that if the temperature of the planet increased by just six or seven degrees Celsius, then ninety-nine percent of all living things would die out within weeks. (Flags or no flags.) There would only be beetles, or something, left. They thanked her politely for the information.

She didn't get any of those jobs.

Worst of all was her experience with the Galwally branch of a major supermarket. They must have been absolutely desperate for staff, Brenda thought. Because they hired her straightaway, even though she told them the nonstop beeping of the electronic tills made her want to attack somebody. Most likely an impatient customer. And that she was allergic to nylon and might not be able to wear the blue and orange uniform.

They told her not to worry, that she would soon get used to the job, and that it really wasn't too difficult. Just scanning groceries, stacking shelves and being generally friendly and helpful. But unfortunately, they couldn't budge on the uniform issue.

Had they considered issuing a new uniform, Brenda wanted to know. Maybe an all-black ensemble with a jaunty pillbox hat and wide-leg combat trousers? She'd be happy to design one for them.

"No, thank you," they said firmly, and

could she please show in the next candidate? They were on a very tight timetable.

Brenda was very disappointed that they didn't give her enough time to put some of her ideas to the panel; that they do more to promote fair trade tea and coffee, for example, but she thanked them for the job, all the same.

"How hard can it be?" she told her mother, on the phone that night. "It's only a bit of shelf-stacking. The worst part will be the boredom. And the shame, of course. If any of my arty friends see me with a mop and bucket."

"Don't worry, darling. You'll be promoted in no time," said her mother, kindly. And it will do you good to get out of the flat for a few hours each day, she thought. "Sure, you'll be a manager yourself, in no time. Haven't you a perfectly good degree? You'll have money in your pocket—you'll be set!"

Brenda was thrilled with the possibility of being promoted. She hadn't thought of that, or that she'd finally be taking home a regular pay-packet. She wrote out a big list of ideas, ready to show the manager, and she bought a packet of children's sparkly hair clips to keep her fringe out of her eyes. Yellow plastic sunflowers, they were. (In honor of Vincent van Gogh, who was her favorite artist and greatest inspiration.)

She ironed her uniform and tried it on. It was a little too tight across the chest and hips. Well, that was her own fault. She'd told the panel she was a size ten, when they asked her. But, bloody hell! She wasn't going to tell a row of complete strangers that she was actually a size twelve! Talk about loss of dignity, she fumed. When you were a skivvy on minimum wage, the whole world was entitled to know the exact circumference of your womanly curves. The Blue Donkey Gallery in Galway hadn't wanted to know the size of her backside, thank God.

With a mixture of dread and excitement, Brenda circled the first day of her new job on the calendar. She turned up at the supermarket, in her too-tight uniform, and was shown the tea room and the warehouse. She was introduced to lots of people, and she forgot all their names at once. The warehouse was a bit scary, all bare concrete walls and pitch-dark shadows. Brenda didn't like the warehouse. Luckily, they had already allocated a position for her, on the shop floor.

She was sent to the fresh fruit and vegetable section and told to stack two cages of bright yellow honeydew melons and dark green watermelons on the shelves.

"Tidy up the straw and wipe down the island," said the supervisor.

"The island?"

That was the name for the display stand.

"Right you are," she beamed, and set to work with gusto. She toiled away for half an hour, thinking that melons were a lot heavier than paint brushes. In fact, they were very heavy indeed, and the tight uniform made her uncomfortably warm. She was exhausted by the time the cages were empty, and then the supervisor told her they wanted all the potatoes moved from one island at the front, to another island at the back of the section.

"Why?" Brenda wanted to know, beginning to hate the very word, *island.*

So they could put strawberries and cream at the front of the section, of course.

Brenda hauled her cages and her industrial-sized tub of wipes over to the front section, and started all over again, keeping her head down in case she was recognized by Tom Reilly-Dunseith or any of his friends.

She had potato dust on her face when she was finished. And then she had to go to the warehouse for kiwi fruit and mangoes. Brenda didn't even know what mangoes looked like. She didn't know anyone who had ever eaten a mango. She made a mental note to tell the manager that he was wasting his time bringing this fancy stuff halfway across the globe.

While she was walking up and down the dimly lit aisles, looking for the elusive fruits, some of the teenage staff turned out the lights for a joke. There were no windows and it was suddenly so dark, Brenda couldn't see her hand in front of her face. She couldn't remember the way back to the door, either.

She had a panic attack, stumbled and fell over a bin containing an absolutely filthy mop, which she thought was a zombie-murderer lying in wait for her. She rolled across the floor with it, screaming the place down.

Then, the lights came back on and the pranksters were clinging to the shelves, killing themselves laughing. Brenda had to go to the staff room and splash cold water on her face. She wasn't supposed to be there, unless on an official break, and the supervisor caught her and told her off. And another thing—had she found the mangoes yet?

Thankfully, it was time for a tea break. Sod the bloody mangoes, thought Brenda, as she selected a hot chocolate at the vending machine and sat on a delivery of barbeque charcoal to drink it. She couldn't believe it was still only 10:45 AM. All too soon, it was back to work.

Most of the customers that morning appeared to be pensioners, all ferried to the supermarket on cut-price buses. They didn't seem to know where anything was, and they all pinched Brenda's arms to ask her questions.

"What's on special offer, love?"

Brenda didn't know.

"Have you tights to match my coat, love?"

Brenda didn't know.

"Would this kind of fruitcake cause constipation?"

Brenda didn't know, and she didn't *want* to know.

"Stop pinching me, for heaven's sake," she said to the elderly woman, who was a lot stronger than she looked. "My poor arms are black and blue."

"It's a pity of you," replied the outraged lady. "I'm going to report you to the manager. You have a shocking attitude problem."

"I'm sorry, but I am only asking you not to *pinch* my *arms.* This is a supermarket, not a kinky brothel!"

"You cheeky article!"

"It's just, you're very *strong.* What are you looking for, anyway? *Spinach*?"

"Right! That's it! Manager! Where's the manager? I'm going to have you sacked."

"Oh, oh . . . Hi! Missus! Come back! I'm sorry."

But the outraged woman was off on a mission to rid the store of cheeky articles. The manager was found and a shouting match ensued between the three of them. Brenda won.

She was fired, of course.

She decided it would be better not to tell Nicolas that she had lost her temper completely at that point and started wrecking the nearby displays. It was all just too unbearable: getting the boot after less than three hours. She'd only earned twelve pounds, for heaven's sake. And for that princely sum, she'd endured potato dust in her eyes

and quite painful arm-pinching and a dirty mop falling in her face. And now she was getting sacked because she didn't know enough about constipation. And the uniform was making her skin itch like mad.

She'd grabbed melon after melon, both yellow and green, and heaved them up into the air, in all directions—as high as her strength would allow.

"Come and get your hands on my lovely, juicy melons!" she'd screamed, as she sent the terrified shoppers running for cover.

"Come and devour my priceless melons of delight!" they heard her cry, as the huge soft fruits exploded on the tiled floor, and babies began to cry and four pensioners fell over in the scramble to get away.

Some people were cut with broken glass, as they stood filling their little plastic containers with grated carrots in jelly and bacon-flavored croutons, when the biggest melon in the store came thundering through the glass roof of the coleslaw display. Brenda herself was chased around the store by the security guards, pulling over the displays of washing powder and tins of biscuits, as she made her way to the manager's office and locked herself in.

"Dunnes Stores is way better than this!" she roared into the in-store loudspeaker system, as the guards tried to force the door open with a wooden plank. *"Dunnes, Dunnes, Dunnes, we want Dunnes! We want Dunnes!"*

(The manager was speechless with rage. This madness was taking place in one of the biggest branches of the biggest supermarket chain in the UK. He told someone to call an ambulance, so they could blame the whole thing on Brenda's mental instability, in the court case, should anyone take legal action.)

She didn't tell Nicolas that the staff had been quite kind at the end, as they waited with her in the carpark for the ambulance to arrive and gave her a cup of tea with lots of sugar in it. Someone said that working in a supermarket could be very stressful. It was the nonstop beeping of the electronic tills, Brenda told them. It was a kind of psychological torture, especially to someone like her, who lived on her own and wasn't used to noise of any kind.

Brenda pretended to be calming down and, when the guards let go of her arms, she ran away across the carpark, like a greyhound let off the leash. When she got home, she discovered her lovely sunflower clips had fallen off.

After much deliberation, the manager decided not to get poor Brenda into trouble with the police or the mental health people, and he let the matter drop. He was a decent sort of man and, anyway, he was too preoccupied with trying to calm down the hysterical woman who had triggered off the whole thing. He offered to buy her a new coat, as he wiped the melon seeds off her lapels, and he wondered again if he should take early retirement.

•22•

Two's Company, Three's a Crowd

Two days after Brenda posted her latest letter to America, Sadie left the house at lunchtime. She knew that Arnold was meeting some colleagues for lunch in the Europa Hotel. Sadie had bought him a new shirt and tie for the grand event.

She'd been dithering for weeks, putting off the moment when she would have to stand up for herself. She'd eaten dozens of toasted bagels spread with raspberry jam and chilled chocolate profiteroles with hot custard. Strangely enough, the bagels and profiteroles had no effect whatsoever on Sadie's personal life. Except to make Arnold say some very hurtful things: like he would have to have the furniture reinforced with steel girders if Sadie got any fatter. (She was nearly 182 pounds, now.)

So, very reluctantly, she made her way into the city and went quietly up the stairs to his office. It was on the second floor of a Victorian house on Eglantine Avenue. Sadie tried every key until she found the right one. No one saw her go inside. She locked the door behind her. There was no sign on Arnold's desk of the framed picture she had given him of the two of them on the beach in Portrush last year. Her plan was to hide in the office until she heard something that would prove his infidelity. A phone call or piece of conversation. Then she could decide what to do next. She had been looking in his desk and checking his pockets for months, but she had discovered nothing. That was why she was forced into this ridiculous position today. She quickly scanned the office. There was only one hiding place.

Sadie pulled the large cupboard in the corner out from the wall and set a small chair in the space behind it. With her mouth in a hard line, she stepped into the corner and pulled the cupboard back into place. She sat down on the chair and shifted around until she felt comfortable. It was quite a squash. She took a paperback and a bag of butter toffees out of her handbag. She popped a toffee into her mouth and she began to read.

At two o'clock precisely, Arnold returned to the office. Sadie held her breath as the door opened with a rattle, and the overhead lights flickered on.

"Come here, you wicked temptress," he said, to someone Sadie could not see. "I was dying to kiss you all through that boring lunch. You were a witch to wear that tiny skirt. You did it on purpose. I could hardly concentrate on the speeches. Wasn't it absolutely the most boring lunch in the history of double-glazing? I thought it would never end."

"I know, I know," whispered a woman's voice. There was some breathless kissing and then Sadie's eyes opened up like saucers, as the man who had married her twenty years ago said, "I must have you now, Patricia. I can't wait any longer. Up you go on the desk. Quickly! Oh, quick as you can!"

It sounded like his companion jumped up on the desk as if she did this kind of thing every day. Sadie looked up at the ceiling, just in time to see a red blouse land on the chandelier. Arnold was panting like a puppy. A zip was opened.

Patricia giggled. "Come on, then! You naughty, naughty boy! Do you want to see my pretty new stockings? With bold black lace right at the top?" Some brochures slid off the table, and there was a clatter.

"Mind the lamp," said Arnold. "That's a valuable antique."

When it was over, Arnold poured some whiskey into two tumblers, and Patricia lit two cigarettes. Behind the cupboard, Sadie sucked her toffee with her eyes tightly closed.

"I've got a surprise for you, Patty-Pat," he said, when his breathing had returned to normal.

"Oh, goody! I just love surprises. What is it? Tell me, tell me!"

"I've sold a lot of conservatories recently."

"Is that all? You sell conservatories all the time."

"I've made a tidy little sum on commissions. There's daft people in this city with more money than sense. There was this one old bat, for example. Always going on about dead bloody writers."

"I know! Tell me the surprise, you tease," the woman laughed.

"Calm down, gorgeous. I'm taking us to Paris for a couple of days, by way of celebration."

The woman sitting on Arnold's blotter screamed with delight.

"I knew it! I knew you were up to something. When do we go? I need time to shop for new clothes! Reach me down my blouse, will you? What will you tell Sadie Sponge and the Bitter Lemons?"

"Oh, don't spoil the moment! Honestly, sleeping beside that woman is like having a kip by a bouncy castle. Go on," said Arnold. "Do your Sadie impression. It cracks me up."

"Sadie Sponge! The *hideous* creature from the crypt!" said Patricia, in a doom-laden voice. They both laughed until they were out of breath.

"That's brilliant! You sound just like her. More!"

"I'm coming to eat you with my big sharp teeth! My appetite cannot be satisfied. I am going to eat the whole world," growled Patricia, as she stomped around the office, wearing only her lacy red knickers and her black stockings.

"Stop it! Stop it," begged Arnold. "I'm getting a pain in my side. Oh God, you should be on the stage. Here. Get dressed before the area manager turns up!"

"Tell me more about the trip, Arnie, baby."

"We fly to Paris in October. And don't bother buying new clothes. Well, maybe some lingerie, if you like. But it's not necessary. You'll be naked for forty-eight hours. And I'll tell Sadie Sponge I'm going to a conference on environmentally friendly products for the home. The Frogs are really into all that stuff. I'll tell her we're thinking of branching out into other markets. She'll believe anything I tell her!"

"She's a real dope!"

"Oh, she is, she is! A real dope! Another whiskey?"

"Mmmm . . . yes, please. Just a little one—I still have to go back to work, you know. We're expecting a delivery of candle-sticks this evening. When will I see you again?"

"I'll call you. Keep your mobile phone switched on."

"I missed you at the weekend. There was a great film on, at the cinema. I had to go on my own. I wish we could get rid of Sadie Sponge and be together always."

"I've told you before. I couldn't afford the help. My parents can't manage on their own. As soon as they shuffle off this mortal coil, I'll give old Sadie the heave-ho. I'll in-herit a bundle of dosh. And then you can move in. The house is in my name only. Though Sadie doesn't know that."

"And she can spend the rest of her days as a live-in care assistant. With her face in a box of biscuits. She's had plenty of experi-ence in both departments."

"Now, now. Little minx! Don't be cruel. She's not a bad old stick. When all's said and done."

"But she's not me. You love me, don't you, Arnie, baby?"

"You know I do, Patty-Pat! You know I

love only you. Why, you've got the best pair of legs in Northern Ireland!"

Patricia left the office at three o'clock, and Arnold read his paper for the rest of the afternoon. He answered four telephone calls and made a pot of coffee. It was a leisurely business, selling windows, when all was said and done. When five o'clock came, he wondered aloud what Sadie had prepared for his evening meal, as all his romantic exertions had given him quite an appetite. Steak and chips, with a beetroot and tomato side salad, perhaps? Pork chops and apple sauce? Or maybe some nice, juicy sausages? Ho, ho, ho! He switched off the lights and the office was plunged into darkness. He locked the door and descended the stairs.

After a while, the cupboard in the corner began to tremble. Sadie slithered out from her hiding place, and her face was as dark as a thundercloud. Cigarette smoke still hung in the air. She thought that Arnold had given up smoking years ago. He often complained of clients blowing their smoke all over his expensive jackets. Sadie turned her face away from the desk and left the office.

Arnold noticed something strange about

Sadie that evening. She was late home, for a start. He never arrived home before Sadie. She was always there with his supper ready, the fire lit if it was cold outside, and his parents seated at the dinner table. She mumbled something about the bus breaking down and gave them cold meat slices and shopbought salad for tea. Arnold looked up at her as he shook the bottle of salad dressing. He saw that she was chewing very slowly and strangely and staring at him in a most peculiar way.

"Would you like a piece of French stick?" she asked him in a small voice, as she wrenched and twisted the bread into pieces.

"No, thank you," he said. And he swallowed hard.

·23·

The Great Conservatory Is Finished

At the end of July, the grand building was completed. Even though Arnold Smith had hired extra builders to finish the job faster, Henry thought the sounds of the hammers and the saws would be in his head for the rest of his life. There was dust in the back of his throat and he was suffering from palpitations.

David Cropper came to visit and declared the work a triumph. Perfect conditions for filming, he announced. Perfect. The light was just right. The Brontë Bunch came to view the conservatory and they were all thrilled. Aurora introduced them to David Cropper. Their exclusive society was the talk of the city, he told them. The date for filming was set, and their costumes were all ready. Aurora practiced reading aloud until her voice was in danger of collapse.

Henry was in love with the girl in the flower shop. He went there every week to buy something for Aurora. He found out her name was Rose Thompson and told her his was Henry Blackstaff. They were both old-fashioned names. That fact made him absurdly happy. He had fantasies about looking after Rose, in a pretty cottage somewhere, with a fairy-tale garden around it. The two of them sitting in a willow arbor, watching the sun set behind a privet hedge. Sharing a tender kiss surrounded by the lingering perfume of lavender.

Sometimes, if the shop was not busy, Henry and Rose would talk about flowers and plants, and which ones lasted longer and which ones were easy to care for. They realized they shared the opinion that imported flowers were all very well, and beautiful in their own way, of course, but they were killing the native flower market off completely.

"Most people in this city wouldn't even be able to name a native flower," said Rose. "And that's sad, because they're so easy to grow."

"And the perfume. Well, the hothouse flowers have no perfume at all, compared to the local varieties. Frail little things, they are," said Henry, sniffing some miniature roses and thinking of Aurora. "All image and no substance. I remember roses when they were as big as side plates, full of rainwater and earwigs. All the gardens around here had some."

"Mmmm," said Rose, who wasn't sure that was an appealing image for her customers.

"But the perfume," said Henry, "the perfume was intoxicating. The air was heavy with the scent of them on a summer's evening."

"Oh, yes. Pure romance," she agreed. "There's nothing on earth as beautiful as a rose garden."

Henry always found something to buy, in the end, and the windowsills at home were full of blooms of every color and size. Aurora thought it was very sweet, but she wouldn't let him put any flowers in the conservatory itself. She said it would spoil the formal atmosphere.

Then she changed her mind and decided some elegant plants with big leaves would take the bare look off the walls. Well, it was David's idea, but Aurora thought he was absolutely right. She told Henry about her plan but he seemed distracted.

"Are you listening to me, Henry?" asked Aurora, when the filming was almost due to begin. "I said, I think I will order some large-scale plants for the conservatory. It looks a trifle bare in here, with only the books and the cane chairs. Some potted palms and an aspidistra? What do you think?"

"Aspidistra? Yes. Very suitable."

"What is the name of that place you always go to?"

"What?"

"Honestly. You're miles away. I said, what is the name of the florist you like?"

"Rose Thompson—I mean, Thompson Flowers." He was thinking of Rose's green eyes and her white ankles. She looked just right, expertly snipping the stems off flowers with her scissors and pushing them into florist's foam with her long, thin fingers.

"Well, do you have the telephone number of the shop, Henry? Honestly, I haven't got all day. Actually, could you do it for me? I'm seeing David tonight for a last-minute discussion."

"Yes, yes. I think I have a receipt somewhere. I'll do it."

Henry telephoned the next day and placed an order for some plants in keeping with the period of the house. Did Rose have anything in stock, he asked. Only, the plants were needed right away. Rose said she would bring them round at lunchtime.

The camera crew arrived to set up their equipment and take light readings. There were lots of people running in and out of the house with cables and wires and spotlights. In the middle of all the upheaval, the plants were delivered in a small van. Henry's heart skipped a beat when he saw that Rose was standing on his doorstep, with a huge palm in her arms. He rushed out to help her.

"Thanks a million," she said. "This pot is really heavy."

"I'll show you where they go, although I'm not sure of the arrangement. I'll ask my wife where she wants them. Excuse me for a moment."

"Okay. I'll bring in the others."

When the plants had been arranged, and rearranged, and Aurora was satisfied, she went upstairs to change. Henry and Rose were left standing in the hall.

"Thank you so much," said Henry. "It all looks great. They're filming this afternoon, you know. For television."

"Really? Wow! Well, I hope it all goes well, Henry." She reached for the door handle.

"I . . . I meant to ask you about your name, before. Was it just coincidence that you liked flowers?"

"No," she laughed. "My mother was a keen gardener."

"I see. She must have taught you about horticulture, then?"

"Yes, she did. Well, I must be on my way. Don't forget to water the plants."

And off she went, reversing the little van and disappearing out the gates, and leaving Henry's heart in turmoil. He stood at the hall door, looking out at the road for a long time after she had gone.

The Brontë Bunch arrived in two and threes, clambering out of cars and taxis in full Victorian costume. Henry kept himself busy serving Earl Grey tea and tiny salmon sandwiches in the kitchen. He made sure he trimmed off all the crusts, as Aurora had specified.

As the afternoon wore on, Mrs. Johnson felt faint, and had to be revived with a paper fan. Someone tried to take off her cloak but she waved them away with a weary hand in a crochet glove. Henry wasn't sure if her faint was genuine, or if she was just getting into character. Aurora and David Cropper were deep in conversation in the conservatory. Aurora was wearing her lace-trimmed bonnet, and her black gown with its miles of petticoats. David Cropper was weak with lust, wondering if Aurora was wearing a laced-up corset underneath. He prayed that she was. Her waist was positively tiny. She read an extract from *Wuthering Heights,* to test for acoustics, and David listened as if she was telling him the secret of eternal life.

·24·

Penny's Choice

Penny was in a trance. That's what it felt like. Like she was living inside a transparent shell. She could see people and hear what they were saying but she felt nothing. She knew she was going to have an affair with Richard Allen, the estate agent, and she was preparing herself for the consequences. Dulling her conscience, practicing calm and gathering courage.

She had phoned him up to arrange a

viewing, and they'd chatted on the phone for half an hour. Penny told him she'd like something unusual, and he told her about his own apartment by the river, with a ten-foot-high window in the open-plan sitting room. When Penny said she'd love to see something fantastic like that, he'd laughed, and said it could be arranged. Yes, she thought she might be able to have a little fling with Richard.

She would dress provocatively, flirt with him, flatter him. Men loved to be flattered, to be admired. To open doors for women and carry heavy things for them. They didn't like Women's Libbers at all, no matter that it was 1999. She would ask him to explain the various mortgage deals, even though she knew them inside out, and didn't need one anyway.

Millie was always telling her she was very attractive, that she could have done a lot better for herself. Well, Penny was going to test that theory. She'd see if her pretty clothes and her womanly curves had any effect on the well-groomed and highly confident Mr. Allen. She was going to do everything she could think of to make him want her.

And if he did want her, what then? She was going to go to bed with Richard, even though she could barely breathe sometimes, with the shame of what she was planning. But she had to make love to him. There was no other way of finding out if the passion she wanted really existed, or if it was all a trick of the publishing industry. And if she felt desire or pleasure or anything at all, she was going to leave Daniel, and move away from the city. She knew there was little chance of her and Richard having a future together. And she didn't want them to have a future. It was Daniel that Penny loved. It would always be Daniel. But she didn't want to live with him anymore, with all this frustration seething inside her. No, she would find some little apartment by the seaside and live on her own.

And if she felt nothing, then she would know that her strange marriage was her own fault, and she would go on working in the cafe, and dream no more of love and foolish things.

Penny was going to get herself tidied up, as Millie put it, and phone Richard, and talk to him. Come on to him, that's what they said, nowadays. She had done it once before, she told herself, and she could do it again. She could have seduced that plumber, if she'd had enough time. If the telephone ringing hadn't destroyed the charged atmosphere.

She was consumed with the story of Clare Fitzgerald and her lost handbag. Her future with Peter, and all that might have been. His address on a cassette, placed in a beaded handbag, left behind on a bus. One careless action, changing the course of history. Peter had left Clare a note, and Mr. Muldoon had just put it in a drawer and forgotten about it. Seventeen years, it had lain there, in the dust. Penny was terrified by the story and convinced that it must be significant in some way. Was the tea house an unlucky place? Millie hadn't said that straight out, but she'd hinted at it more than once.

·25·

The Affair Begins

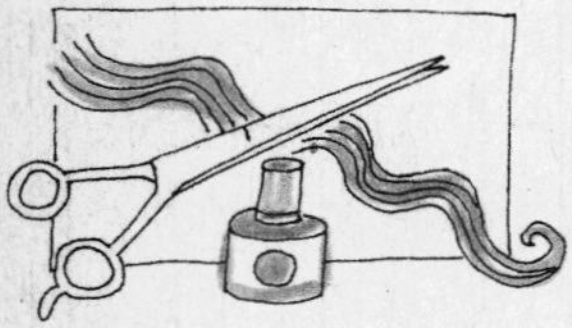

It was the first Saturday in August. Penny began the day as she always did, with a round of baking, serving and tidying-up. But at one o'clock she sat down near the counter, delicately sipping a large cappuccino, and ignored Daniel's pleas for help in dealing with the lunchtime rush. At two o'clock, when Daniel was in the storeroom looking for tea bags, Penny walked out of the tea house and left the place unattended. She took her checkbook with her. She intended to spend a lot of money. When Daniel came out of the kitchen with a pot of tea and a plate of currant scones, she was not there. A little knot of fear formed itself in his stomach.

Penny walked into the city center, and picked out a hair salon that looked modern and busy. She went in and waited patiently for one hour on a leather sofa, all the time watching the other customers as they were groomed by the stylists. A young apprentice summoned Penny to the sink to wash her hair and asked her if she was going for a completely new image. She seemed to think this was necessary.

The stylist who came to view Penny's hair frowned and bit her lip with concentration. She ran her fingers through Penny's long brown hair with a hopeless air. The hair was very dry and thick, she announced. Cutting in layers, keeping the hair long, a blunt bob or blond highlights were all ruled out. Penny said that she was too busy to take better care of her hair. She needed something nice and easy that would take care of itself. She was a career woman, she explained, to cover her embarrassment. The stylist, who was twenty years old, gorgeous, and a mother of two who worked for ten hours a day, eventually decided that Penny's hair was a lost cause. It would all have to come off. Penny reluctantly agreed.

She closed her eyes as the hot, soapy water washed her old life away. She kept them closed as the scissors began to snip, and pieces of tinfoil were placed on her head and painted over with hair-coloring gel. Thirty minutes ticked by. Then, her hair was washed again. The hair dryer buzzed, and the overpowering smell of hair lacquer enveloped her.

"There," said the girl, whose name was Carrie. "What do you think of it?"

Penny examined her new image in the mirror and nodded her head. She could not speak. She looked years younger than thirty-five. Wisps of mahogany-tinted hair curled themselves round her cheekbones.

"If you don't mind me saying, you could go through to the beauty-treatment room and get your eyebrows done. If you're not in a hurry. They're very thick, and they could look so nice if they were properly shaped."

"I will, indeed. Thank you for the advice."

"We sell cosmetics as well. If you're getting ready for a special occasion, I mean. Why don't you have your face professionally made up? It would really finish off the look. You have great bone structure." She tried to end on a positive note.

Penny nodded and smiled and gave the young girl a generous tip.

In the beauty room, Penny's eyebrows were tamed with a session of waxing and plucking that brought tears to her eyes. The beautician, whose own eyebrows were as thin as fuse wire, rubbed some cooling gel onto Penny's bright red brow, and brought her a cup of tea. When the swelling began to subside, Penny submitted to a pale foundation, smoke-colored eye shadow and glittery, bronze lipstick. Her eyelashes were thickened up with a heavily laden eyelash wand. She had to blink several times to get used to the weight of the mascara. Her eyes were suddenly huge and sexy. The effect brought a lump to her throat. The beautician told her she was beautiful. And it was true. Penny Stanley was indeed a beautiful woman.

She chose a small compact of foundation, a pot of gray eye shadow and a bronze lipstick in a pretty gold case. They gave her a complimentary makeup pouch with a gold rope handle, to keep her new purchases in. Daniel would have been disgusted to see the way Penny simpered over such a silly trinket. But to Penny, it symbolized all the glamour and loveliness that her own life had never provided. Finally, they gave her a business card with the names of her stylists penciled in for future reference.

When it was all over, she went to the desk to pay. Daniel's Aunt Kathleen used to say that the best things in life were free, but that was only half-true.

She had spent just one hundred and forty pounds, but she felt like a millionaire. When she went back outside to the busy street, she saw that people noticed her and gave her admiring glances. Spending money was great fun, she decided.

Filled with a new confidence, she went window-shopping for a while. Then, she pressed the buzzer of an exclusive boutique near the Europa Hotel. It was nearly closing time, but the assistants let her in.

After a quick flick through the rails, Penny chose a new outfit. A gray wool trouser suit to match her eye shadow, a black vest and shoes and a tiny little handbag. She decided to keep the new clothes on, so the assistants snipped off the labels with a pair of scissors.

"You do realize, madam, that you cannot return these clothes, now that you have worn them out of the shop. There's no going back."

"I know," said Penny, and she handed over another check. She transferred her new cosmetics pouch into the dainty handbag and closed the clasp. It made a satisfying snapping sound. She left the shop with her old clothes in a carrier-bag and waved good-bye to the bemused staff.

She dropped her old clothes into a skip on University Street. A group of builders fell silent with admiration as she went by. She walked along the street in her new suit, and the wind stirred the leaves on the chestnut trees.

Penny felt young and free and alive. She sat on a bench in the Botanic Gardens, clutching her new handbag. It was made of black velvet. She thought of Clare Fitzgerald. She wound the strap around her wrist several times so that she would not lose it. It was six o'clock. She was meeting Richard at the wine bar at eight. She began to feel hungry, despite her nerves.

Penny had dinner in an Italian restaurant beside Queen's University. She was tempted inside by the pink lights in the windows and the smell of garlic drifting along the street. A small queue was forming behind her on the steps of the restaurant, as Penny was beckoned inside by the manager. The waiters were charming and handsome and lively as they rushed around the restaurant with their round silver trays held high.

"Table for two?" one said, looking at his watch.

"Just for one, I'm afraid," said Penny, smiling sadly. "But the night is still young."

"Certainly, madam," said the waiter, and he brought her to a discreet little table beside a small artificial tree covered with fairy lights. Penny sat down graciously and ordered a glass of wine. It was nice to have someone else do the cooking for a change. She savoured the smells of simmering tomatoes and red wine gravy, and Parmesan cheese and olive oil.

"I'll have the crab claws and salad," she

said, after a lengthy perusal of the leather-bound menu.

When her plate was empty, she asked the waiter for an espresso coffee and a glass of sparkling water. She wished Daniel was with her. How nice it would be to hold hands at this little table and pretend they were on holiday in Rome!

There were grapevines hanging from the ceiling and a mural of the Italian countryside on the walls. The tablecloths were green-and-white checked, and the napkins were green, and there was a statue of a beautiful woman, made out of snow-white marble, beside the bar. Penny noticed everything. She was used to observing things, and being quiet, and eating on her own. She wanted to remember everything about this day. At ten minutes to eight, she paid her bill and left the restaurant.

With her handbag clutched tightly in her hands, she pushed open the door of a wine bar on the better end of the Lisburn Road and went inside. The interior was dimly lit. Would Richard remember their date? Would he turn up? He'd seemed quite keen on the phone, when she'd told him she had decided to buy an apartment. It was Penny's idea they meet for a drink. Richard thought it was a nice idea to meet in the wine bar to discuss Penny's options. He was an easy-going man, who believed in going with the flow.

Dark blue tapestry seats and mahogany tables; brass lamps above the modern art on the walls; rows and rows of dust-covered wine bottles on rustic shelves. The drinkers were mostly male and quietly spoken. They looked her over as she went up to the bar, sat on a high stool and ordered a glass of wine. She made a little show of looking at her watch so that the men in the bar would think she was waiting for someone. She did not want them to think she was here on her own. That was asking for trouble. She drank the wine and ordered another.

At ten minutes past eight, a well-dressed man came into the bar and signaled to the barman that he wanted a drink. It was Richard. He smiled at Penny. She smiled back and continued to smile at him. He sat down beside her.

The bar was filling up and the music was turned up just a little.

"Hi," he said. "You look beautiful. You've

changed your hair—almost didn't recognize you. You look fabulous."

"Thank you," she said.

"I'm glad I came out tonight. Even if I don't make a sale."

Penny smiled. "I bet you say that to all the girls," she said. But it was very nice, all the same.

The barman knew Richard well. When Richard went to the Gents at ten o'clock, the barman came over and told Penny to watch it. He told her that Richard was fond of the ladies and unreliable. He was only after a bit of fun. Penny was delighted. That was just what she wanted, she said. A bit of fun.

She told Richard she was married. She wanted to lay her cards on the table, from the beginning. He didn't seem to mind. He said he had sensed something in Penny's voice, on the phone—that she wasn't only interested in the price of the riverside apartments.

She reminded him that she owned a cafe, and he told her about a cafe he had once sold to a celebrity chef; and the way property prices were increasing in some parts of the city and going down in other areas. They chatted about the general lack of celebrities living in Belfast; good and bad television programs; the way the weather could suddenly change when you had gone out without an umbrella; the new types of cars that were becoming popular in the city; holidays they had been on, food they liked and what restaurants gave good value for the money. They didn't mention politics or religion. It was dangerous to talk about those two subjects with a person you had just met. Richard paid for all the drinks, and occasionally he rested his hand on Penny's arm and she didn't brush it away.

At eleven o'clock, Penny and Richard left the bar together. Richard offered to show her his apartment. So that she could see one from the inside. To appreciate the view of the Lagan river. Neither of them commented that it was a bit late in the evening to go viewing apartments.

They hailed a taxi.

It seemed to Penny the most natural thing in the world, to go in through the heavy front doors of the apartment building with Richard and skip lightly up the steps to the second floor. He unlocked the door and stood back to let her go in ahead of him.

From the lounge, they could see the lights of the Waterfront Hall shining out across the water. The people inside the huge, glass concert hall were talking and laughing and walking up and down the stairs to different levels. It was like a human ant farm. They stood together, watching it for a while. Richard rubbed Penny's back gently. Her stomach turned over, not with lust or love, but with nerves.

The apartment was very well coordinated, with all the furniture and the decor in matching shades of cream and chocolate. Penny asked him if he'd chosen the furniture himself.

"It was the show home," Richard explained. "I bought the furniture along with the flat."

"Had you nothing of your own when you moved in?"

"Just the hi-fi and my clothes. Typical bachelor, I'm afraid."

The words tripped easily from his lips but she thought he said them with a trace of sadness. "Indeed."

"Make yourself comfortable," he said. He went into the tiny, modern kitchen to make coffee. She heard him fiddling with the buttons of an expensive espresso machine, and she stifled an urge to laugh when he scalded himself slightly with the frothy, hot milk. Those machines were difficult to operate unless you used them every day.

Penny thought of Daniel, his lovely face, his ice-blue eyes and the way he danced with her on the night they met. She thought of their wedding day and how much she loved him then, and how much she had been looking forward to going to bed with him in the bridal suite. She stood beside the huge window and gazed down at the water. There were tears in her eyes.

"Kiss me," she said, when Richard returned from the kitchen, with two glass cups of latte and a plate of fancy German biscuits on a tray.

He set the tray down on a small table, took off his jacket, tossed it onto the sofa and crossed the room in a matter of seconds. He brushed her arms gently with his fingertips and Penny closed her eyes. Then, he took her in his arms and kissed her expertly. Richard Allen was not nervous where women were concerned. In fact, he was full of confidence in his lovemaking abilities. It was only when engagement rings were mentioned that he began to get worried.

They kissed for a long time, and the coffee went cold and Penny did not think of Daniel anymore.

•26•

The Lovers

Daniel was eerily quiet the next day. Penny bathed and dressed at a leisurely pace and came down the stairs for breakfast, not at eight o'clock in the morning, but at one-thirty in the afternoon. He stared at her new hairstyle, and her newly made-up face, and said she looked lovely, but he asked her nothing else about the previous day. His main feeling seemed to be relief that she had come back at all,

Penny thought. He brought her a cup of tea and a scone, as he always did. To her utter amazement, he did not ask her where she had been all night, or why she had come creeping into the tea house at six that morning, just as dawn was breaking.

As the day wore on, she began to believe that he just didn't know what to say. He had married her for the business. Well, she'd known that for many years now, hadn't she? At five-thirty, she told Daniel she was going away for a couple of days, for a holiday, and that she would be splashing out a bit with the checkbook.

Daniel's face turned very red, but still he said nothing.

"Aren't you going to ask me where I'm going?" she asked him.

"Are you going to tell me?"

"Daniel, we need to talk. Really talk. Please."

"I'm going out myself, actually, for an hour or so," he said. He locked the door and closed the blinds. Penny could not recall one time in the last seventeen years when he had closed the shop before nine o'clock at night. Even on Christmas Eve, he stayed open to feed the flocks of people walking the streets with tinsel scarves, on their way to and from the celebrations.

"We need to talk, to save our marriage, Daniel. It can't go on like this."

"We'll talk when you come back."

"We can talk now. I won't go if you don't want me to."

"It's okay. You go and have a good rest. You deserve it."

He went out through the back door, and Penny didn't try to stop him. She packed a few things in a small bag, locked up the shop and hailed a taxi to take her to Richard's flat. He was taking her to the countryside for a couple of days. They were going to go for long walks, have dinner in a gourmet restaurant and share a bed in a small but expensive hotel. Penny was struck by that thought. She was a married woman, with a lover, but she still had very little sexual experience.

Millie Mortimer was delighted that Penny was having a little break. She said that Penny deserved to enjoy herself, after all her years of slavery in the cafe. She lent her friend a nice, warm coat and a fancy pair of bedroom slippers. Penny didn't tell Millie about Richard. She only said that she was going away for a couple of days to think about her marriage. Which was the truth, after all.

Richard was waiting for her now. It was too late to undo their plans. Penny sat back in the taxi, clutched her overnight bag and checked her new hairstyle in the driver's mirror.

·27·

The Crawleys Get a Shock

Two weeks before the day of the royal visit, Alice remembered the brooches. They still had to buy new brooches to complete their splendid outfits. They had some money put away and were discussing whether or not to spend it on new jewelry, when Beatrice suddenly wanted a slice of chocolate gateau.

"Come on," she said. "Daniel might know of a place that sells nice things that don't cost too much, if you know what I mean."

"If anyone does, he does," agreed Alice. "You lock the back door and I'll switch off the radio."

Penny was out, which was very unusual, but Daniel had a great idea when he heard the problem.

"Why don't you wear some of your late mother's jewelry?" he said. "Preferably some pieces from the war years. You could show them to the queen and tell her about them. Something for her to look at besides all those war photographs."

Beatrice thought of her mother's trunk in the attic. It was full of old clothes and shoes, and things they could not bear to give away when Mrs. Crawley died. She was sure there was a box of costume jewelry in it.

"We'll fetch it down from the roof space and have a root through. You never know what we might find," she said. "Thanks, Daniel."

Daniel smiled. It was easy helping other people. The Crawleys ate their cake and went home to begin the search.

After much heaving and hauling and cries

of "Look out!" the trunk was dragged down the ladder and into Beatrice's bedroom. The two sisters sat on the bed to rest, and then they opened the ancient leather trunk. It was dusty and covered in cobwebs but inside time had stood still.

Their mother's things were as clean and bright as they had ever been. There were dresses and coats and slips and stockings.

"Wasn't mother such a tiny little thing," said Alice. "This jacket wouldn't fit a fly."

Beatrice found the box and lifted it out. "At least jewelry fits all sizes. I hope there's something we can use. Great idea of Daniel's."

There were necklaces and bracelets and earrings, and right at the bottom of the box, two large brooches. One was shaped like a dragonfly, set with turquoise stones; and one was a posy of red tulips and golden leaves. Beatrice held them up to the light from the window. The glass stones glittered and shone.

"I think we've found our finishing touches," said Beatrice. "I'll have the red and you have the blue. We must show Penny, next time we're in."

"What's that piece of paper in the bottom

of the box? There's a corner of it sticking out."

Alice reached under the silk lining of the box. She drew out a piece of paper, yellowed with age. She unfolded it and smoothed it out on the bed. It was a birth certificate. William and Eliza Crawley were registered as the parents of twin girls, Beatrice and Alice, born at home, in Belfast, in 1941.

"But that is incorrect," said Alice. "We were born in 1940. Six months after father went to fight. They must have made a mistake."

Beatrice did not move. She coughed, nervously.

Mental arithmetic silenced the sisters. They looked at the date on the certificate, and neither one trusted themselves to utter the truth. Once spoken, it could never be taken back. They must have been conceived when William was away fighting in the war. So, that must mean their biological parents were not married. At least, not to one another. Beatrice thought of countless occasions when she had called some of the badly behaved children of Belfast "rotten little bastards." And of how soul-destroying it must be for children to be condemned like that, when they were still trying to make sense of the world.

Alice was thinking of her first day at grammar school, fifty-five years earlier. Some of the girls were giggling and elbowing one another, when the teacher called out the names on the register. Alice *Crawley.* Beatrice *Crawley.* Did the other girls know, even then? Had they heard their parents gossiping at the tea table? *Well, if that pair weren't made on the wrong side of the blanket, I'll be a monkey's uncle!* Some awful, cheap slur like that. Poor Eliza, how did she bear it, all those years? Everyone looking at them, every time they went out of the house. It was because of their different appearance, she knew that now. She had always known it, in her heart.

"We were quite small when we first went to school. Smaller than the others," said Alice. "Although we soon caught up."

The glass brooches glittered in Beatrice's hand, a gift from Eliza's lover. The brooches knew the answer: a German-born man by the name of Leo Frank was their real father, his genes succeeding where William's had failed. Leo's Israeli origins were plain to see, in the faces of his twin daughters.

Beatrice put her hand up to her neck and coughed again. "We are not the children of William Crawley, war hero," she said softly, and a tear rolled down her cheek.

"You mean, Mother had an affair?" Alice's face was white.

"It looks that way. Mother always told us she lost the certificate during a house move. We are one year younger than we thought."

"Oh, Daddy, dear Daddy," whispered Alice. "I don't believe it! It's just a clerical mistake they made in the office, some silly girl with only half her mind on the job."

Beatrice shook the box and a tiny photograph fell out. It was faded and cracked. The picture showed their mother in her nurse's uniform, standing on the steps of the Royal Victoria Hospital, beside a tall man wearing round spectacles and a tiny black hat on the back of his head. On the back was written: *Eliza and Leo, 1941.* The man had his arm round their mother's waist. Eliza's stomach was slightly swollen. Beatrice and Alice had the same dark eyes and long straight nose as the man in the photograph.

Alice said, "That's one photograph we won't be giving to the City Hall."

Beatrice said, "You know this means our father might have been a man of the Jewish faith? Look at that little hat he is wearing—I think they call it a yarmulke."

"You mean, he was a Jew?" said Alice, and she put her hands up to her mouth.

"I think we must consider that to be a definite possibility," said Beatrice, gently.

"But how can this be? Mother was a good woman. Perhaps she was the victim of a savage attack. One reads such awful things in the papers."

"Alice, look at the photograph. Mother is smiling. Can you not see the resemblance between that man and ourselves? I'd prefer to be the result of a love affair, wouldn't you? Not something terrible, such as an attack. You have heard of such affairs happening in wartime. People are vulnerable to temptation when their spirits are low," whispered Beatrice. "For all Mother knew, she would never see her husband again."

"But that means Mother was a sinner, fallen by the wayside, cast out into darkness." Alice was beginning to panic.

"Stop it," said Beatrice, dabbing at her

eyes with a tissue. "Stop it, please. Don't say things like that about Mother. I couldn't bear it. I really couldn't." They went downstairs and sat in the parlor drinking cup after cup of hot, sweet tea.

"I feel different now. Are we different? Are we Jewish?" Alice asked.

"No. We were raised as Christians and that is what we are." Beatrice was sure about that. "Although, they do say the Jewish people are a hard-working race, with strong family values. And of course, they put great store by education."

"Oh! Yes! And we were teachers! Should we tell anyone?" asked Alice.

"Oh, no. Definitely not. I don't think so. After all, what would be the point? We have no surname, no clue as to his identity," said Beatrice. "He may not have been the one who—who—he may not be our father." Beatrice didn't want to suggest that Eliza might have known other lovers as the bombs fell. Alice missed the point.

"But there cannot have been too many Jewish people here during the war. Perhaps there is a list somewhere? Of refugees? We may have a family somewhere."

"No. They didn't want us to know about

this. We will go on as if nothing has happened."

It was then Beatrice noticed a tightly folded piece of paper on the ground—it must also have fallen out of the box. She opened it up. It was a telegram.

"What does it say?" urged Alice.

Beatrice hesitated. She feared it would confirm what was already too obvious. It did.

Congratulations, my darling. We wanted a baby and now we have two. You choose the names and keep our children safe. I want only to come home to you and hold you in my arms forever.

Your loving husband, William.

"He was a true hero," whispered Beatrice. "Never, not even once, did he make us feel we were not his children."

"That's true. Men of that caliber just don't exist anymore!" Beatrice said tearfully. "I miss him so much!"

"We both miss him, sister dear."

They held each other close and wept for a little while.

Then, Alice almost had a heart attack with delayed shock. "Oh, my God," she said. "Are we half-*German,* do you think?"

•28•

A Present for Brenda

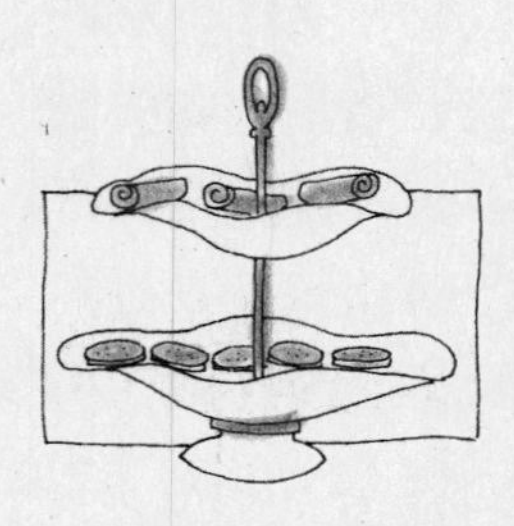

Mrs. Brown stood ringing the doorbell of Brenda's flat. In one hand, she held a large, brown paper carrier-bag.

"Surprise!" she called, when Brenda opened the door, blinking repeatedly in the harsh daylight.

"What is it, Mum? I'm busy working on my paintings for Galway."

"I know you are, sweetheart. And that's why I've bought you a lovely present. I think it may be valuable, though I got it for twenty pounds in a sale."

"Oh, great! Is that it, in the bag?"

"Of course. Now, let me come in, will you? It's heavy."

Brenda was thrilled. Things were definitely looking up in her life, she thought. About time, too. It had taken her hours in the unemployment office to have her benefits reinstated, after her dismissal from the supermarket.

Mrs. Brown closed the front door behind her and trotted up the narrow stairs after her daughter. Brenda was hopping from one foot to the other, in the tiny hall, with sheer excitement. But when her mother opened the bag, Brenda wasn't sure what to think. It was a very ornate frame, gold-colored, with carved fruit and flowers at the corners.

"Ta-da!" cried her mother. "Now, what do you think of that?"

"Mmmm," said Brenda. "I don't usually have my paintings framed, Mum. That's why I paint the sides of the canvas, you see? It's my trademark. And I don't think I have one that would fit those dimensions, either. Mine are all square-shaped."

Mrs. Brown was upset that her great surprise had fallen a bit flat. She pursed her lips and dropped the lovely frame back in the bag. "Never mind. I thought you'd love it. You could have painted something to fit in it, and it would have been the main attraction in your exhibition."

"I don't know . . ."

"Sure, aren't Vincent what's-his-name's pictures all framed in gold? Honestly, Brenda! I thought you'd be pleased."

"I am pleased, Mum. It's a lovely present."

"Do you want me to take it away? I suppose I can sell it on."

"No, no. Not at all. Here, give me it. It's a lovely treat for me. Very fancy, indeed. Will we have a coffee to celebrate?"

"That would be lovely. I bought you this as well." And she produced an antique cake stand from the bottom of the bag.

"Thanks, Mum! This is really smashing." Brenda wanted to be sure she sounded grateful. She reached out her hands for the gifts.

"Oh, good. I knew you'd be pleased." Mrs. Brown was convinced she had chosen the right gifts. She handed them over.

The two women went into the kitchen and

Mrs. Brown sat down at the little table while Brenda made the coffee.

"I'm sorry, I haven't a biscuit in the house," said Brenda. Mrs. Brown pulled a packet of peanut cookies and a box of mini-rolls from the pocket of her anorak.

"When have you, ever?" she smiled. "You're a true artist, Brenda. You've no notion of the real world at all."

"Well, I think that's not such a bad thing," replied Brenda. "I find the real world a bit of a disappointment. So, tell me, have you been busy recently?"

"Oh, yes. I have. I've sold seven car-bootfuls of your father's old junk. I've made a fortune." Mrs. Brown opened the box of rolls and the glossy packet of cookies and placed them on the cake stand.

"Mum, he'll go berserk."

"Well, I only sold the stuff he didn't want anymore. Records, out-of-date clothes, books, ashtrays. And since he moved out of the house and set up home with that harlot from Dublin, nothing I do is his business anymore."

"I suppose so," Brenda sighed. "I'm still getting over the shock. Are you coping okay on your own, Mum?"

"Not too bad. I've been to a Daniel O'Donnell concert with the girls from work. Daniel's a great tonic for a broken heart."

"That's nice."

"And we're going to a new line-dancing club at the weekend. You know, we're thinking of organizing a trip to Nashville."

"Mum! You're a fast mover!"

"Well, at my age you can't afford to mope about for ten years when your husband decides he doesn't love you anymore. I refuse to turn into a gibbering wreck."

"He'll be back, you know, Mum. This fling won't last. He'll be down on his knees at the front door in less than a month, begging to get back into the house, I promise you. Harlots never make good housewives."

"We'll see. Meanwhile, I'm going to get out there and enjoy myself. And if you'd any sense, you'd do the same, instead of being cooped up all day in this poky wee place. Now, will you let me take a couple of these pictures of yours? I'm going to a boot sale in Lurgan tomorrow. There's always a few well-heeled people about Lurgan."

"I won't even dignify that with an answer."

"Suit yourself. Well, I'm off."

"Won't you stay awhile?"

"Can't. The decorators are coming to paint the lounge at eleven. I'm having the whole place brightened up. Maybe you'd do a nice wee landscape for me, when you get the time?"

"Okay—cheerio, then."

"Bye, love. Here's a few quid for you, pet." She handed Brenda forty pounds. "And don't spend it all on paint. Do you hear me, now? Get yourself a few square meals next door."

"Thanks, Mum. I love you."

"Good job someone does. Right! I'll be off. Be sure and lock the door behind me. I don't trust this neighborhood."

When her mother had driven off, Brenda knelt down on the floor and examined the picture frame in more detail. It was hand-carved from real wood. Could that finish be genuine gold leaf? Covered in thick, sticky dust, it was, with threads of canvas hanging off the back, where the original painting had been torn away. Brenda began to think that her mother was right. This frame might be worth money; it did look like the real thing, not a molded reproduction. She would clean it up, and use it, after all.

In mounting excitement, she found a ruler

and measured the sides. She would make up a canvas to fit this frame, and hang it in a quiet corner of the gallery in Galway. Somewhere, where it would not distract from the other, unframed pieces. A little piece of whimsy, perhaps, that the critics would remember when they were writing their reviews?

She made another cup of coffee and nibbled her way through the rest of the peanut cookies, wondering what she would paint. It was a good omen, the timely arrival of this golden picture frame.

·29·

The Crawleys Meet the Queen

Alice crossed off the days on the calendar until the 26th of September arrived. The Crawleys were due to attend their special lunch at City Hall that afternoon. They got ready in complete silence, and stood side by side before the hall mirror as they pinned on their mother's brooches. A sudden tooting from outside told them the taxi had arrived.

"Come on," said Beatrice. "The sooner

we get this over with, the better. Now, remember, think twice before you open your trap. If this gets out, we're finished in the rambling club."

"Don't worry. Wild horses wouldn't drag it out of me. I just hope there aren't too many snobs about the place. Have you noticed how these special occasions seem to bring out the worst in people?"

They sat in the back of the car as if they were on their way to be executed.

"Where are you off to, the day?" asked the driver. "All done up like you are?"

"City Hall, please, driver." Beatrice did not want to talk.

"City Hall? Anything special?"

"No. Just a spot of lunch. And please keep your eye on the road."

The guests were mingling in the gardens. Speculation was rife as to who would be the guest of honor. Alice carried her handbag over her arm and struck up a royal pose beside the war memorial. One journalist with poor eyesight came rushing over, thinking she was a mystery VIP and was very embarrassed when he discovered she was only a humble pensioner. Beatrice took her sister by the arm and marched her over to the main entrance where they stood in line with their tattered invite at the ready.

The guests went into the banqueting hall and took their seats with the maximum of fuss and confusion. There was almost a scuffle at the top table as the mayor's wife and another female councilor fought over the chair nearest to the VIP section. There were some unpleasant accusations, regarding possible tampering with the seating plan.

There were so many fresh flowers on the tables, there was barely room for the cutlery. Beatrice hoped the flowers had been carefully checked for spiders. Wouldn't the queen think it was just typical of the muck-savages in Belfast if a big, fat spider fell out of the carnations and landed on its back in her soup? Alice glanced around the room, checking for unattended packages, and prayed their big day out wouldn't be spoiled by a bomb scare.

The lord mayor was perspiring heavily in his formal robes. His decorative chain was getting heavier by the minute, and his best trousers were much too tight. He'd have to go on a diet, one of these days. Or buy new ones in a bigger size. (Would expenses run to a new suit, he wondered.) He tapped the microphone and called for silence. The guests were so tense by now they were clawing the edges of the tablecloth and leaving marks on it. They all held their breath, and Alice gave Beatrice a good prodding with her elbow, to get her to look up. Beatrice told Alice that if she prodded her again, she would find herself flat on her back, on the patterned carpet.

The mayor coughed to prolong the agony. He was painfully aware of the rumors that were going around. He knew that everyone expected the queen to appear, and he had tried his best to get her there, but she was just too busy that day. Something about a dog show in Leeds. And so, he proudly announced that they would all be joined by none other than . . . the reigning Ulster beauty queen, Miss Northern Ireland herself.

"Miss . . . Miss . . ." He'd forgotten her name. All these dolly-birds looked the same to him: big white teeth and long thin legs. Like horses, they were. He liked his women petite and wearing housecoats. "Miss . . . Northern Ireland!" he roared into the microphone, causing a screech of feedback.

Suddenly, she appeared from a side

room, waving prettily, in a 1940s dress. She wore red lipstick, high heels and an RAF hat. There was a moment's stunned silence as she made her way up the room, swinging her pelvis from side to side, in a bizarre fashion. As if she was on the catwalk.

Someone giggled, and Beatrice realized it was her sister, Alice. She began to cough and clap, to cover up the strangled sounds of Alice's mini-breakdown. Then, the rest of the crowd recovered and began to clap, too. The tension that had been building for months exploded. The applause was tremendous, and the reporters surged forward to photograph the beauty queen. She smiled the most enormous smile the Crawleys had ever seen. Two whole rows of bleached white teeth, they could all see back to the very molars. The guests were temporarily blinded by the flashes of the cameras.

"Tell me this is not happening," said Alice, and then it was Bea-trice's turn to collapse in hysterical laughter.

"Cover your ears, Alice. I'm going to swear like a drunken docker," said Beatrice. And she did, six times.

The meal was served, and every delicious

mouthful was painful for the sisters to swallow. Their faces ached with the effort of smiling at everyone. Alice wished she could think of an excuse of some kind, so they could both go home. But she couldn't. She felt like someone had taken her heart away and replaced it with a peach stone. Her only consolation was noting that the mayor's wife, Georgina, looked even more depressed than she did. And that Georgina's enormous black hat, with artificial lilies on it, resembled a crashed hearse.

Miss Northern Ireland listened politely while the speeches were being read out, but the proceeding had lost all credibility.

"You can call the royals a bunch of idiots, if you like," said Alice, "but who else has anything even approaching their dignity? This whole thing has been a washout."

When it was all over, only half of the guests clapped, and the other half poked at their dentures with the complimentary toothpicks. Beatrice thought of her dear father, William, reading the telegram, in an army tent somewhere in France; the telegram that told him of the twins' birth. She shed a tear or two of disappointment then, and the guests correctly assumed she was thinking of a deceased relative, and they looked away, to spare her any embarrassment.

Alice was hiding in the toilets when the photographic exhibition was duly declared open. While she crouched in one of the palatial stalls, she overheard one of the guests reveal that she had stolen her three-hundred-pound shoes from a shop in Bangor, and another one boasted that she was having a lesbian affair with her tennis coach. Strangely, these snippets of scandal cheered Alice up a little bit.

When the sisters finally met the guest of honor, they were thoroughly bored. They were lined up against the wall like POWs and photographed with jolly television presenter Frank Mitchell and Miss Northern Ireland, whose name still escaped them. The photographer filled the frame with the lovely face of the beauty queen in the RAF hat, and Frank and the Crawleys were squeezed in round the edges.

When Beatrice saw herself and Alice, the next day, in the *Belfast Telegraph,* she said that the two of them looked like their mouths were full of vinegar. Their beautiful hats were sliced off the top of the picture. Beatrice laughed every time she looked at the newspaper, but Alice was outraged.

"If it wasn't for war and culture and pride and nationality, and stupid bloody *flags,* our dear father wouldn't have had to risk his life on the front line," she said to Beatrice, "while poor Mother found comfort in the arms of another man."

"Well," said Beatrice, "if you think about it, if it wasn't for the war, we might not be here at all . . ."

After that, they made a pact not to worry about it anymore. Some things were just too deep and profound for the human heart to understand.

And when one of the neighbors called round to congratulate them for appearing in the newspaper, and said, "We showed the Germans, all right. We gave them a right pasting," Alice left the room.

·30·

Connemara Memories

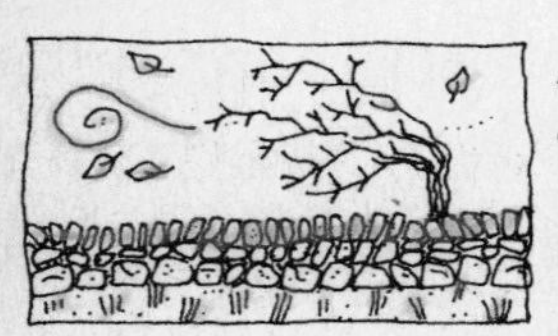

As Aurora and David viewed the tape of the documentary, in the sitting room, Henry slipped away from the house. He wandered around the park for a couple of hours and then he went to the tea house. Rose was sitting there, on her own.

He hesitated for a few moments and then went over.

"Excuse me," he said. "I hope you don't mind me interrupting you, but I'd like to buy you a coffee, to thank you for all your hard work with the plants."

"Oh, it's you, Mr. Blackstaff."

"Please call me Henry."

"Thank you, Henry. That's very kind of you."

He ordered coffees and bagels, and sat down again. He had no intention of saying anything personal; he was merely enjoying this chance meeting, but she was so easy to talk to. He found himself asking her all kinds of things.

"Your accent—you're not from Belfast?"

"No. I'm from Connemara."

"How did you ever come to live in this part of the world? I mean, it's supposed to be very beautiful there."

"It is. Totally unspoiled. But there's the rub. There aren't too many factories, you see—nowhere to get a job. I came here to live when I met my husband. He has a small business in the city center. He sells gadgets and electronic things. He's mad for anything modern, silver and small."

"My wife is the exact opposite. She lives for the past. Dusty old books and that sort of thing. Have you been married long?"

"Four years. Actually, we broke up awhile ago."

"Oh dear. I'm so sorry. I had no right to ask . . ."

"That's okay. I'm not going to fall to pieces or anything. I knew it was going to happen eventually. We had nothing in common anymore."

"Indeed," said Henry, and his heart swooped like a bird in flight.

"He asked me to give up my flower shop and work for him. Selling burglar alarms. That was the last straw. I knew then, it was the end." She smiled sadly. "You must think I'm terrible. Just to walk away from my marriage so easily."

"Not at all. I think you're very brave. If there's really nothing left between you. Are there any children?"

"No. John said we should wait until the business was established. You?"

"No. We never got round to having children. There were too many other things to do. And then, one day, we woke up, and we were ancient." He knew he was saying too much, but the words were coming out, and he could not stop them.

"Stop it! You're not ancient at all. Just

well-preserved. A hardy annual, in gardening parlance."

Henry laughed. "What will you do now?"

"I'm going home to Connemara. I like Belfast, but it doesn't feel like home. A friend of mine owns some holiday cottages right on the beach. And I'm going to stay there for a bit, and keep an eye on the place for her, until I decide what to do next. I have a sister in Australia. I might go there. I haven't made my mind up. I'm staying with a friend until I sell the shop."

"Tell me about Connemara."

"Well, everything is gray and it rains all the time. Not many trees. Stone walls everywhere. But sometimes I really miss the silence, and the mist coming in from the sea. I suppose you have to be born there to understand what I mean. Most people say it's lonely, and they wouldn't live there for a pension, but I like it."

"So why don't you do that, then? Live there?"

"I could do. All I need is a house to live in, some money to live *on* and a charming companion to live *with*! Now, if I could find myself an easygoing man of independent means, who likes the quiet life, then I'd be set up. You don't know anyone who fits that description, do you?"

Henry's face flushed very red. She was joking, of course. But maybe . . . "What would you do then, if you found such a person?"

"Simple. I'd spend the rest of my life planting trees. You know, of course, that this entire island used to be covered in trees? I'd plant hundreds of trees. And millions of flowers. Wildflowers."

The television program had been a great success. Aurora was thrilled with the resulting publicity. David Cropper became a great friend, and the two of them were planning a series of radio programs for schools and colleges.

Henry pottered about the house, feeling like a resident ghost. Aurora's conservatory repelled him somehow, like it didn't want him there. He was beginning to think it had a personality of its own, and he refused to have his morning coffee in it. Aurora teased him about it, endlessly. She spent all her spare time in the conservatory, reading obscure novels under a linen parasol.

Henry invited Rose to Muldoon's Tea Rooms for lunch several times, and they talked and talked about everything under the sun. He knew so much about her. Little things. Like, when she was fourteen, she jumped out of a first-floor window in school, to hide from the nun who would have caught her smoking. She broke a leg and never smoked again. He told her about his bookstore, his monkey-puzzle tree and his greenhouse, but did not mention his novels. He was finished with fiction. He wanted a real life, with real things happening in it.

• 31 •

Brenda Is Galway-Bound

Brenda Brown had been sitting in the tea house the day Henry and Rose had the conversation about Connemara. She listened carefully to Rose's description of it. She wasn't proud of herself for listening to someone else's private conversation, but Rose made the place sound so nice that she couldn't help it. Brenda was writing another letter to Nicolas Cage, but her concentration was flickering on and off like a faulty light, with excitement.

October 10, 1999
Dear Nicolas,

How are you?

Please write to me and tell me if you received the painting. It would make me so happy to know that you got it. Just a postcard, or anything.

You know that gallery I was telling you about, the one in Galway? Well, they've been so nice. They understand what I'm trying to do. I think people in the southern part of this island are more advanced, culturally, than their northern counterparts. The only things that sell in Belfast are kitsch little landscapes.

Well, I'm not going to paint boring watercolors of Portstewart Strand. That's the junk food of the art world: easy and quick. The owner of this place, a Mrs. Penny Stanley, has one such painting upstairs and it's absolute rubbish. She showed it to me last year. I can't believe her husband paid good money for that rubbish.

If things go well for me in Galway, I may never come back.

If you get this letter, think of me on

December 15th. That's the date of the exhibition opening.

I found out recently that my father is getting married to another woman, and I now recall an argument he had some time ago, with my mother, about a Dublin tart. But I thought they were talking about pastries. Poor Mum. The neighbors have taken to walking their dogs by our house, hoping to catch a glimpse of her crying in the front room. But she's been a real trouper.

She's started using her maiden name again.

I mentioned the idea of changing my name to the owners of the Blue Donkey Gallery, but they said not to worry. Brenda Brown is fine, and names don't matter, they said.

A few uplifting pieces for the window display, that's what they want.

Take care of yourself.

Lots of love,

Brenda

PS. Please send me a signed photo.

I'm a genuine fan.

·32·

The Crawleys See the Light

Several days passed. Alice wept a little when she said her prayers each night. Beatrice looked at the portrait of her father many times and searched in his blue eyes for some evidence that he was disappointed in his children. But she saw only love. They went over and over the possibilities, and cried, and prayed, and ranted and raved. But in the end, they had no choice but to accept the fact that their biological father was almost certainly a German gentleman of the Jewish faith. Their mother had had an affair, with a man called Leo, a refugee from Nazi Germany probably, and her husband had forgiven her. And if he could forgive and forget, then so could they. Alice cheered up a little when Beatrice pointed out that the British royal family had some German blood in its veins as well.

"Queen Victoria's husband, Albert, was a German, wasn't he? They had a huge family together. The German race must be incredibly fertile," said Beatrice. "In a way, we have become international, which is better than provincial, at the end of the day. They say a good mix of genes makes a person stronger." Eventually, after days and days of sadness, they felt something close to contentment.

They told no one, not even their minister in the church. They still attended morning service every Sunday, but when he preached about sin and sinners and corruption in the modern world, they said nothing. They did not clap or nod their heads in agreement.

"Let him who is without sin cast the first stone," whispered Alice.

They gave up writing letters to the newsagent's. He was stocking more filth than ever, to spite them, they felt. It was only a waste of postage stamps. Even the charity work had lost its sparkle, a little. No one in the congregation was all that impressed anymore when Alice and Beatrice collected the most money for each project. In fact, some people even went as far as to say, why wouldn't they collect the most money? They had nothing else to do all day. No grandchildren to pick up from school, no big family dinners to arrange, no husbands to tidy up after. As outraged as the sisters were, they had to admit it was true.

"Oh, bugger this," sighed Beatrice, one wet Sunday afternoon. (She had taken to swearing, like a duck to water.) They were sitting at the table after enjoying a superb roast of beef and Yorkshire pudding. "Don't let's bother with the washing-up. I want to do something else. Something exciting."

"Well, what else is there to do on a drizzly Sunday in Belfast?" Alice was puzzled.

"Get your coat on, Alice," said Beatrice. "We're going in to the city center, to book ourselves on a holiday to Israel. Sure, what are we saving our pensions for? Haven't we got one foot in the grave, and no children to provide for? We are going to have the trip of a lifetime!"

"What will we do in Israel, of all places?"

"See new sights! Eat new foods, and meet new people. And say a few prayers while we're there, of course."

They chose to fly out to Israel for Christmas. Alice developed a taste for bagels with cream cheese. Beatrice decided she preferred apple strudel. They began to say hello to strangers on the street. They were all a part of the human race, Beatrice would say, from time to time; people were all related to one another in some way.

·33·

Sadie Gets Rid of the Bitter Lemons

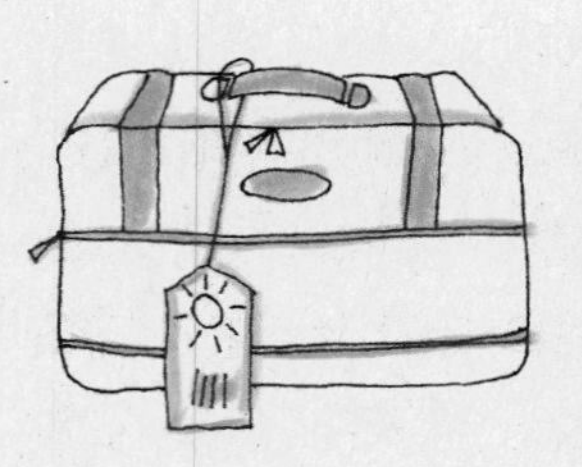

Sadie's revenge was slow to gather momentum, but her planning was sheer genius. First, she was going to make Arnold look ridiculous in front of his fancy woman, and then she was going to get rid of his parents and all their money. And then, she was going to embarrass him professionally, and then she was going to kick him out of the bungalow in Carryduff for good.

She had spent hours in Muldoon's, perfecting her ideas.

She was a regular in the cafe these days, on first-name terms with Penny and Daniel. She watched them closely from the little table for one where she always sat. She noticed that Daniel was not as dedicated to the cooking as he once was. If the sandwich Sadie wanted was not available, he would just say so; not go rushing to make it up specially. Quite often, he got Sadie's order mixed up or gave her the wrong change. He seemed very tired, and he yawned a lot. His hair was getting so long he could tuck his fringe behind one ear. He really needed a rest, by the look of him, thought Sadie. Most of the time, he was the only one working in the tea house.

Penny, on the other hand, was full of life and energy. She had blossomed since having her hair cut so dramatically. Gone were the cheap and glittery hair accessories and earrings of the past, and the gypsy-type blouses and skirts she had worn for so long. Nowadays, she wore high quality makeup and perfume, and expensive, plain linen trouser suits. She drifted in and out of the cafe as she pleased, arriving back with several carrier-bags from expensive shops one day, when Sadie was having lunch.

Another day, Sadie heard the two of them arguing in the kitchen. It was hard to catch all the details but Sadie thought it had something to do with a silver necklace. An expensive necklace that Penny had been wearing for a few days. Where had she got it? Daniel wanted to know. And where was she at the weekend?

Sadie was shocked to hear Penny taunting her husband. Couldn't he guess? Couldn't he work it out for himself? What did he care, anyway? Wasn't he happy enough with his cakes and pies and his rusty old kitchen? That sort of thing. Sadie almost forgot to eat her strawberry cheesecake, so intently did she spy on the Stanley marriage.

Then Sadie saw Penny getting into a car on the Lisburn Road, driven by a good-looking man in a fancy suit, and it all made sense. Penny was having an affair with another man, and Daniel was too distracted by the worry of it to concentrate on his baking. The poor wretch. Sadie wondered if the whole of Belfast was driving around, having flings and fancy pieces on the side, and if she was the only one left with any morals. Daniel really should do something about his wife's behavior.

Sadie was determined to punish Arnold for what he had done to her. She wanted him out of the house by Christmas. She'd given him time to mend his ways and plenty of it. Nobody could say that she hadn't.

During that long, dreadful summer, there was a little part of Sadie that wanted to forgive Arnold: to excuse the awful things he had said about her to Patricia, as the idle boasts of a middle-aged man trying to impress his younger mistress. (His poisonous, gold-digging mistress.) Poor Arnold, she reasoned: Patricia Caldwell was only bewitching him with her lacy red knickers, to get her bony hands on their luxury bungalow. One hundred and fifty thousand pounds it must be worth. Patricia would never make that kind of money, selling ashtrays and potpourri in her little shop. Well, thought Sadie, she'll get this house over my dead body: I'll commit mass murder and arson before I let that happen.

Then, she calmed down again. No, no, she always relented. If I lose control, I'll lose everything. I'll end up in prison, and I'll bet they don't serve cherry cheesecake in Maghaberry Women's Wing. And then she would go over her plans again. It was nearly time to put them into action. She'd been to see a lawyer as well. He'd told her not to worry; Arnold could not throw her out on the street. He was only bluffing. Anything he had on paper would not stand up in a court case, after twenty years of marriage.

Sadie had fantasies in the wee small hours of the morning, where Arnold would confess everything and say he was sorry. So sorry, he couldn't say how sorry. He would weep with shame. He would kneel on the carpet and beg for her forgiveness; declare that he had been a blind, stupid, cruel, monstrous fool.

But Arnold didn't do that. He refused to eat fried food and had muesli instead. He admired his trimmer waistline in the hall mirror before going to work each morning. He spent all his free time in the study, making illicit calls to Patricia on the telephone. And so, Sadie sighed with resignation and crossed off the last few days until his trip to Paris, on a wall calendar from Nicholl Fuels with a picture of an oil tanker on it.

On the day that Arnold was due to go to the airport, Sadie snipped two buttons off his best suit with a pair of nail scissors and flushed the buttons down the lavatory. She burned his new shirt with the iron and kicked his passport under the bed. She slipped a couple of raunchy men's magazines from the newsagent's into his overnight bag, hidden under a towel at the bottom.

"Oh dear," she said, coming into the kitchen, where Arnold was sipping his morning cuppa. "Two buttons have fallen off your new jacket, darling. I never noticed till right this minute!"

"Bloody hell, Sadie! How did that happen? Have you looked in the wardrobe?"

"Yes, my love. They aren't there."

"Damn and blast! That suit looked so good on me, too."

"I'm afraid that isn't all . . ."

"What is it, woman? I'm in a hurry."

"I left the iron on your new shirt too long."

"You've not burned it?"

"I have, darling. I'm so sorry. I was looking for the missing buttons."

"Sadie, you twerp! Do you expect me to fly to Paris in a burnt shirt?"

"Oh, Arnold, forgive me! It's just, I'm going to miss you so much, I can't think straight."

Arnold had to wear another, inferior, suit and shirt, and this irritated him greatly. Then he noticed his passport was not on his bedside table and, by the time he found it, he realized he would miss the plane. In his haste, he cut himself shaving and stubbed his toe on the hall table while rushing out to the car. He drove at breakneck speed to the airport.

Patricia was very upset. She was waiting in the airport bar, in tears. She thumped him with her clutch bag when he arrived, gasping, at the terminal building. They had to wait for three hours for the next flight, which gave them plenty of time to argue. By the time they checked into their Paris hotel, dinner was over and the bar was closed. Patricia was outraged when Arnold unpacked his bag and she saw the offensive magazines he had brought with him.

"Is that how you see me? As a cheap tart? How dare you bring this smut on our lovely holiday," she barked. Arnold had never heard Patricia shout before. She sounded disturbingly canine.

"I don't. I didn't. I have no idea how it got there. I swear it."

"Who packed the bag? Did Sadie Sponge do it?"

"Of course not. There's three packets of contraceptives in there. How could I explain that to Sadie? A person doesn't usually need condoms at a double-glazing convention, for God's sake! Not unless their sales figures are so low that desperate measures are called for. Ha ha ha!"

"Oh, shut up! Why don't you just admit you brought pornography to Paris?"

"For the last time, I did not bring it! I'm telling you the truth, Patricia."

"I don't believe you, Arnold. Why should I believe a word you say? You're a liar!"

"I beg your pardon?"

"You heard me. You're a big fat liar. You've lied to your wife for months. More than a year, for heaven's sake. You said she was a real dope. That she would believe any old hogwash. Is that what I am, Arnold? Am I a real dope, too?"

"Look! Are we going to get frisky, or not?" said Arnold, feeling suddenly weary. He sat down on top of the magazines. If a bit of fun was off the menu, he was going to lie in a hot bath, with a large whiskey.

"You what? You're the limit, Arnold Smith. You really are. You take that smut into the bathroom and have fun with it. I've never been so insulted in my life." She had gone off the idea of model-ing her sexy lingerie. In fact, she began to think Arnold was a bit arrogant.

Arnold scuttled off to the bathroom, where he sat on the laundry basket and sulked for a while, waiting for the bath to fill.

At midnight, they had a cup of watery French tea and collapsed into bed, exhausted. Patricia turned her back on Arnold, and when he slipped his hand under her nightdress, in a desperate bid to consummate the trip, she nipped the skin on the back of his hand as hard as she could and left a tiny, purple bruise.

Earlier that evening, in Belfast, Sadie poured Maurice and Daisy a very large gin and tonic apiece and set out some pretty bowls of nibbles on the coffee table. She drew the heavy curtains in the sitting room. They were all sitting comfortably in front of the fire, politely ignoring an enormous pile of ironing in the corner.

"When the cat's away, the mice will play," she chuckled, as she picked up some ice cubes from the bucket with her little tongs and dropped them into the glasses.

"Well, this is very nice," sniffed Daisy, reaching for a peanut.

"What's up?" Maurice wanted to know. "What are we celebrating?"

"Oh, nothing," said Sadie. "I just felt we deserved a treat." She flicked around with the remote control until she found the travel program on the television, that she had circled in the *Radio Times*. She wanted to make sure the atmosphere was right.

Daisy looked at the blue skies on the screen and she sighed.

"Oh, how lovely," Sadie said. "Sometimes, I wish I'd been born a Greek. Or a Spaniard. Or an Italian. Anywhere really, where there's a bit of sun. It doesn't seem natural to have to pay hundreds of pounds on some package holiday just to see the sun."

"I know what you mean," said Daisy.

"Some of us would be happy to pay it, if we were fit to go," said Maurice.

"Funny you should say that," said Sadie. "I was watching television in bed the other night, and there was a great program on, about this retired couple from Birmingham. Anyway, the husband had arthritis, just like you, Maurice. And the wife was a bit stiff herself. Anyway, they went on holiday to this Greek island. Oh, it did look lovely!"

"Were they as old as we are?" asked Daisy.

"Older. The resort was specially designed to cater to pensioners, and they had a whale of a time." Sadie ate some peanuts and topped up their glasses.

"Not cheap, I'll wager," said Maurice.

"Of course it wasn't cheap. The whole place being on the one level and all. There's no stairs, you see. Very quiet at night. There's no discos allowed on that part of the island. And a full English menu. All the rashers you can eat. No, it's not cheap, as I said before. But what's the point of having money in the bank if it doesn't bring you pleasure? You can't take it with you. That's what I say. And I got to thinking what you said, Maurice, about wanting to go on holiday before it was too late. . . .The two of you should go! What's stopping you?"

Maurice and Daisy looked at her in amazement. Sadie did not usually sound so friendly. They said they would think about it. It was really quite strange, because only that morning, they'd been considering going on a little holiday to Portstewart. Life in the bungalow had become very tedious, since Sadie gave up her domestic duties and became a full-time layabout.

"You do that," said Sadie. "Don't you be hoarding your money, to leave it to Arnold and me, and the boys. When you pass on, I mean. We'll be fine. Arnold does very well financially, although he doesn't like to boast about it. And, of course, the boys are well set up in Australia with their gardening business. Making a packet, they are. Those Australians won't lift a finger in the garden if the sun is shining. They're all away charging to the beach with those board-things."

"I'm not sure," said Daisy.

"I think you deserve a holiday. Sure, it never stops raining in this godforsaken place. If I had any money myself, I'd be out of here like a shot."

"Well, Sadie, I don't know what to say," began Maurice.

"You know what, Maurice?" she interrupted. "I've never told you and Daisy just how much I love and admire you both. It's not in my nature to show affection and to be fawning all over people, but I just want you to know that I love you both very much."

"Oh. Well. Thanks, Sadie," said Daisy. "I always thought we were in your way here."

"In the way? Not at all. Far from it. I only wish the two of you had more of a life."

"What do you mean?" asked Maurice.

"Well, now. It can't be very exciting for you to be stuck with me all day."

"There's not much call for excitement at our time of life," said Daisy.

"Oh, I disagree. You should enjoy your retirement. You've earned it. And I'm not much of a cook, either—not like you were, Daisy. You can't compare frozen cod to what those people are eating in that Greek tavern, there." They all looked at the television screen. A sexy, young waiter was serving a multicolored salad to some laughing tourists. "And you both used to be so active and independent. It's a shame."

"What are you trying to say, Sadie?"

"Just that if you do go away to Greece, I'll look after Arnold. I promise. I'll see he gets everything that he deserves."

And with that, Sadie wiped her eyes with the back of her hand, to show them how sincere she was. Then she turned up the volume on the television and let the travel program do the rest of her work for her.

When Arnold returned from Paris, his parents were in great spirits. There were four new suitcases in the hall and holiday brochures on the coffee table.

"What's going on?" he asked. "Do we have guests?"

"Oh, there you are. Did you have a nice time in Paris? I hope it wasn't too boring for you. Was the food terrible?" Sadie was folding tea towels in the kitchen.

"No, of course not. But what's going on?" He was impatient, now.

"All those chicken giblets and snails and horses' heads. Oh!" She made a face. "Is it true they make sausages out of cows' intestines?"

"I said, what is going *on*?"

"Do you mean the luggage?"

"Yes. I mean the blessed luggage."

"Maurice and Daisy are going on a little trip of their own," said Sadie. "You're not the only globe-trotter in this family. They're off to Greece next week."

"They're what? Who is responsible for this? I absolutely forbid this nonsense. They're in their seventies, for heaven's sake!"

"That's not old, by modern standards, my love. They're going to Greece next week, and they're delighted about it."

"They can't manage on their own. This is ridiculous. I go away for three days and the whole place falls to pieces. Really, Sadie, I'm disappointed in you."

"Now, you haven't heard the whole story. They'll be collected at the front door in Belfast and brought right to the hotel in Greece, and they'll be accompanied all the way by a nurse and several helpers. They won't be on their own. All the meals are laid on. They won't have to do anything except enjoy themselves. Don't worry." Sadie smiled at Arnold as if he was a small child who had grazed his knees.

"A nurse! What is all this costing? That's what I want to know," said Arnold.

"Who cares? They have plenty of savings," said Sadie. Though not for much longer, she hoped. "Oh, and by the way," she added, "could I have some extra money at the end of the month? I'd like to join a gym and get rid of this tummy of mine. Now that I'll have some time to myself . . ."

Arnold was in a bad mood for days. Maurice and Daisy set off on their trip to Greece, and they had such a good time, they decided to stay on for another month. They sent a postcard to the bungalow. They had made lots of friends and were beginning to know their way round the island. Their suite was very comfortable. Maurice said the pain in his knees was easing, and Daisy had developed a taste for the local cuisine. They said they felt they might live forever. Arnold was furious.

Then Sadie left Arnold's golf clubs out on the lawn when she was cleaning in the shed, and they were stolen by a light-fingered passerby, in broad daylight.

"I just came out of the shed, and there they were . . . gone!" she told Arnold when he came home from the office. She was very sorry indeed, she said, over and over. She couldn't believe she could be such a *dope.* But Arnold thought he heard her giggling in the bath that evening.

He told Patricia that Sadie Sponge had

joined a gym, and that she went there every day.

"But so far," he said, "she hasn't lost any weight. In fact, I think she's getting bigger."

•34•

The House on Magnolia Street

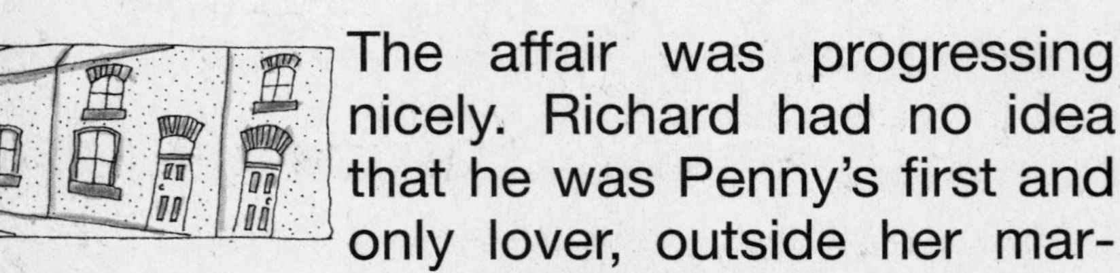

The affair was progressing nicely. Richard had no idea that he was Penny's first and only lover, outside her marriage, although he did think she was very innocent. She always let him lead the way when they made love in the low designer bed in the flat. Richard thought she was very dignified. Mysterious, too. Penny always got dressed and undressed in the en suite bathroom. She wasn't like his previous lovers, pulling their underwear off and on in front of him. She was polite. He liked that in a woman. She seemed very pleased and contented every time they went to bed together. They usually fell asleep holding hands.

In another life, Richard might have proposed to Penny. He was very fond of her. Maybe he was falling in love with her. He told her she was very sweet and charming, but he was careful not to mention the word *love.* That would mean commitment, and that wasn't Richard's style. If he did ever find himself at the altar rails, there would have to be a very wealthy bride walking up the aisle toward him. Richard didn't want to sell houses forever.

Meanwhile, Penny was the perfect lover. She laughed at his jokes and did not ask him about his personal life, or where his parents lived, or when she would see him again. She took care of the birth-control side of things, without lecturing him about it being his responsibility. She was gentle in bed, patient and relaxed, caressing his muscular back and kissing him softly. She was very quiet, too. No screaming his name out loud and scratching his back with her fingernails, like that girl from North Down he'd dated two years earlier. Richard respected Penny for that. These liberated women could be a real turnoff, especially when they asked him to do unusual things. He had no time for adult films, strip clubs, stag weekends, binge drinking or sex toys. Richard Allen was an old-fashioned lover.

Penny enjoyed their liaisons in the stylish flat. Richard was always attentive and sexy, playing his part well. They went to the theater, for drives along the coast and for meals in country pubs. Sometimes Richard paid, and sometimes Penny picked up the bill. It was well worth the effort she spent on her makeup and clothes. She enjoyed their time together but it was nothing like the sexually charged encounters she saw in the movies.

Brenda Brown often said she would give anything for one tender kiss with Nicolas Cage and die happy afterward. Penny didn't feel like that about Richard. Maybe the kind of love she wanted only existed on the silver screen.

Sometimes Penny stayed the night at Richard's place and sometimes she went home in a taxi, at midnight. She told lies to

Daniel. It was the only way she could think of to lessen the hurt she was causing him. He had his suspicions, of course, but he couldn't prove anything.

The taxi drivers knew Penny and they assumed she was having an affair. But she was a nice reliable customer and she always gave a good tip. They asked no questions on the trips back and forth to the expensive apartments beside the river.

"Does your husband never wonder where you are?" Richard asked her, after they had been seeing each other for eight weeks.

"If he does, he never shows it."

"Really? He doesn't ask at all?"

"No. We rarely speak to each other these days. We're more like business partners, to tell you the truth. I take what I need from our joint account and I just tell him I'm going out."

"And he lets you spend the money?"

"He doesn't like it. But he doesn't stop me."

"Are you going to leave him?" Richard was nervous.

"Maybe. Maybe not. Probably not. But don't worry, darling. I'm not going to turn up on your doorstep with all my belongings in a bin-bag."

"I didn't mean that."

"Yes, you did. And I don't blame you one bit. You've got a great setup here, and the last thing you want is some hysterical housewife bringing her whole life in on top of you." She touched his hand affectionately. They were eating a salmon pie from the supermarket at a little bistro table in the dining room.

"I'm not ready for a serious grown-up relationship, that's all."

"I'm here tonight because I love spending time with you, and talking to you and going out for nice meals with you. I'm not trying to move in here, or maneuver you into a position where you're afraid to finish with me." She poured another glass of wine for them. "It will end between us, no doubt, when the time is right."

"You're a special woman, Penny," said Richard, who had never known a female to be so calm and self-possessed.

"That's certainly true," said Penny with a smile.

"What does your husband do when you go out?"

"He works in the shop. He tries out new recipes . . ." Penny didn't want to think about Daniel. She wanted to enjoy these lovely evenings with Richard. She planned to bring them to an end soon. Richard was great fun to be with, but the feelings that Penny wanted to experience, the feelings that Brenda talked about, were not there. She thought she had felt it, the night she met Daniel, and look how that turned out.

"What did you say was the name of your business?" Richard was thoughtful.

"Muldoon's Tea Rooms."

"On Mulberry Street?" He had stopped eating and was scratching his head now.

"Yes. That's it."

"How long have you and him been living there?"

"Seventeen years. But, Richard, I don't want to talk about—"

"Wait. This is so odd. I think I sold him a house."

"You must be mistaken," said Penny casually. "We live above the shop. Always have."

"No. I am quite certain. Years and years ago, it was. Fourteen, fifteen? I sold him a little house on Magnolia Street. Wait now . . . Was it definitely Magnolia Street?"

"Well, it can't have been him," said Penny, taking another delicious forkful of salmon pie.

"It *was* him," said Richard.

"Oh, come on, Richard! In any case, how can you possibly recall a sale that far back?"

"I remember, Penny, because he paid me in *cash.* Well over the asking price, too. Strictly speaking, I shouldn't have put the sale through without checking him out legally. But I was a bit short of money at the time. Very determined, he was, to have the place."

Penny suddenly put her fork down, a strange feeling sweeping over her. She got up and walked over to the large window, where she could look down and see the lights shining on the river.

"Magnolia Street isn't that far away from where we live now. You don't happen to know the address of this house, do you?" she said, quietly.

"I can check the house number from my records. I've kept all my work diaries. They're right here in the apartment. It was a real dump, as I recall. Hadn't been renovated in years. He could have got a new-build in the suburbs for the money he was spending. I did try to tell him . . ."

He went to his desk, to find the right diary. Penny sat down on the leather armchair and drained her glass of wine. If she found out that Daniel owned a house on Magnolia Street, after he wouldn't even consider a new fitted kitchen for the cafe, then she really would leave him. She'd throw him out of the tea house and phone the builders the very same day. Suddenly she was possessed by rage. It seethed like a boiling cauldron.

"Here it is," said Richard, in a triumphant voice. "I never forget an easy sale."

·35·

Sadie Cancels Christmas

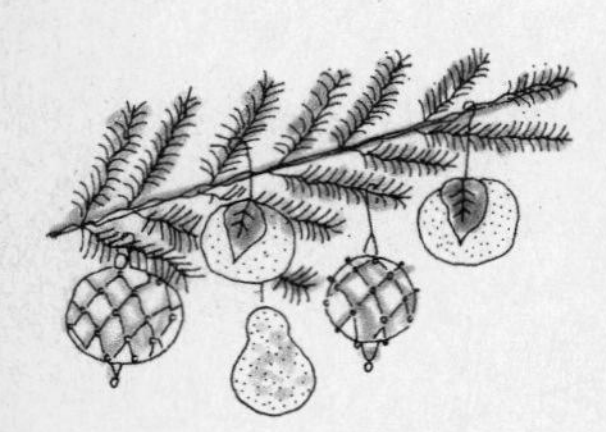

Sadie left the bungalow every morning, regular as clockwork. She had a track suit and sneakers in her basket. But she never went near the gym. She considered gyms to be dirty and uncomfortable places, full of stale air and aggressive people. She caught the bus into the city and wandered round the shops, treating herself to little things. New wool gloves, or a romantic paperback, or fancy packets of upmarket crisps. At lunchtime, she went to the tea house on Mulberry Street and ordered lunch. She sat, all by herself, at her usual table and enjoyed the delicious food with a clear conscience. Daniel had introduced a turkey-and-stuffing toasted sandwich for the run-up to Christmas, which was proving very popular. So was his Christmas Platter, which consisted of a mince pie, a slice of iced fruit cake and a large cup of coffee with fresh cream on the top.

Sadie went browsing in every shop in the city that sold candlesticks until she found Patricia. Arnold's wicked temptress was serving customers at the counter, with a scowl on her painted face. They must be short-staffed, thought Sadie. She watched Patricia scolding a terrified young assistant who had stuck the wrong prices on a batch of pottery chickens. Sadie took a deep breath, put on a pair of sunglasses, picked up a glass bowl and went to stand in the queue.

"£39.99," said Patricia, rudely. Not so much as a *please.*

"It's a lovely bowl," said Sadie.

"Indeed," said Patricia.

"It's the very thing I was looking for," said Sadie.

Patricia thrust the bowl into a carrier-bag and held out her hand for the money.

"Oh, I'm terribly sorry. But would you mind wrapping it up in tissue paper? I'm afraid I might break it on the bus." Sadie smiled apologetically.

"Right," said Patricia, and she took the bag back, with a sigh.

"Thank you very much," said Sadie. "I'm having a big party this Christmas, you see. Can you believe it's November already? All my husband's family are coming for the day. And I want the house to look just perfect. I'm going to fill the bowl with scented pine cones and set it on the coffee table. I just love Christmas, don't you?"

Patricia seemed very irritated by this question. Her red lips disappeared into a thin line.

On the day that Maurice and Daisy were due to fly into Belfast Airport, Arnold took the day off work and polished the car until it shone. He would pick them up at six o'clock in the evening. He hoped their gallivanting days would now be over.

"The sooner those two come home, and everything returns to normal in this house, the better," he said, as he rubbed and rubbed the bonnet with a chamois.

"I think you'd better come inside, dear," said Sadie, from the front porch. "Your father wants to speak to you on the telephone."

Arnold's face was a tonic when he heard the news. A proper tonic. Maurice and Daisy had spent their life savings, leasing a small apartment on the island. It was some deal they had cooked up with a local businessman, but it was all legal and aboveboard, Maurice assured his son. Maurice would live there with Daisy, for the "duration" (as Maurice liked to refer to their natural life span) and then the apartment could return to this local man. Of course, it was money they could never get back, but it was the only way they could get the splendid apartment with sea views on three sides. They couldn't afford it, outright. Not to worry, they still had the proceeds of the sale of their old home to live on. Thank God, they hadn't touched that money when they moved in with Arnold and Sadie, five years ago.

They could live very cheaply there, Maurice said. The food cost next to nothing. They had cashed in the policy on their life insurance, too. They had gone to the market on a shopping spree and bought lots of summer clothes. They had made some new friends, not just British and Irish ex-pats, but local people, too. They were all getting on like a house on fire, not a bit of racial tension. They were not coming back to Belfast. Not ever.

Arnold had to kneel down on the hall carpet—not to beg Sadie to forgive him for his affair with Patricia Caldwell, but to get his breathing to return to normal. His inheritance faded away along with the color in his cheeks.

"A lease! They're spending their money on a lease! They're going to die as paupers. This is all your fault!" he shouted, as Sadie set the table for supper. "You sent them on the blasted holiday in the first place. I can't believe this is happening."

"What about their life insurance?"

"They've cashed in the policy for extra spending money!"

"Oh, isn't Maurice clever?" said Sadie. And she meant it. She knew that Daisy and Maurice could look after themselves, perfectly well, given half a chance. "Of course, Maurice was a very successful accountant, before he retired."

"Holy cow! I was going to retire on that money." The full realization hit Arnold like a ton of bricks. A small fortune of a windfall, gone—on a whim of his dotty father. The lovely things Arnold could have spent that money on. . . . Classy hotels abroad, with staff who knew how to treat guests with respect. Visions of Patricia, lying on various beaches around the world, in various bikinis. Maybe even other women. *Really* beautiful women. Eating out, in all the best places, rubbing shoulders with celebrities . . . he'd wear a cravat. Sadie Sponge's voice reared up through his daydream like the Loch Ness Monster.

"I think it's a lovely idea," she soothed. "Isn't it great they still have so much life in them? I shall miss them both dreadfully."

"Don't tell bare-faced lies! You hated the pair of them."

"I did not. They were a sweet old couple!"

"They kept you on the go all day. You never got to sit down," he ranted.

"Not at all. I was happy to help," she said, innocently. But it was a kind of victory, getting him to admit it like that.

"Well, I'm not blinking-well standing for this! I'll have them both sectioned under the Mental Health Act, and brought home, and their assets frozen. Hell's bells! What's the phone number of their doctor?"

"Arnold, dear. They are competent adults and they can do what they like. That's why they went to Greece in the first place, because their assets *were* frozen." She began to giggle. "And will you please stop swearing and calm down."

"I won't calm down!"

"You want to watch your blood pressure, at your age. You'll work your way up into a heart attack. You've been looking dreadful, lately. You're as pale as death. I hope you don't mind me saying so." She got up and patted him on the head.

"But—the money! The *money* they've spent. Wasted on a *lease.* I can't bear to think of it . . . I wonder if there's a get-out clause. I'm going to fly out there—today."

"Well, I don't think you should bother, my

dear. After all, you don't want people to think you're a gold-digging parasite of a son, just waiting on them to die . . . Do you?"

But Arnold did not trust himself to say any more.

Patricia was not as passionate as she had been in the beginning of their relationship. She had forgiven him for ruining their Paris trip, she said, but her desire for him was on the wane. Arnold's magazines had made her feel cheap and tawdry, not the glamorous and sultry mistress she once thought she was. She stopped wearing her lacy thongs and suspenders, and threw her PVC blindfold in the bin.

And then, there was this calamity of Arnold's nest egg disappearing on a lease, in Greece. He went on and on about it. Life savings, life insurance policy, house-sale money, all gone. All neatly tied up forever. Apparently, the Greeks had very good lawyers; they weren't all just waiters and shepherds, after all. It was very boring to listen to. And Patricia didn't want to hear about it. She'd had a lot of plans for the Bitter Lemon Fund, as she liked to call it.

She began making excuses not to see him: a headache, a family occasion, a conference on time management.

A little voice in the back of Arnold's mind told him that Patricia was going off him because his inheritance was slowly seeping into the Greek economy, but he refused to believe it.

Sadie was neglecting the housework. That was another thing that worried Arnold. The grass was not cut, weeds grew over the garden paths and the shrubs were untidy. There was dust on the bathroom windowsill and on his aftershave collection. She was always forgetting to post his mail and collect his dry cleaning. The ironing lay undone on the sofa, in a huge tumbling pile. More often than not, he had to iron his own shirt in the morning, because Sadie was getting ready for the gym. He was no good at ironing, and Patricia often said he looked like he had slept in his clothes. His socks were not rolled into neat balls in his sock drawer and his shoes were not polished. Arnold began to appreciate all the little things Sadie had done for him over the years. Especially the sock balls. It was such a nuisance to have to look for two matching socks in the morning. But no matter how much he nagged her, she was not prepared to organize his socks anymore. He began to look quite untidy.

"In fact," said Patricia, one evening, as they were having dinner in a pub near Saint Anne's Cathedral, "you're starting to look positively disheveled."

Arnold thought he caught her smiling at another man when he came back from the Gents.

When December arrived, the Christmas decorations had already been up for weeks. Shop windows all over the city were filled with gifts and goodies and little Santas with long white beards and round wire spectacles. The supermarkets played compilations of carols and classical music. A huge Christmas tree was erected in front of the City Hall, and decked out with red and yellow lights and tinsel. The members of the city council managed to put their various squabbles behind them for long enough to organize a lavish Christmas banquet. And the divided communities of the city were finally united in their begrudgery of it all. Millennium or not, those boys were getting away with far too much.

Arnold had a deluge of phone calls from housewives who wanted a new conservatory, after they saw Aurora Blackstaff's on the front cover of *Ireland's Homes and Interiors,* with a gorgeous ten-foot spruce tree inside it, absolutely dripping with barley sugar canes and strings of fresh cranberries. That was the way things were going in suburbia, Arnold noted. The women wanted a traditionally decorated tree in the sitting room for the family to enjoy and another whimsical one in the conservatory. Just for themselves.

They should feature a Christmas tree in the next Walley brochure, he decided. He faxed the idea to Head Office and they were delighted with him. They sent him a crate of champagne by return of post and got to work on a new brochure straightaway. The flood of new orders cheered Arnold up and gave him the motivation to sort out his personal life.

He wanted Sadie to revert to the superb housewife she used to be and Patricia to return to her role as his willing sex slave, on permanent standby to attend to his manly needs. It was frustrating for Arnold when the two women in his life were not behaving properly. He went shopping for lavish gifts for the two of them, to sweeten them up. He bought Sadie a bread maker, a fancy see-through vacuum cleaner, an electric hedge trimmer and some electronic scales for the bathroom. He bought Patricia a bottle of expensive perfume, the naughtiest black bra and suspenders he could find, a set of massage oils and a black leather dress. He wrapped the gifts in his office and stashed them neatly beside the door, ready for Christmas Eve.

He arranged to spend Christmas Eve with Patricia and he booked a romantic meal for two in a little restaurant on Botanic Avenue, for four o'clock in the afternoon. If things went well, he would be home with Sadie by seven-thirty, ready for a big family get-together on Christmas Day itself.

He thought Christmas would be a good opportunity to get Sadie back to work around the house. Arnold's relations were always invited for Christmas Day and Sadie usually spent weeks polishing the house from top to bottom, and baking cakes, pies and pastries for the freezer. She always filled the house with fresh greenery from the garden, and homemade salt-dough angels and stars. He would speak to her that evening, he decided, as he stuck a big pink bow on the bread maker. Pink was Sadie's color, he thought. Pink, like a cartoon elephant. Like marshmallows and candy floss. Patricia's color was black, like the black of a wicked witch's cloak.

Sadie was watching a drama on television when Arnold came home, and did not even look at him when he asked how the Christmas preparations were coming along.

"I can't be bothered with all that stuff anymore," said Sadie. She was sitting on the sofa, with her feet up on a cushion.

"You what?" he said. "The turkey, the goose, the fruit cake—"

"Well, nobody really appreciates it, do they? It takes a whole day to bake a cake and another day to decorate the damn thing. No. I'll get some sausage rolls and party nibbles from the supermarket and heat it all up in the oven. Ready-made pasta salads. Potato croquettes from the freezer."

"Tell me you're jesting!"

"A buffet. That'll do. As long as there's plenty of booze, they'll be happy. You know your relations are a bunch of old soaks. Now, hush, I'm watching *Midsomer Murders.* You know it's my favorite."

"Sadie, I must insist—"

"Oh, here comes the murderer now, and she doesn't know it's him. Oh, you stupid girl, he's got the knife in his pocket! Look out!"

"Sadie. Switch that rubbish off. You can't mean you're not doing the traditional turkey lunch? Have you gone insane?"

"Oh, Arnold. You *are* old-fashioned. Nobody in the street is cooking a turkey anymore. Mrs. Kelly next door is having a dressed salmon delivered from the deli. And her friend, Jessica, has booked the entire family into the golf club for lunch."

"I don't care. I *want* a turkey."

"Honestly, you should loosen up a bit. You're turning into an old man before your time. You know your trouble? You've no imagination."

"I *want* a turkey dinner."

"I want to be a size ten, Arnold. But it's not gonna happen."

"This is outrageous—"

"Now, *shush,* I want to hear this. Isn't John Nettles just divine? Oh, I wouldn't mind finding him under the tree on Christmas morning. I'd soon get the wrapping paper off him!"

"Don't be smutty, Sadie. You wouldn't know what to do with him."

"I certainly *would.* I'd have a good go, anyway."

"Oh, Sadie! What about all the decorations?" he asked feebly. "The little biscuit angels?"

"I'm having a few scented candles and pine cones in a big glass bowl. Minimal and restrained. That's the fashion, nowadays. I'm not killing myself anymore."

Arnold went out to the shed and sat on a deck chair, beside the plastic Christmas tree. Sadie had no time for either him or the tree. She had dismissed them both as old-fashioned. She had bought some willow twigs in a big pot and was planning to hang five stars made of crystal beads on them. That was their Christmas tree now. Some twigs and stars! And a bowl of candles! That was the full extent of the Christmas decorations.

Everything was going wrong. Just that morning, Patricia had told him she thought they should take a break. She wasn't getting any younger, she said. She was tired of being the mistress. She wanted to be the wife for a change. She wanted a big house to decorate for Christmas and fill with family and friends. She was tired of living on her own in a bed-sit, waiting for the phone to ring. Her lovely apartment had suddenly become a *bed-sit.*

Maurice and Daisy were staying in Greece for Christmas. Arnold wanted them to come back to Belfast for the holidays but they told him they couldn't face the crowds in the airport. They were meeting some friends in a local restaurant for lunch and then hosting a small cocktail party in their apartment. Maurice was going to play a selection of songs from the 1950's. Daisy had bought a new dress for the occasion. She said it would be lovely to spend the day with people their own age, people with the same interests. Arnold was devastated.

His sons sent a big card and said they were staying in Australia, and going to a pool party with their girlfriends. Arnold peered at the enclosed photo of some near-naked girls lying on a sunny beach with his two sons. It would simply be a waste of his dwindling energy, telling them to come home.

Never mind, he consoled himself, there was still the office party to look forward to. And the presentation of his award for Employee of the Year.

Sadie was delighted that her campaign of subversion was going so well, but she wasn't finished yet. Arnold's confidence was waning. He was deflating slowly, like an old balloon. The next part of her plan involved the public face of Arnold Smith. The crisp, white invitation to his office party was tucked in a corner of the hall mirror.

WALLEY WINDOWS AND
CONSERVATORIES OF DISTINCTION INVITE

Mr. Arnold Smith and guest

TO THEIR CHRISTMAS PARTY TO BE HELD

December 21st, 1999
8 p.m.

AT THE EUROPA HOTEL
FORMAL DRESS

Sadie was going to wear a pink trouser suit and a pair of sandals with diamonds on the toe straps. She was having some red streaks put in her hair and had bought a new handbag with embroidered roses on it. She was going to wait until Arnold went up to the microphone to accept his prize, and then she was going to make her big announcement.

·36·

Merry Christmas, Nicolas Cage

Brenda was enjoying one of Daniel's Christmas Platters, a blob of cream still on her top lip as she wrote the letter.

December 14, 1999
Dear Nicolas,

How are you? Have you decorated your mansion for Christmas yet? Have you got white fairy lights strung around your swimming pool? I bet you have.

My mother bought me a lovely frame for my exhibition. I haven't decided what to put in it yet.

I'm feeling really happy today. The gallery in Galway got in touch, first thing this morning. The Blue Donkey Gallery. They said they are all ready to stage my show tomorrow. They have the walls freshly painted and a stack of promotional postcards printed up. Everyone who was invited has said they will attend.

Maybe Belfast artists are becoming fashionable at last. If you ever received the painting I sent you, hang onto it. It could be worth money some day!

I have sixty-nine canvases ready for the exhibition. I have used canvases with deep sides, and painted the sides as well, so they won't need to be framed. That's very contemporary, you know. And cost-effective.

There'll be local musicians to play soft Irish ballads, and there will be designer nibbles as well. I've got a new dress and high-heel shoes for the occasion. All I have to do now is pack the paintings into crates, ready for the journey.

Wish me luck. Merry Christmas.
Love,
Brenda

PS. Please send me a signed photo.
I am a genuine fan.

Brenda posted the letter right away. She was sure that Nicolas would reply to her soon. Even a movie star of Nicolas's magnitude could find the time to send a postcard, surely? Should she have written *Love, Brenda* at the end of the letter? Oh, never mind! It was Christmas! She spent the rest of the morning packing her precious paintings into wooden crates and filling the spaces between them with polystyrene balls.

Her beautiful dress from Monsoon, with the blue and silver bugle beads on it, she hung on a padded hanger from the picture rail. A fortune, it had cost her, even though she had found it on the sale rail. She checked her new shoes for SALE stickers and set them on the floor, beside the dress. She didn't want to turn up at the exhibition with a big yellow sticker on each sole, declaring ONLY £4.99; that had happened before. Twice. She dyed her dark hair raven-black, in honor of Nicolas Cage, when he played the part of Sailor Ripley, in *Wild at Heart.* The blue-black sheen of it made her look paler than ever. Pale and interesting, she hoped. Finally, she was ready. She sat down on the tattered sofa, with a celebratory gin and tonic, and wondered how she would spend the afternoon.

She had one large piece of canvas left. She would do another painting, maybe one of Nicolas himself? Strange, but she had never painted him before. That was it! She would stretch a piece of canvas across the back of the golden frame and staple it in place! She had plenty of staples left, thank God. Why had she not thought of that, the moment her mother pulled her surprise gift out of the carrier-bag? It was the perfect, *perfect* thing to do. She would paint a string of fairy lights around the edge of the picture and call it *Merry Christmas, Nicolas Cage*. Sure, she had a really nice tree right here in the flat, this year, for inspiration. (Mrs. Brown had supplied the decorations.)

She had a scrapbook full of magazine

pictures, postcards and reviews. She chose one of him wearing his snakeskin jacket, in *Wild at Heart,* staring at the camera with his big, poetic eyes. She sketched it out on the canvas with a long piece of charcoal. She poured herself a large gin and tonic when she was finished the drawing and sat back to contemplate the canvas. She decided to paint it in full color, not in her usual palette of blues and grays. She got her jar of paint-brushes from the kitchen and selected the tubes of color she needed for the painting, from the big toolbox she kept them in on the sitting room floor. She laid everything out neatly on the coffee table and studied the exquisite contours of Nicolas's face for a while. When she was ready to begin, she poured herself another drink.

"We'll show, them, Nicolas," she told the canvas. "You and me, together. We'll save the world with our joint talent and show them that the only important things are art and music and films and love. And they'll all stop fighting and arguing over trivial things, and everything will be perfect." She smiled then, already tipsy, with four gin and tonics inside her. She topped up the glass again, from the big green bottle of gin on the mantelpiece and reached for a brand-new paintbrush.

"God bless those auld credit cards," she said, as she began to paint.

At five o'clock, the painting was finished, and it was very good. Maybe it was the best painting Brenda had ever done. An excellent likeness. She collapsed onto the sofa to admire it. She was tempted to put it in the show but, sadly, the paint would still be wet in the morning.

But, never mind, she told herself. On the day of the show, the world would know what a huge talent Brenda Brown was. Then, all the galleries who had turned her down would be killing themselves with regret. They would be begging her for pieces of work, and she would take great satisfaction in telling them that, sorry, she was moving to the Irish Republic and would no longer be exhibiting in the north.

Almost without thinking about it, she pulled the phone, by its cable, across the carpet toward her and began to flick through the *Yellow Pages.* Art Galleries. Art Galleries. She found the page and dialed the number of the first gallery she recognized.

"Hello," she said. "It's me, Brenda Brown from Belfast Town, here. I just wanted to tell you that I am having a major show in Galway tomorrow and I will also be moving there to live. So I won't be able to show my work in your gallery in the future. Unfortunately. I'm sorry about that, now."

"Oh, dear! Thanks for letting us know," said an amused voice. "Good-bye."

"Just a minute! Are you familiar with Vincent van Gogh's *Portrait of Doctor Rey*, painted on wood, in 1889?"

"I am." A sigh.

"Did you know that Vincent gave that painting to Doctor Rey as a gift? And that the good doctor nailed that painting over a hole in his chicken shed? And that it was rescued years afterward, when Vincent was recognized for the true genius that he was. And it was sold for millions of dollars?"

"Have you been drinking, Miss Brown?"

"Well, in my humble opinion, all the paintings in your gallery should be nailed onto a chicken shed without further ado. But they won't be worth anything in a few years. They'll still be on the side of a shed and you'll still be a back-street gallery in a one-horse town, and I'll be famous. And married to a movie star. Good-bye." And she slammed down the phone.

Brenda wasn't sure how much of this speech the gallery owner heard before he hung up the phone, because she was quite drunk, but she felt exhilarated. She put her Placebo CD in the stereo and turned the volume up as high as it would go. She replenished her glass of gin, saw that she was out of tonic water and plonked a few ice cubes in, instead. She ran her finger down the list of galleries in the directory and found another one that had rejected her, and she dialed the number and took a deep breath. Why not burn a few bridges, she thought. I don't need this town anymore. I'm finished with Belfast. She had to shout over the level of the music, but she managed to call seven galleries before she gave up and replaced the receiver with a shaky hand.

At six o'clock, she carried her painting of Nicolas Cage to her little bedroom, and hid it carefully under the bed, beside her shoebox of letters.

"I'm sorry about this indignity, Nicolas," she told the picture. "It's a little dusty in there, and I'd rather you were in the bed, not under it, if you know what I mean. But there are thieves everywhere these days. You'll be safe in here, from burglars, till I get back. *If* I come back."

Finally, she lay down on the sitting room floor, beside her lovely Christmas tree, and sang along to the music, drinking the last bit of gin, neat, out of the bottle, watching the room spinning and the fairy lights twinkling off and on, off and on, in a delicious drunken haze. She slept for half an hour before waking suddenly with severe hunger pains. A rummage in the kitchen cupboards proved futile. She phoned her mother and invited herself over for supper. Mrs. Brown had just made a nice pot of Irish stew and some pink and green meringues with vanilla butter-cream.

"Get a taxi over, love, and I'll pay the fare when you get here. You might as well stay over."

Bliss.

Brenda drank some strong black coffee and combed her blue-black hair. She suddenly felt gloriously certain *he* would turn up at her exhibition.

At nine o'clock, she phoned a taxi and staggered down the stairs to spend the night at her mother's house.

"Good-bye, Belfast," she announced, as the front door closed behind her. "I'm finished with you! Hello, Galway! Hello, Nicolas Cage!"

Well, Brenda might have been finished with Belfast, but Belfast wasn't finished with Brenda.

·37·

The Other Mrs. Stanley

Penny got out of the taxi and paid the driver. She waited until the blue Mercedes reached the end of the street before she moved a muscle. Then, she turned and looked up at Daniel's house. It was not a palace. Richard was right about that. A little Victorian terraced house, covered with decades of coal dust. There was a narrow passageway leading to the back garden. The tiny patch of grass at the back was neatly clipped, though, and there was a single lilac tree in the center of it.

She opened the gate and went up to the bay window. The curtains were old but clean. She tried to see through them but she couldn't. She tried the doorbell. There was no answer. The front door was firmly locked.

The street was quiet. There were no people about, not even a stray dog. Still, there might be someone watching her through the lace curtains of the house across the road. She walked quickly through the passageway to the backyard.

She searched about, hoping there might be a key. Failing to find one, she lifted a stone from the flower bed and broke a pane of glass in the back door. She reached in and found that the key was in the lock. She twisted it slowly and opened the door. Then, with her heart thumping she went inside.

She walked from room to room, looking for something significant. A clue that would tell her why her husband had bought a house in the same city where they lived and kept it a secret from her for fifteen years. All of the furniture in the sitting room was old and worn, and nothing special. There was a nice dresser in the kitchen, with some plates and cups on it, and some loose tea leaves in a black and red tin.

Penny went upstairs. In the front bedroom was a brass bedstead, with an old eiderdown on it, and some bottles of Apple Blossom perfume on the dressing table. Penny saw at once a white envelope leaning against the mirror. She went over and lifted it. It was addressed to a woman called Mrs. Teresa Stanley. She opened it.

My Dearest Teresa, if you ever come back to the house, and I am not here, please wait for me. I bought the house for you, so you won't have to go away again. I own a little cafe on Mulberry Street but I come here for a short while some afternoons. I want you to know that I forgive you for leaving me all those years ago, and that I still love you with all my heart, and that I hope every day that you will come back to me. It is not too late for us to get to know each other again, and I will take care of you, and look after you always.

All my love,
Daniel

Penny read the letter over and over. It was inconceivable that Daniel had a wife already, but there it was in black and white. He had been married to someone called Teresa. Maybe he still was. No wonder he didn't want children. He was besotted with this Teresa creature. He didn't love Penny at all. He had married her for the business, nothing more. *I own a little cafe on Mulberry Street.* Well, thought Penny, we'll see about that. She put the letter in her pocket and left the house silently.

When she returned to the shop that afternoon, Daniel was rushing about the kitchen in a fluster.

"Where have you been?" he cried. "You can't keep disappearing like this. I've tried to be patient with you, Penny, but I'm trying to run a business here."

"Get out," said Penny, quietly.

"What?"

"I said, get out of my shop."

"Are you feeling all right, Penny?" He set down the teapot he had been holding. This was new territory for Daniel Stanley. He had come to think of Penny as part of the business, like the water heater or the toaster, as indeed she was. "It's those magazines," he cried. "They've put your head away. You shouldn't read them. Magazines are destroying the institution of marriage!"

"Oh, you!" she shouted at him. "I don't believe you're right in the head!"

"Penny, what is going on?"

"I am giving you fifteen minutes to pack your bags and get out of my family business. I know about the house on Magnolia Street. Does number fourteen, *Magnolia Street* ring any bells? And I know about your long-lost wife, Teresa; and I am absolutely fed up with you, and your pointless penny-pinching. Now get out to hell!"

Daniel suddenly found it hard to breathe. His eyes were wide with panic. "Please, we can talk—"

"It's too late for talking. Our marriage is over. It isn't valid anyway, you fool! You're a bigamist. A criminal! You have no right to be here. You'll get nothing in the divorce."

Daniel looked as though he had been slapped across the face. He stared at Penny for what seemed like an eternity.

"Divorce? Penny, please listen to me—"

"No. No more lies. Just go before I call the police." She took the letter from her pocket and placed it on the table.

His blue eyes were pools of dread. "I can explain about all this. How did you find out?"

"I doesn't matter how I found out. It's true, isn't it? You've lined your pockets for seventeen years out of my dear father's cafe. And you've used the money to buy your other wife a house. You've used me as an unpaid skivvy and wasted my youth. I hate you!"

"Penny, please, don't do this to me!"

"I hate you. You've made me into a pathetic excuse for a woman. I blame myself for most of this. Millie Mortimer told me not to get married so soon after we met. I should have known that there was something wrong with you—in your thirties and still single. Only, you weren't single, were you? You were married to Teresa!"

He had his hands up to his face. His voice came out in a whisper. "Teresa is my mother."

Penny laughed in his face. She wanted to kill him. "You liar! Do you never stop? Your mother was called Kathleen."

"No. Kathleen was my aunt. I swear it."

"I don't believe you."

"Look, there are customers waiting. Let

me get rid of them and we'll close the shop and I'll tell you everything."

"No, it's far too late for that. I don't care what you say anymore. I've nearly gone out of my mind, wondering what was wrong with you, all these years. Wondering why you didn't want me more, why you wouldn't give me children. I want you to leave this minute and take all your secrets with you."

"Please, Penny!"

"It's over between us, Daniel. I've been having an affair. I want a divorce. I'm going to a lawyer to get a divorce."

"An affair! How could you?"

"Because I'm a *normal* person. Didn't you even suspect? All the late nights I've had? The new clothes? I've been with another man. And he doesn't find me so unattractive he prefers to read cookery books than make love to me! Now, *get out.*"

"You can't just end it without listening to me! And, Penny, we have the business to think of."

"You can keep whatever money you've managed to wring out of this place. Think of it as a settlement. A final settlement. And if you think for one second I am going to let you take this shop away from me, you can forget it. I'll burn it to the ground, rather than let you darken the door, ever again."

She went into the cafe and asked everyone to leave. They did not have to pay for their meals, she said. Could they just eat up and go? There was a family crisis. Grumbling, astonished, curious, the customers left the premises. Penny locked the door. When she went back into the kitchen, Daniel was gone. She locked the back door and sat down on a chair, shaking all over. Then, she made three calls. She called Millie to tell her that Daniel was a bigamist. She called a local builder and told him to come round, first thing in the morning for an estimate. And finally, she made an appointment to talk to a solicitor.

·38·

Daniel Tries to Make Amends

Daniel walked all the way to Teresa's old home, with tears streaming down his face. All his life he'd been living in two tenses: the present, where he went to work in the tea house, and the past, where he waited for his mother to come back. Now, those two worlds had collided, and everything was ruined. He let himself into the house and sat on the sofa until it grew dark. Then, he heated some milk and made a hot drink. He drank his cocoa in a trance.

Penny was leaving him. She had left him. It was all over. He thought and thought of how she could have found out about the house, but he could not work it out. He wept again.

She had a lover. He was angry about that. Why did women set so much store by romantic love? And why did it take her so long to have an affair, anyway? She could have left him any day she wanted, in the last seventeen years. She could have divorced him years ago. But she did not. So, she must have loved him.

Still, his mother loved him, and she had gone away. Women were unpredictable creatures, he knew. They were strange and impossible to understand. And yet, when they were not around, life seemed bleak and empty. The years ahead stretched out before him. There would be no one to talk to at the end of the day. He must not let Penny leave him.

He would go back to the tea house and tell Penny the truth and make her understand. He would take her away to a hotel so that they could talk it all through. Penny would like that. She liked pretty things. What was the name of the hotel that Penny talked about? The one in the magazine? The Lawson Lodge?

The hotel that Penny admired so much confronted him like a guilty secret. It was the very opposite of his meanness, and all the years of thrift that Penny had endured with him. He began to weep. He took from his wallet the shilling that Father Mulcahy had given him for his missing mother, when he was four years old. He turned it over and over in his hand.

And suddenly, it all made sense. His mother had not left him because she did not love him. She went away because her heart was broken; because her husband let her down and left her with a stack of bills she could not pay. She went away because the neighbors whispered about her behind her back and said bad things about her that were not true. She went away because she had no friends. The other women who lived on the street did not like her because she was beautiful and slim and unattached. It was not Daniel's fault that she had gone away. She must have remarried and not told her new husband that she had a son already. Why had no one explained all this to him before?

He was no better than his father. The truth winded him like a boxer's punch. Penny was leaving him. He would be alone again, and this time, it was all his fault. There was no one else to blame. What time was it? Ten-thirty in the evening. He went out and walked until he came to a pay phone. He asked the operator for the telephone number of the hotel. He dialed the number.

"I'm sorry for calling so late," he began. "I just wanted to ask you, is it too late to book a room for Christmas? I mean, do you have any rooms free over the holiday period at all? I want to surprise my wife with a last-minute holiday."

The lady on the other end of the line was businesslike. She registered no surprise at the late hour. "Let me see," she said. There was a pause. "We do have a room available, as it happens. Just the one, remaining. But it's very expensive. It's the bridal suite, comprising en suite luxury bathroom, and sitting room with a real log fire. It's three hundred pounds per night."

"I'll take it," he said, his voice a husky whisper.

"Certainly, sir," she said. "What night were you thinking of? We're open right through the holiday period."

"Could I possibly have it for three weeks? From December eighteenth, through to January seventh?"

The receptionist in the Lawson Lodge sat up in her chair and set down her coffee cup on the mahogany counter. She seldom managed to get so much business, so easily.

"That will be fine, certainly. Thank you, sir. I hope you will have a pleasant stay with us, and take full advantage of our packed program of seasonal events. Can I have your credit card details, please?"

"I don't have a credit card, I'm afraid. but I'll send a letter of confirmation, and a check for the full amount, first thing in the morning. Could you tell me the address?"

She told him. "That will be fine, sir. Thank you very much. Is there anything else we can do for you?"

"Yes," he said. "Can you put a Christmas tree in the suite, and decorations, and some chocolates, and champagne?"

"Certainly, sir. All those things come as standard in the bridal suite."

"And some perfume. Something expensive," he said. "That's everything. Oh, my name is Daniel Stanley."

"Thank you, Mr. Stanley. I'll phone to confirm, when I receive your letter."

"Ah, I'll phone you. I'm very busy at the moment. Always out and about . . ."

"Very well. Thank you. Good night."

He replaced the receiver gently. He felt good. Spending money was not that difficult after all. It wasn't so hard, once you put your mind to it. He did some quick calculations in his mind. He had a couple of hundred thousand pounds in the bank. His life savings. But half of it belonged to Penny. More than half, if he was honest. Penny had worked hard to earn the money. He would pay for the holiday, and give all the rest to Penny. He would beg her to stay, and tell her he would do anything she wanted. He could not bear to be alone again. The money would not keep him company when she was gone. He loved Penny. He was frightened to think how much he had loved her all this time and not realized it. He hurried back to the little house.

He would give Penny tonight to cool off and he would go round in the morning. He would tell her everything. It was a lifetime too late, but she might still have some feelings for him. She might still forgive him, and give him one more chance.

•39•

Millie Mortimer Is in a Rage

Millie Mortimer came tearing up Mulberry Street as if the hounds of hell were after her. Hurrying along in her wake was her bewildered husband, Jack. He carried his heavy toolbox with him, and he called out to Millie to slow down. He hated Millie meddling like this in other people's affairs, but it was useless trying to tell her what to do. She was like a whirlwind when she got going. He was grateful, at least, that it wasn't himself on the receiving end of Millie's vicious temper. Jack Mortimer would never be stupid enough to have an affair behind Millie's back.

Millie hammered on the door and when Penny turned the key, she burst into the shop like an explosion. The door nearly fell off its hinges.

"Where is the evil wretch?" she cried, standing in the middle of the floor. "I'll kill him. Daniel Stanley, get down here and take what's coming to you. Jack! Bate him up!"

"He's gone," said Penny. "I put him out and I told him not to come back. Not ever. He's gone for good."

Jack was giddy with relief. He had arm muscles as big as grapefruits. It wouldn't have been a fair fight.

"You're right about that," said Millie. "Jack, get yourself in here."

Jack was hovering by the door, not wanting to get involved in Penny's marital problems. Why couldn't women be less emotional about things, he wondered.

"Get out there to the kitchen and change the locks," said Millie, "and put two bolts on the back door. And put shutters on all the windows."

"That'll cost a lot of money," he said.

"Oh, men! Never mind about the money. Do you want that waster to break in here tonight and strangle poor Penny in her bed? There's nothing he wouldn't do to hang on to this place, I tell you! Get what you need from the hardware shop and tell Mr. Cook that Penny will settle up with him in a couple of days."

Jack took some measurements and left the building without speaking to Penny. He simply nodded his sympathy to her as he was going out the door. She noticed that he seemed to have lost a fair bit of weight. Millie's bathroom makeover must have been a success.

Millie made tea and paced up and down the kitchen, smoking furiously.

"I knew it. I knew it all along. I just knew there was something wrong with Mr. Daniel-I'm-So-Perfect-Stanley. A bigamist! Well! The nerve of him! You, Penny, on your hands and knees all these years, working your poor fingers to the bone so that he could buy his other wife a house! And she's not even in it, you say? She's missing? Well, if that doesn't prove he's a headcase, I don't know what will. I'll reach for him the next time I see him, as God is my judge. I'll turn him inside out and feed him to the dogs."

Penny was too numb to stop Millie ranting.

"You tell all this to a lawyer, Penny. Do you hear me? I'll be a witness to the fact that you gave that man only love and devotion. Have you got the letter he wrote to his other wife? Keep it safe now. And don't even think of letting him keep that money. You, that never had a decent stitch on your back since the day you got married. That penny-pinching slug! You'll get that money back in court. And if they can't get it back for you, I will. We have our own way of doing things in this part of the world. Oh, the weasel!"

Jack returned, laden down with locks and bolts and shutters, and got on with the business of turning the tea house into a fortress. It took him two hours.

When Jack and Millie left the shop that night, with a box of cakes and thirty pounds for their trouble, Penny sat in the tea house for a long time. She did not feel alone. It was her shop, and she had taken it back. She would divorce Daniel with as little delay as possible. She didn't care about the money. She would borrow some money to redecorate the tea house and she would start all over again. Mary Soap, the cleaning lady, would help her, and she could employ some new staff. She would tell Richard all about it the next time she saw him. But tonight, she felt very tired.

There was a bottle of brandy in the cabinet upstairs, a gift from Millie the Christmas before. Penny went upstairs and opened it. She poured a generous amount into a glass, and she sat gazing through the window at the strings of fairy lights in the street outside. She was hungry but the very thought of having to prepare a meal for herself was just too much. She telephoned for an Indian take-away.

Sometime after four o'clock in the morning, full of brandy and curry and tears that would not fall, Penny fell asleep on the sofa.

·40·

The End of an Era

The room was deserted but the lights were still on. There were several wooden crates beside the door. There were jam jars full of linseed oil and turpentine on the mantelpiece. There was a torn copy of the *Yellow Pages* on the floor and an empty bottle of gin on the coffee table.

There was a beautiful beaded dress hanging on the picture rail and a pair of high-heeled shoes on the floor.

The digital clock on the stereo said 5:00 A.M.

There was a pine Christmas tree by the sitting room window, with secondhand fairy lights winking prettily on it, as well as some antique baubles from a car-boot sale. The Christmas tree made a heartwarming splash of color in the dreary little room, and that was why Brenda had forgotten to switch it off. She'd also forgotten to switch off a small portable room heater. Her only thought, as she left the flat that night, was that a very famous person might just turn up at the exhibition in Galway the next day . . .

But the flex on the extension cord was old and damaged. And it was very hot now, because it had been working hard all night, keeping the little glass lanterns on the tree flashing, as well as the heater.

A thin wisp of smoke curled out from the cracked socket on the wall, and then a tiny flicker of red flame appeared on the frayed flex.

The fire started slowly, burning the shabby hearth rug, and the worn carpet underneath it. The flames were small and graceful, barely moving as they struggled to find a foothold. But when they reached the pile of turpentine-soaked rags in the fireplace, they exploded into life. The digital clock display faded to blackness, and the fairy lights went out with a pop. The flames began to lick at the wallpaper, working their way along the wall, blackening and obscuring Brenda's sketches and meager possessions.

The beautiful blue and silver dress surrendered to the fire and fell off its padded coat hanger, with a shower of sparks. The cheap sofa and the wooden coffee table were alight in minutes, filling the tiny flat with dense, black smoke. The wooden crates beside the door only protected the paintings inside for two minutes, before they fell apart and spilled their contents into the inferno. Every single painting was burned; thousands and thousands of Brenda's dabs and sweeps and strokes, all destroyed in seconds. Her precious sketchbooks, her graphite pencils, her Radiohead and Placebo CDs: everything that made Brenda what she was. Her painting easel was the last thing to be destroyed as the fire raged through the flat and the windows cracked right across. When the sitting room floor collapsed, it made a hole in the connecting wall and smoke began to pour into Penny's flat.

Penny lay asleep on the sofa, curled up in her old cardigan. Oblivious to the fire, she was dreaming of a big house in the country, full of white sofas and thick carpets and blue gingham curtains.

Daniel came hurrying up the street at that very moment, worried that he might have left the oven on. Unable to sleep since he'd thought of it, he had walked to Mulberry Street to warn Penny, and maybe even to talk to her and try to explain. When he saw the fire, he broke into a run. The flats next door were well alight by now. There was nothing he could do to save them. He banged on the door but there was no sign of that mad painter, Brenda Brown, or any of the other tenants. His blood ran cold when he saw smoke at the window of his own sitting room. He got out his keys and fumbled desperately to find the right one, but somehow it wouldn't fit into the lock.

"Damn you, Millie Mortimer," he shouted, sensing Millie's hand in the locks being changed. He thumped the door, and even tried to force it with his shoulder, but it was double-bolted and wouldn't budge. He tried the knocker, and rang and rang the bell. He would have kicked the windows in but they were shuttered against him.

"Penny, Penny, wake up!" he called.

But she was deep, deep in a drunken sleep and couldn't hear him. She didn't move as the smoke drifted across to her.

"Penny, there's a fire!" he shouted. *"You've got to wake up!"*

But Penny slept on.

"Damn my miserly soul for not buying a smoke alarm! Oh, God! Help me! What will I do?"

Flames were licking round the edges of the room. Penny coughed but did not stir. Daniel called out for someone to help him.

"Help! Help me! Anyone?" But no one heard him, and even if they had, they couldn't get in. Jack was very good at his work. The tea house was impenetrable. Only the strings of fairy lights along the street stirred in the breeze. Daniel sprinted round to the back of the shop and went tearing up the alley as fast as his legs would carry him. He was over the wall in seconds and trying the back door, but it too was firmly secured. He looked up at the window of their bedroom. He could see no movement and couldn't see if it too was shuttered. He threw a stone up at the dark glass. Nothing. Then a bigger stone. A small hole appeared in the glass, and a pattern of cracks, but still no Penny. In desperation, he began to climb up the drainpipe, cutting his arm badly on a protruding nail. Ripping off his coat, he wrapped it round his hand and pushed in the glass in the window. There was no shutter, thank God. Using all his strength, he pulled himself over the sill. He felt for Penny in the big double bed she had slept alone in, for the last few months. She was not there.

He ran into the spare room at the front of the building, but again, the room was empty. It was hard to breathe with all the smoke that had begun to build up in a thick blanket at the ceiling. He crawled into the sitting room on his hands and knees and found Penny on the sofa.

"Penny, Penny darling! Wake up! You've got to wake up. There's a fire." He prayed hard that it was not too late.

With a shake of his head, he lifted Penny off the sofa in his strong arms and stumbled with her down the stairs and through to the kitchen. He drew back the bolts on the door and carried her out through the yard and down the alleyway.

"I'm sorry, Penny!" he wept. "I'm so sorry. This is all my fault—I should have replaced the old wiring in the kitchen years ago!"

He saw that some of the neighbors were now on the street. Someone would have called the fire brigade. He laid Penny down gently on the footpath at a safe distance from the burning building, and she felt the cold ground underneath her and opened her eyes and coughed again.

"What's happening?" she whispered.

"Thank God. Thank God," he said softly.

"I'm frightened," she said. "What's happening?"

"It's a fire. The shop is on fire. I'm with you now—it's me, Daniel." He knelt beside her, holding her hand.

"Daniel . . . what are you doing here?"

"I couldn't sleep."

"Oh, Daniel! We've got to save the tea house." Penny tried to struggle to her feet.

"Never mind the tea house! Thank God you're alive! Penny, sweetheart, just wait for me here—the fire has spread to the next-door house—"

"Oh, no, no! Brenda! Oh, Daniel, what about Brenda?"

"Just stay here, Penny, and let me see what's happening . . ."

He returned in a few moments, relief evident in his face.

"It looks like no one has been hurt. Brenda's flat is badly burned but Brenda was actually seen leaving in a taxi fairly late last night—she probably didn't return. They've called the fire brigade and an ambulance. We'll have you checked out, and you can come home with me—to Magnolia Street."

"What will the other Mrs. Stanley say?" said Penny, and she began to weep.

"Penny, I'm telling you the truth about Teresa. She was my mother. I didn't tell you about her because I was ashamed. She went away and left me with Kathleen when I was a child. I bought the house for her, hoping she would come back. So as she'd know where to find me. Kathleen was my aunt and I hated her."

"Where is Teresa, then? Why did she leave you?"

"She couldn't cope on her own. She was broke. She probably married again and didn't want me in the way. Please, Penny, don't let it all end like this. I've been mad, insane. It's true I married you for the business, for the money—I'm sorry!"

"You didn't feel anything at all for me, on our wedding day? On our honeymoon?"

"I felt guilty."

"Is that all? Guilt?"

"I loved you a little bit. You were young and pretty."

"If you only knew how much I cared for you, Daniel, that day!" Penny sobbed.

"But I love you so much now, Penny. And I have, for a long time. I just never realized how much. I'll die if you leave me. All these years I've wasted. Please let me make it up to you. I'll give you everything I have. Please! I've booked us a holiday in that nice hotel by the sea. We can start all over again."

Penny was too tired to think, so she clung to Daniel, and together they watched their beloved tea house burn to the ground. One of the neighbors gave her a blanket to keep her shoulders warm. By the time the fire engines came screaming down Mulberry Street, there was nothing of the tea house left to save. The firemen verified that

Brenda's flat had not been occupied. Penny was laid gently in the ambulance and taken for a checkup in the Royal Victoria hospital. Daniel went with her. She wanted to be with her husband, she said, when the policeman told her the building would have to be demolished. That was all that mattered now.

• 41 •

AFTER THE FIRE

December 15, 1999
Dear Nicolas,

It's all over. (Sorry this notepaper is not my usual brand.)

My career is in tatters, before it even managed to crawl out of the gutter of broken dreams. Sorry if I sound a bit poetic; I've been drinking gin all day. In fact, I was drinking gin all day yesterday, too. That's what did for me. I should have switched off that blasted heater.

The flat burned down. Faulty wiring, they said. With all that turpentine in the room, well, my paintings didn't stand a chance. They are no more. Gone, all gone. No one was hurt, but only because the other occupants of the building were out at the time. I could have killed them all.

All of my paintings and everything else I possessed went up in smoke. My lovely beaded dress from Monsoon. My high-heeled shoes.

My silver frame for your photo. Which you never sent. All gone. I wasn't insured, of course. And now I'm homeless.

The gallery said they were very disappointed when I rang them. They had invited a lot of important people to the opening night. And a little musical group to play ballads. And all the designer nibbles were ready and now who's going to eat them?

They've told me to contact them when I am ready for another exhibition.

But, I've lost heart in the whole thing. I am never going to paint again. My soul is suffocated, and my heart is withered, and my paintings are somewhere in the universe; reduced to a light-memory, spinning away to the outer edges of space.

I'm staying with my mother. See phone number below.

Love,

Brenda

Brenda went out to post the letter, even though she was so sick with gin and disappointment that she could barely stand up straight. Her mother was wonderful, of course, and her father turned up on the doorstep, with a big bouquet of pink roses and white daisies for his tragic daughter. Her two sisters came to visit and brought Brenda some spare clothes.

"Nothing survived the fire," Brenda told them, over and over. "I went there this morning, with the hired van, and the whole building was just a black shell."

It was unbelievable. Nobody could believe it.

"All ruined?"

"Just ashes."

"What will you do, pet? Where will you go?" Her father offered to take her to Dublin for a holiday, but Brenda turned him down.

"I'm in the middle of a personal crisis, Dad," she whispered. "I have to make some life-changing decisions. But thanks, anyway. It means a lot."

"What decisions?" everybody asked then.

But Brenda was hard to understand. She kept muttering something about bad omens and bad luck, and wondering why the fire had to happen that particular night, of all nights.

"I was going to be famous, you see? Like Liam Neeson. There was a group booked to play ballads, lovely Irish ballads. And fancy nibbles. Italian, I think. Nicolas might have turned up. That's why I bought the fancy dress. And the high-heeled shoes."

"Nicolas who?" asked one sister. Mrs. Brown made a face. Don't ask.

"And I wonder, is that what I did wrong? Buying those silly shoes? Was I too sure of myself?"

"Brenda, you're not making sense," said the other sister.

"Was it fate? I think it was fate. The exhibition was never meant to be." Brenda shook her head, sadly. "You see, in a lot of my paintings, there were cracked windows in the background. And I never knew why they had to be cracked. It was just something I sensed. And when I looked at the flat today, there they were—the cracked windows! It was a prediction, do you see?"

"Holy smoke, Mum, do you think she needs a doctor?" Both sisters, this time.

"I'm going to my room, now, to write a letter," said Brenda, and she left the room quietly.

December 16, 1999
Dear Nicolas,

You must know by now that I am in love with you.

I can't help it. I love you, and I have done ever since I saw you impersonate Elvis, singing "Love Me Tender" to Lula Fortune.

I know the media portray you as a playboy, but that is not the truth. The real you is sensitive and kind, and crying out for a gentle person to share your life with. And that person is me. That is why I have never fallen in love with anyone before. That is why you have never settled down with anyone before. Fate was saving us for each other.

Please write to me.

I know you would like me if you met me.

Even if we don't fall in love, I'd be content just to be your friend.

I sent you a painting and you didn't even say thank you. I sent you lots of letters and you didn't answer one of them. Why? All I wanted was a little picture of you and your autograph. A small connection to you, that's all I wanted. To touch something that you had touched.

Please call me.

I am a genuine fan.

Love,

Brenda

The phone rang a few times that day, and every time it did, Brenda ran to the hall table and grabbed the receiver with both hands. It couldn't be him, of course. He wouldn't have received the letter yet with Mrs.

Brown's phone number on it, but Brenda had lost all track of time.

"Nicolas?" she begged.

But no, it was only one of Mrs. Brown's many friends from the line-dancing club, checking on the arrangements for the trip to Nashville. Would Brenda like to go with them, they offered kindly, when they learned of the disaster. There was a spare seat.

But Brenda would rather take part in a Miss World competition, on prime-time television, wearing a big cardboard number on her wrist and a wet-look bikini, than go to Nashville, on a bus, with her mother's friends. (Dolly Parton and Slim Whitman for seven days straight.)

She sat in the front room all day, just looking at the busy patterns on the carpet. She couldn't eat or sleep. She wished, a thousand times, that she could just turn back time and unplug the faulty extension cord. Please, please, please, she whispered, with her eyes closed tightly. God help me. Please. But it didn't work.

As the evening wore on, she decided to go out and have a couple of drinks to settle her nerves. She got off the bus just outside the Crown bar on Great Victoria Street and went inside. She was a girl on her own, but that didn't worry Brenda. She was dressed for a night of serious drinking, not for a night of flirting with attractive men. She wore a full-length overcoat that had once belonged to her grandfather, her mother's gardening brogues and an old 70's suit of her father's. She wore an extra-thick layer of eyeliner, just to let people know that she was a fashionable chick, not a homeless tramp. She brought a writing pad and envelopes with her, just in case. She got a few looks when she pushed open the heavy doors and went up to the bar counter, but nobody said anything, or spoke to her.

"What'll it be, miss?" asked the barman, rubbing his hands on his old-fashioned white apron.

"Double gin and tonic, please, barman."

"Certainly, miss. Ice and lemon?"

Brenda nodded.

When the drink was served, she turned around and leaned her elbows on the bar, sipping the ice-cold gin. She studied the floor for a while, and then she gazed round the bar, at the different faces of the other drinkers. And then she saw one of her old bosses, Patricia Caldwell, sitting by the window, having an argument with some poor man in a crumpled suit. Brenda took a deep breath, and a general feeling of resentment that had been simmering for two days, suddenly found a focus. She ordered another drink, and a pint of Guinness as well, and climbed up onto a barstool, watching Patricia in the mirror behind the bar.

December 17, 1999.
Dear Nicolas,

This is the last letter I am ever going to send to you.

I have been arrested. It's six o'clock in the morning. I'm writing to you from the police station on the Lisburn Road.

I threw a whole pint of Guinness over a woman in a pub.

Patricia Caldwell, her name was. She used to be my boss. She made me work in the stockroom, unpacking deliveries. Me! A fine art graduate! (First Class Honors.)

After two weeks there, she sacked me for having what she called an attitude problem.

(That old chestnut.)

So anyway, there she was, gasping in the seat, drenched in Guinness, and I said to her,

"Remember me? I'm Brenda Brown, talented artist and friend to the stars. I just wanted to tell you that I was the one who put a brick through the window of your tacky little gift shop last year. Or was it the year before? You capitalist bitch!"

She called the police. The bouncer held my arms behind my back until they arrived. The shame of it. They actually got a doctor in to see me in the cells. I told him I was an artist and that you were a personal friend of mine. (He prescribed antidepressants.)

Anyway, I'm not sorry. I'm glad I broke the window, and I'm glad she knows it was me, and I'm not sorry, not one bit. I'm a Belfast hard woman now, resorting to violence. Hurrah!

I don't know if they are going to press charges.

Rock and roll, eh?

Love,

Brenda

PS. My career is over so I don't expect we'll get to meet now, but I hope you have a wonderful life and that you have everything you ever dreamed of. My feelings for you remain undimmed by time or disappointment.

PPS. Don't bother sending me a signed photo, as I'm moving house. However, I remain your number one fan.

PPPS. Wild at Heart *is still my favorite film, in spite of all the other weirdos in it. I love your nose and ears in that film. Please don't ever have plastic surgery.*

PPPPS. I am changing my name now, definitely.

All my love, forever, Brenda Brown (that was)

They let Brenda go at eight o'clock, and she posted her letter, and idled along the Lisburn Road, looking in the windows of the trendy coffee shops there. Some of them were very nice, color-washed and genteel, but it wasn't the same as Muldoon's. The atmosphere was too contrived. She went again to Mulberry Street and stood looking up at the wreckage of the shop. There were several skips on the street, waiting to be filled with the debris that had been her life.

Penny and Daniel could have been killed and so could the other residents of the flats. Brenda was so grateful that they hadn't been. Although she'd lost everything, it could have been a lot worse. Penny and Daniel arrived then, in their little car, and Brenda tried to walk away without being seen. But Penny rushed after her and gave her a big hug.

"Everything is fine," Penny cried. "We're going to rebuild the cafe and make it far better than it ever was! We're going to have a glass roof and a new kitchen."

"Oh," said Brenda. She'd thought Penny would strangle her on the pavement.

"And we want you to be our very first customer when we reopen."

"I'm really very sorry about the fire, Penny."

"Not at all. It could have been something in our own place that caught fire. In fact, that's what Daniel first thought! It was all falling apart, anyway. The insurance will pay for some of it."

"Well, I'm glad you're taking it so well."

"Oh, that reminds me, Brenda—our

builders are also working on the flats next door, and they found some things in your flat that survived the fire. They showed them to me and I said I would hold on to them for you. Wait there, I'll get them. They're in the boot of our car." She hurried across the road to fetch them.

"I was told there was nothing left, Mr. Stanley," said Brenda to Daniel.

"Well, there is. They found them under the bed yesterday, apparently."

Penny came back with a slightly singed shoebox full of red envelopes, and the portrait of Nicolas, miraculously unharmed, except for a few cracks round the edges, where the paint had dried too quickly in the heat. Penny was delighted with herself for being the one to give Brenda back her treasured possessions.

"There," she said. "Wasn't it great luck that I was having a chat with the foreman when they found these? They might have gone in the skip otherwise!"

Brenda stood on the footpath, waiting for the bubbles of excitement that usually filled her when she was dreaming of Nicolas. But she felt cold and empty inside, like the cave she had once visited on a school trip to Fermanagh. Outside the dimly lit flat, the whole Nicolas Cage thing seemed a bit sad. His lovely face, the thick bundle of letters that she had written with such passion, failed to move her at all. She knew then, the love affair that had never been was over. She was twenty-five. It was time to grow up.

"Well, Penny, it must seem very ungrateful of me to say this," she began, "but I don't think I want them back. I've decided to stop being an artist. I'm going to be an ordinary person and get an ordinary job."

"But, Brenda, this is so good." Penny held the picture up to get a good look at it. "Aren't you going to start again, like we are?" Daniel put his arm round Penny and smiled at her lovingly. Brenda didn't think she had ever seen them embrace before.

"I'm going to start again, I daresay, but it won't be here. I'm going away. A job has come up, and I'm going to take it. I wish you both the very best, though," she added, and she shook their hands solemnly. Daniel patted her awkwardly on the arm, and Penny kissed her on the cheek.

"Thank you, Brenda," said Penny. "Without you, we might never have found out just how happy we were."

Brenda smiled and nodded her head.

Slowly, very slowly, she walked away, rubbing her arms as if she were very cold. She didn't look back once.

"What will I do with these?" Penny called after her, holding the picture and the box aloft.

"Throw them in the nearest skip."

"Oh, Brenda!"

"Good luck now." And she was gone, around the corner, onto the Lisburn Road. On her way back to her mother's house to rest.

"There's no way I'm dumping these," declared Penny.

"What will we do with them, Penny?"

"I'll think of something. Give me a minute, Daniel."

"We have to go shopping for clothes. We've nothing to wear on our holiday."

"I know!"

She opened the shoebox, took out a handful of letters and posted them.

"Penny! You can't do that!"

"Why not? There's stamps on them and all," said Penny, shoveling in more letters.

"You heard her. She said she's finished with all this stuff."

"She doesn't mean it, Daniel. She's just disappointed. Wait till Mr. Cage gets all these letters in one go. Then, he'll take notice of poor, wee Brenda."

"Aye. He'll have her charged for stalking him."

"Not at all. He'll be delighted with the attention."

"He won't."

"Wait and see." And she put the last bunch in the postbox.

"Are you going to send him the picture, too?"

"No. I'm going to keep that and hang it in the shop. I'll see if I can't get Brenda a few commissions. Get her back on her feet again. She'll be back to see us when we reopen, don't you worry."

·42·

A Poem for Brenda

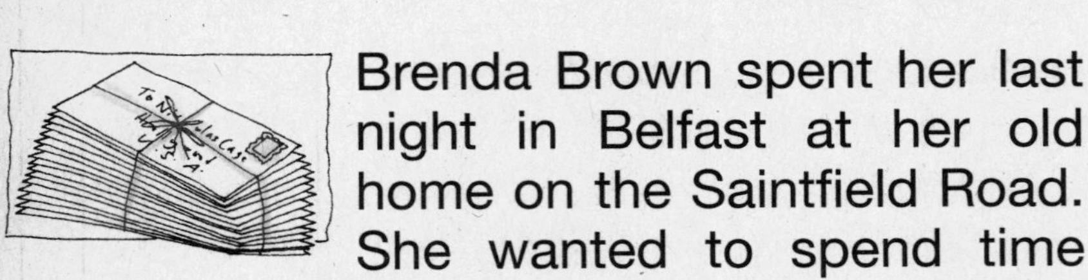

Brenda Brown spent her last night in Belfast at her old home on the Saintfield Road. She wanted to spend time with her mother before she left the city forever. They shared a lovely meal of roast chicken with all the trimmings, followed by vanilla ice cream with wafers and a bottle of white wine each. Her father and sisters were invited, too, and for a while it was just like old times.

Brenda was so hungover from a week on the gin, she could hardly keep the wine down, but she needed something to numb the pain. She was so shocked by the loss of her paintings, it was hard to function normally, but Mrs. Brown did her best to cheer Brenda up. They sat in the kitchen talking when the others had gone home.

"Now, I said I wouldn't interfere, but are you sure you won't stay?" Mrs. Brown asked gently.

Brenda thought about it for a while, as she sat warming her toes on the radiator. She could rent another flat, get another job, start making the repayments on her credit card bills, take the antidepressants like the doctor suggested and start painting again. One painting a week, for a year, and she would be ready to ring the Blue Donkey Gallery. And she could apologize to Nicolas Cage's representatives for bothering him and assure them she would not write to him ever again. But she knew, in her heart, that she didn't have the energy to do all those things.

"You're very kind, Mum. But that's all behind me now."

"Nonsense. You're only a youngster."

"Mum, that was two years' work that went up in smoke. Two entire years of my life."

"So? You can't throw in the towel over a few paintings. Just now, when you were starting to get the recognition."

"I know that, Mum. But I've been doing a lot of thinking this last couple of days. It's time to move on. That fire was an omen."

"You and your auld omens! What if Nicolas Cage writes back to you?"

"Listen, Mum, you've got to promise me one thing."

"Anything, love."

"Promise me you won't tell anyone where I'm going. Not the bank, or the landlord, or the Blue Donkey Gallery, or Clare Fitzgerald, or Penny Stanley even, or Nicolas Cage himself. I must have been out of my mind when I sent him that painting. I'm never writing to him again. I'm not a genuine fan, Mum. I'm a crazy-head. That's what I am. A stalker. Stars laugh at people like me. We're pathetic. Why would someone like him contact a dole-ite loser like me? I'm damn lucky he didn't get me lifted."

"Now, don't be saying that. Where's the harm in a few fan letters?"

"You don't understand, Mum. People that famous don't write to their fans. For all he knew, I could have been hiding in his dustbin with a bread knife. I'm in pieces about the fire, but in a way, this is my chance to begin again. You know, I might even give up alcohol—I think it makes me reckless."

"Are you sure about this job, pet? It doesn't sound like your type of thing at all."

"Yes. I'm sure. I'll write to you, and I'll get in touch with Dad and my sisters when I'm over all this. And I'll pay back what I owe when I'm on my feet again. But you're the only one who knows where I'm going, and I want you to promise you'll not tell anyone where I am. No matter what. Promise me now."

"I promise. Now, you should get some sleep. You're worn out. Go on, I've put a hot-water bottle in the bed for you."

Brenda put on her pajamas and lay down under the quilt in her old room. She lay awake for a long time. She wrote a poem to pass the time—on blue paper. Her red-letter days were over.

A POEM FOR BRENDA

Good-bye to The Big Smoke.
This IS my last day.
I've bought my bus ticket
And I'm on my way.
Good-bye to my flat.
Have you not heard the news?
It burned down last week.
(There were 3 fire crews.)
Good-bye to my dream
To the Ulster's van Gogh.
My paintings are ashes.
The big show is off.
Good-bye, my career,
I had so much to give.
Now, I'm tired of giving.
I just want to live.
Good-bye to the bills,
The police and the shrink.
The dreams and the music.
The dole and the drink.
Good-bye to the flags
And the curbs painted bright,
And the bonfires that burned
Long into the night.
Good-bye to the labels,
I don't want them on me.

Single, white female.
Non-voter. RC.
Good-bye, the job market,
With prospects so sour.
And grim little jobs,
Paying four pounds an hour.
Good-bye, Bradbury Graphics,
You were my favorite shop.
Your glass fountain pens,
Thirty-five quid a pop.
Good-bye, all my letters.
Every single, red page.
I thought you might love me,
My sweet Nicolas Cage.
Good-bye, house in Hollywood.
Good-bye, turquoise pool.
I thought I'd be famous,
But I was a fool.
Good-bye, Clare Fitzgerald,
You were my only sale.
Good-bye, 'Tricia Caldwell,
You put me in jail.
Good-bye, Penny Stanley,
You were my only friend.
Good-bye to the tea house,
For this is the end.

When Mrs. Brown looked in on Brenda, later that evening, she was fast asleep with a smile on her face. She kissed her daughter on the forehead and pulled the covers up to her chin. Maybe Brenda was right, she thought. It certainly seemed to be a very stressful occupation, this whole art carry-on. Maybe it was time for Brenda to grow up and get a proper job.

Brenda slept for eighteen hours and woke up ready for her journey. The two women hugged each other in the sitting room when it was time to part. Brenda wanted to walk all the way to the Europa Bus Station on her own, taking in the sights as she went.

"Don't worry about me, Mum," she said, as she set off for the bus station, with a small suitcase under her arm. "I'll be all right."

·43·

SALESMAN OF THE YEAR

When the day of the party arrived, Arnold had a lie-in, so that he would look well rested for the occasion. He checked and rechecked his suit for missing buttons and spent one hour polishing his shoes. There was a rumor going round the company that the chairman was going to give him a gift of some kind, as well as the trophy. He went to the barber's for a proper shave and a haircut. He spent all afternoon rehearsing his speech. Sadie kept out of his way by going to the cinema to see a double-bill matinee. She sipped cola and munched popcorn in the dark and steeled herself for the night ahead.

There was a light drizzle as the guests began arriving in taxis. The hotel foyer was brightly lit with thousands of fairy lights. Glasses of chilled white wine were served. The guests stood around the marble entrance hall and stairs, talking in small groups. Sadie thought she saw boredom on the faces of the other wives, as their husbands discussed light-sensitive glass and electronically controlled blinds. She went to the ladies' room and checked her lipstick.

When they were all seated in the function room, Mr. William Walley, the chairman of the company, said grace, and the meal was served.

"Don't over-do on the roast potatoes," Arnold hissed at Sadie. "People are watching. You big pink elephant! What possessed you to buy a suit that color?"

"Oh, shut your bloody face," hissed Sadie. "You're only in a mood because that dirty little trollop is giving you the runaround!"

Arnold's face turned cerise pink with impotent rage.

"What did you say?" he said, through gritted teeth.

"I know all about it," she said, cheerfully. "I'm not an idiot, darling. Pass the gravy, would you?"

Arnold's appetite suddenly died.

At last the plates were cleared away, and the speeches began. Mr. Walley spoke gravely, from a small podium, of the dwindling number of Irish homes which still did not have plastic windows. The market for new windows was shrinking fast, he warned.

"I wish you were," muttered Arnold to Sadie.

"And so we have to change our marketing strategy," went on the chairman. "We have to promote our extensive range of conservatories instead. A good conservatory adds to the appearance and to the resale value of a home. It is an investment, in other words. The Walley company is leading the way in Ireland, with our state-of-the-art, double-height model and full range of low-energy heating appliances." There was a smattering of applause. Some of the women yawned.

"And so we come to the presentation of our award for Salesman of the Year. Or should I say, Sales*person* of the Year . . . ha, ha, ha! This is the moment when we recognize the efforts of all our hard-working employees, and one in particular. This year the award goes to a man who has done more than any other to promote replacement windows. Not only has he sold more windows and conservatories than anyone else, he also came up with the idea for our new brochure featuring a Christmas tree. And I'm happy to say that the new brochure is proving very popular with the consumer. Congratulations to you . . . Mr. Arnold Smith!"

There was lots of clapping and cheering as Arnold made his way to the front of the room. Mr. Walley gave him the trophy and shook his hand warmly.

"Thank you, thank you," he said. "This award means a lot to me. And I would just like to thank—"

"Before you get started," interrupted Mr. Walley, "I want to tell you about our new idea to motivate the staff. This year, and every year from now on, the best salesperson will receive a luxury holiday for two, as well as our prestigious award. Arnold Smith, here are two tickets for a three-week cruise, for you and your good lady wife to enjoy. Raise your glasses, everyone. Here's to Arnold Smith, and Walley Windows! Merry Christmas, everyone!"

Arnold was too pleased with himself to carry on with his speech, but he didn't have to. Sadie had left her seat and was making her way to the front. She took the microphone from Mr. Walley's hand. The guests were intrigued. They sat up and strained their necks to get a good look at the plump little lady.

"I'd just like to say a few words myself, if that's okay," said Sadie, as the applause died away. "My name is Mrs. Sadie Smith. I used to be very proud of that title and of my clever husband. But nowadays, unfortunately, Arnold calls me Sadie *Sponge,* on account of my rather generous waistline."

A gasp of shock was heard from the women in the audience. The men giggled nervously. They sensed Sadie was going in for the kill.

"Well, it wasn't Arnold's idea, exactly.

That was the brainwave of his rather nasty mistress, Miss Patricia Caldwell, manageress of Davison's Gift Emporium on Lavender Street."

Arnold rushed across to Sadie and tried to take her away from the podium, but she held on tight and he couldn't budge her. Thirteen stone of scorned womanhood was impossible to shift. He tried to laugh it off, but the audience was wide-eyed with fear and delight.

"Oh, yes," Sadie continued. "My husband is a bit of a dark horse, don't you know? He loves to travel. In fact, he's just been to Paris, where himself and Patricia had a lovely weekend! He brought me back a sweet little cone of pink bonbons! He'll love this cruise. Yes, indeed. And so will Patty-Pat!"

There was silence in the room, but all eyes were on Arnold, who had taken a couple of steps backward. This time Mr. Walley himself decided it was time to bring the proceedings to a close. But Sadie was ready for him. She'd heard a few other interesting things as she lurked behind the cupboard in Arnold's office.

"I'll tell you all another little secret about

my husband. He's planning to leave Walley Windows and set up on his own. He's been pinching prospective clients for weeks now, doing deals with suppliers. Oh, he's very clever!"

"Is this true?" asked Mr. Walley, quietly.

"Not at all, the woman's crazy with jealousy," stammered Arnold.

"So, you're admitting to this other relationship, are you?"

"Would you all like to know what he calls you?" continued Sadie. "You see, it's a little game of his and Patricia's—to think of funny nicknames."

"Sadie, I'm begging you, don't do this!"

"Well, Arnold, I think I *will* do it. Seeing as you were planning to throw me out of my own house and leave me destitute."

Angry chatter filled the function room.

"Where's Charlie Drummond from Omagh? They call you Dummy Drummond, because you're too quiet, apparently. Where's Nora Kennedy? Or should I say, Nora New Nipples? I believe you've had a boob job? And Brett Garson? Poor Brett, you should see your doctor about that flatulence. Then, they might stop calling you British

Gas! Now, let me see . . . oh yes, Mr. Walley!"

"Sadie! No!"

"Great Big Walley! That's you! Ho, ho, ho!"

Sadie wracked her brains to think of some more. But it wasn't necessary. Dummy Drummond was climbing onto the stage, and he had his shirtsleeves rolled up. He might be a man of few words, but he had never liked Arnold Smith, and now seemed as good a time as any to give him a good thump.

But Arnold was already fumbling his way down the back stairs and out the fire exit. He fled to his beloved car and screeched out of the carpark with Charlie pounding along in his wake. He didn't hear Mr. Walley firing him, or Sadie laughing her head off, or Nora New Nipples weeping in the toilets.

Sadie turned to Mr. Walley and said: "Over the years, my husband has sold a lot of windows. He's worked very hard. And I've been very proud of him. But sadly, we have now decided to go our separate ways in the world. We are, therefore, going to donate this lovely holiday to charity. Thank you and good night."

Mr. Walley snatched the envelope containing the tickets for the cruise from Sadie's hands. The chairman was a family man and was very upset that no one had informed him of this sorry state of affairs. Sadie waved to all the guests and left the room with her head held high. Everyone began to clap again, more out of embarrassment than anything else.

Sadie packed her husband's bags and left them on the doorstep of the bungalow. He came to collect them the next day.

"You know what?" she said. "I was just eating a packet of chili flavor tortilla chips and a pot of roasted pepper dip, and if I had to choose between this savory snack and your good self, I would choose the chips without a second's hesitation. And by the way, I'm keeping the house. You may only contact me from now on through my solicitor. Good-bye."

·44·

Operation Grasshopper

If only Arnold could have let things lie, Sadie would not be standing on the fire escape of Patricia Caldwell's flat at midday on a freezing cold Christmas Eve. But there she was, hiding behind a rack of laundry that someone had set out to air. Out of habit, Sadie felt one of the towels to see if it was dry. It was frozen solid.

She knew Arnold and Patricia were in the flat because she had been watching the building all morning and no one had gone in or out. She had eaten all the ham sandwiches in her basket, and the two mince pies, and she was numb with cold and had a cramp in one leg. She would give it another half-hour and then call it a day. From her hiding place, she had an excellent view of the kitchen window. If only someone would open the curtains, she could get what she had come for and go home. She poured herself a small cup of hot chocolate from her tartan-patterned Thermos flask and drank it quickly, warming her gloved hands on the cup. She waved away the steam with her hand and prayed that the owner of the washing was out at work for the day. Explanations would be difficult, to say the least, if her presence on a second-floor fire escape was discovered.

Suddenly, the curtains were wrenched open and Patricia stood there in her dressing gown, a tacky little number with dragons on the front. As Sadie cowered behind the frozen towels, Arnold appeared behind his lady-love and slid his hands up underneath her satin robe. She turned round to kiss him and they locked onto each other like something from a nature program. Patricia was naked underneath her robe, and Arnold was wearing only a tiny pair of black pants that didn't suit him. Sadie felt like a television presenter as she observed them collapsing onto the kitchen table, gnawing at each other like two starving insects: *The female, having attracted the male to her cave with a bold display of sexuality, moves in for . . .* Oh, dear, it isn't pleasant, whatever it is. Sadie dropped her cup into her little wicker basket and fumbled for the camera.

In a way, it was too easy. She had been prepared to wait for days and days to get this picture, maybe even go as far as to pay someone else to do it. But here she was, on day one of Operation Evidence, and she had to admit they were putting their hearts and souls into it. They must be at it ten times a day, thought Sadie, who had never experienced marital relations in the middle of the afternoon herself, let alone on the top of a glass table with spindly silver legs. This was really going to knock Arnold's socks off, she thought. That is, if he ever has the time to put his socks on these days. She saw Patricia's long red fingernails go under the rim of Arnold's black pants and begin to peel them off. He was lying on his back on the table, and Patricia threw off her red robe and clambered up on top of him.

Sadie remembered seeing two grasshoppers fighting inside a glass tank, at the science day in her sons' primary school, and that image came back to her now. Arnold still had a bit of a tummy on him, but his legs and arms were thin. The two people on the table were all elbows, knees and sinews, engaged in what could only be described as an aggressive struggle for sexual supremacy. Sadie had never seen anything like it, not even on satellite television, and she had to admit, it was a little disappointing. It was hardly worth giving up a comfortable bungalow in Carryduff for, at any rate. Dame Edna Everage would have been proud of the faces that Sadie pulled as she watched her husband and his skeletal mistress make love in the minimalist kitchen.

Sadie didn't care for minimalism. It was too raw. The bungalow in Carryduff was full to the rafters with chintz armchairs and floral pelmets and tapestry cushions and pretty baskets of dried flowers. Sadie had spent twenty years creating her beloved home and she wasn't about to let it go without a fight. That morning, she had received a letter from Arnold's solicitor, telling her she had six weeks to vacate the premises, as she had no proof of her husband's alleged infidelity, and no children under the age of eighteen to look after. She wasn't frightened by the letter. Likely some crony of Arnold's from the golf club had sent it. Men like that stuck together when they were getting divorced. But Sadie thought she would be wise to get the evidence she needed, just in case things did end up in court.

And so, she tiptoed over to the window, checked that the camera was ready to use, and that the flash was warmed up. Just as Arnold grabbed Patricia's teacake-sized breasts in his moment of climax, and gave them a good squeeze, Sadie knocked loudly on the window. Patricia looked up and so did Arnold, and even though his face was upside-down, he recognized his turnip-shaped wife immediately. And then he saw the camera.

His wet lips began to form a four-letter swear word, just as the flash popped. He was immortalized making the letter *F,* his top row of teeth biting down hard on his bottom lip. Patricia screamed and leapt off

Arnold's trembling body, causing him quite considerable discomfort in the genital area.

"Get that crazy bitch!" she roared, hauling her bewildered lover up off the cold glass and knocking over a single white orchid in a tall vase.

"Where's my robe, you stupid cow?" he ranted. "I told you not to open the curtains. You, stupid, stupid, little *cow*!"

"Don't you dare call me names! I knew I was mad to give you a second chance. I should have stayed with Jason Maxwell. He's got a Rolls-Royce!"

"To hell with Jason Maxwell! Where's my bloody robe? She's getting away!"

"Use mine!" Patricia screamed.

Sadie had tossed the camera into her basket and was hurrying down the steps of the fire escape in her sensible flat shoes. Despite the fact that she was shaking from head to foot, and absolutely terrified, she couldn't help laughing out loud as she made her escape. She was just fleeing past the wheelie bins at the back gate when Arnold appeared at the back door of the flat. He looked ridiculous in a bright-red satin robe with dragons on the front as he hopped down the freezing metal steps in his bare feet.

"If you don't get that camera, and smash it to smithereens, I'll kill you!" yelled Patricia from the back door. "Bloody, married men! More trouble than they're worth, if you ask me. It's *Fatal Attraction,* in reverse!" She was wrapped in a white quilt, already smoking a long brown cigarette. But Sadie didn't see her. She was already halfway down the avenue and hailing a taxi at the rank on the corner.

"Quick! Get me out of here! Take me to Carryduff!" shouted Sadie.

Arnold was running down the white line in the middle of the road by now, all thoughts of decency forgotten. Sadie got another picture of him reaching for her, through the rear window, as the car gathered speed and pulled out onto the main road. She saw Arnold slow down, then, and throw up his hands in defeat.

"Well, that went very well," said Sadie, to the back of the driver's head.

"I take it you're keeping the house?" said the driver, who was a man of his word and had agreed to wait out the morning . . . for a worthwhile fare.

"You bet your sweet ass, I'm keeping it," said Sadie.

Afterward, when the film was developed and the disgusting pictures safely lodged in a solicitor's office, Sadie renamed the event Operation Grasshopper. Somehow, she felt sorry for Arnold when she thought of the sexual slavery he would have to endure with his new partner. She couldn't understand how he could prefer that rushed and desperate coupling to Sadie's gentle embraces in the big bed that was scattered with cushions and little pillows of potpourri. To be honest, she thought Patricia Caldwell would put the old boy in an early grave. She wished Arnold had been honest with her from the beginning and told her about the affair. They might have parted friends. Who knows, she might even have forgiven him. After all, lovemaking was not one of Sadie's strong points, and Arnold was only human.

But then she remembered his chilling words, when she was squashed behind the stationery cupboard in his office. About keeping Sadie on as the unpaid help until his parents went to their eternal rest, and then showing her the door. And letting that dirty little witch into Sadie's beautiful home.

That was impossible to forgive, and so she hardened her heart against him. She changed the locks and the telephone number and sent his pompous desk and chair over to the flat in a removal van with a note taped to the leather desktop.

It simply said: *Lots of love from Sadie Sponge.*

•45•

The Return of Peter Prendergast

Clare Fitzgerald sat at the big desk in her New York office. It was almost closing time on Christmas Eve. Outside her door, in the main office, they were getting ready for the staff Christmas party. She could hear glasses being set out on a table, and someone was playing "Arthur's Theme" by Christopher Cross on a music-center. Clare knew they would send out for some party food later, but she was quite hungry already. She had a hankering for some cold ham and pasta salad, so she finished the sentence she was writing and shut down her computer. The December issue of the magazine had been a resounding success and she was feeling very pleased with herself. She looked up at the portrait of Brenda on the wall, now lavishly mounted in a speckled gold frame. In the short time it had hung on the wall, it had become for Clare a portrait of Peter. She looked at the picture every morning, every evening, every time he called her on the phone. They had spent hours talking, catching up, falling in love again. They were going to meet up in two days' time. Clare wanted to see him so much, but he had work commitments and couldn't get away any sooner. Now, she had resigned herself to spending Christmas Day on her own.

The article about Brenda Brown, in the arts section, had generated a lot of interest, and there were twenty-four requests for commissions in a folder on Clare's desk. Clare took it out now, wrote a short note to Brenda and placed it in her post-tray. Hopefully, Brenda would not have to stay in that cold little flat for much longer. She was a strange character, but then again, thought Clare, weren't all very talented people a little eccentric?

She opened the Christmas issue and read again her editor's letter to the readers:

Christmas is a special time of year. A time for friends and family to gather round the hearth, a time for flickering candles, evergreen wreaths and homemade treats like our white chocolate fudge. Cut out and keep the recipe on page 212. In this issue, we look at Christmas trees of days gone by, see the collection of delicate, antique feather trees on page 46 and the beautiful aluminum trees of the 1950s which are currently enjoying a revival. And don't forget to have a magical holiday!

She wanted to scan through some rival magazines but her hunger pangs would not go away. Her assistant was in a meeting, and so she slipped on her jacket and went out to the lift.

The delicatessen was crowded. There was a long queue at the glass counter, which was packed with exotic foods from all over the globe. New Yorkers were very hard to please when it came to food and, when they found a good place, they were prepared to wait. Clare took her place in the line.

When she arrived back at work, her assistant waved at her from across the office.

"There's someone to see you in your office," he said, breathlessly. "He says he knew you a long time ago in Ireland. I told him he could wait in there. I'll get you a couple of coffees, shall I? Give me that big sandwich. He'll think you're a pig. He's very handsome, Clare. Put on some more lipstick before you go in."

Clare didn't have to ask who it was. She knew it was Peter.

When she opened the door, he was standing in front of the portrait, looking at it with his back to her. No longer too thin, his shoulders had filled out considerably. The black hair was gone, now graying, and shaved close to his head. But when he turned around, Clare gasped and burst into tears. The big, blue eyes were still the same. The shape of his face, the sensuous lips. She ran across the room toward him and he held out his arms to her, and they held each other for a long time.

"Is this a picture of me?" he said.

"No. But it reminded me of you."

"Where did you get it?"

"It's a long story," she said, as the tears began to fall again.

"I managed to get away, after all," he said.

"How?"

"I swapped shifts with one of the guys."

"That was kind of him."

"Not really. It cost me a lot of money!"

"I'm very flattered. Oh, I'm sorry I can't stop crying! All the time we've wasted!"

"I thought you didn't want me, you know. I guess rejection is very hard for young men to deal with. We're not as tough as we look."

"I know. I know now. So, you're still single. My, my. Three divorces, you said."

"Are you shocked?"

"No. I just wonder why any woman in her right mind would let you go."

"You know why. I was in love with someone else."

"Was it me, Peter?"

"Yes."

"Do you still love me?"

"Yes."

"Can we start again?"

"Yes." He kissed her softly, on the lips.

"Can I take you out to dinner, and you can tell me all about this painting?"

"I'd love that. But you must come to the party first and meet everyone. What are you doing for Christmas, by the way?"

"Nothing. I was hoping an old friend would invite me over to her place."

"Well, consider yourself invited."

Back in Belfast, Henry and Rose were clearing up after the Christmas Eve sale. The flower shop was a mess, but they had done very well. The old-fashioned door wreaths had been a great success. Henry swept up the leaves and bits of ribbon on the floor, and poured water down the sink. Rose closed the blinds and put the money in the safe.

"Thank you ever so much for helping me, Henry. I can't believe you have nothing better to do on Christmas Eve."

"I haven't. Rose, you're doing me a favor. Aurora is having a big party for the Brontë Bunch, and I'd only be in the way."

"Well, I'm very grateful to you. You're very good company."

"Listen, Rose, I took the liberty of getting

us a couple of tickets for the theater. What do you think? But don't feel obliged."

"How lovely! Are you sure Aurora won't mind?"

"Not a bit of her. She'll be far too busy to miss me."

"In that case, let's leave the rest of this for another day."

"We just have time for a bag of chips before curtain-up!"

They put on their coats and scarves and walked into the city center together. They didn't hold hands but they walked very close together, and Henry gave Rose his gloves when it began to snow.

·46·

Sadie's Perfect Christmas

When Sadie woke up at seven o'clock on Christmas Day, she wondered why Arnold wasn't in the bed next to her. She thought he must be opening his presents in the sitting room, the big baby. He could never wait until after lunch. Then, she remembered. She hadn't bought him any presents this year. She had given *him* to his mistress. Let Patricia Caldwell roast his potatoes for him this year. Let her see how hard it really is to look after Arnold Smith. A warm glow began to burn in Sadie's toes and worked its way all the way up to her shiny pink cheeks.

She yawned and stretched her arms and planned how she would spend the day. With no turkey dinner to cook and no ungrateful family to take care of, she could do whatever she wanted. The house was very peaceful. She was all alone at last. It was a good feeling.

First, she had a lie-in, listening to Christmas carols on the radio. The central heating clicked on and the house began to warm up nicely. At ten o'clock, Sadie got up and ran a hot bath for herself, using up all the hot water, and a generous dollop of bath foam. She lay back contentedly in the mounds of scented bubbles and chuckled again and again when she thought of her husband's face when the camera shutter clicked. Let him try to take the bungalow away from her *now*! Lying under that grasshopper, Patricia, grabbing her bosoms in a most ungentlemanly way, he was caught red-handed. As it were. There was no way he could charm his way out of the situation. Let him take her to court now, and she would post a copy of that picture to every person Arnold had ever known. To his pious boss and his stuck-up pals at the golf club, to his jealous colleagues and his even more jealous competitors. How they would gloat over such a picture! She would put it on the Internet, on lamp posts all over Belfast. She would become the worst nightmare Arnold had ever dreamed of.

Then, she decided to relax. After all it was Christmas Day. She stayed in the bath until the water went cold and then she got out and dried herself on a fluffy bath towel, and painted her toenails and brushed her teeth.

At eleven o'clock, still in her dressing gown, she cooked a delicious breakfast of bacon and wheaten bread, mushrooms and tomatoes, lightly fried in sunflower oil. Well, she was trying to eat more healthily. After three cups of tea, she got dressed and went to afternoon service at her local church, enjoying the crib scene with its yellow star glowing above the manger. She listened to the children singing "Silent Night" and she thanked God for giving her precious life back to her. When people asked after her family, she told them the truth, and tried hard to keep a straight face when she saw the shock on their bug-eyed faces.

"The good Lord will give me the strength I need to get through this," she said about twenty times that morning. "These things are sent to try us. The Lord only gives us those burdens he knows we can carry." And so on.

Everyone hugged her and said, Wasn't Arnold a proper scoundrel? Sadie shrugged and said he was a good man really, and it was all her fault for being so old and fat and unattractive. And everyone was outraged, all over again. They promised to ignore Arnold in the street. Wasn't pity a marvelous thing, thought Sadie.

Sadie went home and popped a ready-made meal in the oven. Chicken breasts with red wine gravy. Mashed carrots and swedes. Potato gratin. Potato croquettes. All in dainty little foil containers. Whoever said Christmas was hard work for women? Those days were gone. She covered the table in the dining room with a jolly Christmas tablecloth and added some red candles in various glass holders, a good wine glass and three luxury crackers. While she waited the forty-five minutes until her dinner was ready, she pulled the crackers and drank some wine and listened to the radio. She put on a paper hat, and tidied up the Christmas cards on the mantelpiece. She moved the pot of twigs out to the hall, and trailed her artificial Christmas tree in from the shed. It was a huge tree and it took her a few minutes to put it together. The oven timer rang as she was straightening up the branches. She would decorate it after lunch.

Just then the doorbell chimed and Sadie nearly jumped out of her skin. She peeped out of the bay window. Nine of Arnold's relations stood shivering on the doorstep like cattle waiting to be fed. One small bottle of wine and one wrapped gift between the lot of them. And that was only a box of chocolates, which they always proceeded to eat themselves. Sadie was glad she hadn't spent hundreds of pounds on presents for them, this year. She would get herself a new wardrobe of clothes in the January sales instead.

It began to snow. Tiny, white flakes fell from the sky, sparkling in the winter sun, gathering in the corners of the window panes. Sadie watched her in-laws from behind the curtains, hopping with cold and impatience on the doorstep. She made them wait for three whole minutes and then she answered the door.

"Sadie, my dear, let us in! We are absolutely freezing," they cried, when she opened the door at last. Just a fraction. And she kept the chain on.

"I hope that turkey is ready. We could eat a horse. Why are the curtains closed? Where's Arnold's car?"

"He isn't here. Arnold and I are no longer a couple," said Sadie loudly, so that she wouldn't have to repeat herself. "I will say this only once: he has gone to live with his new girlfriend, Patricia, but he says you are all to call her Patty-Pat. And I just know you'll all adore her. She's just your type. So talented in the domestic arts. What that woman can't do on a kitchen table is nobody's business. You tell her I said that. Do you hear me? In fact, that's where you're having your dinner today. At her place. Here's the address." She gave the nearest open-mouthed relative a piece of paper.

"Now, look here, what's going on?" demanded Arnold's brother, Tony. "Why have you chained the door? Let me in. I'm going to phone Arnold. And Jenny needs to go to the toilet."

"I'm sorry," said Sadie, "but this house, and its facilities, are no longer the property of the Smith clan. I never liked any of you. And you never liked me. So, let's just end the pretence, shall we? The invitation to spend Christmas Day at this address is hereby, officially, withdrawn. There's no turkey and there's no trifle, and there's no free booze. This year, I have only been shopping for one. So this is good-bye. Merry Christmas." And she closed the door firmly and locked it, and drew the curtain, just in case they peeped in the letter-box.

Sadie thought her Christmas lunch was the best meal she had ever eaten. Not once did she have to jump up from the table to get Daisy a glass of water, or Maurice some more stuffing, or Arnold some more gravy. Or to pour endless drinks for Arnold's alcoholic siblings, or worry that they were running out of ice cubes. Or watch them all open their expensive gifts, and show no gratitude. It was hard to believe she had waited on them all, hand and foot, for years and years, and all the time, they were perfectly capable of taking care of themselves.

She had second helpings of the mashed swede, and she had to admit, it was better than her own. There were spices in it and everything. For dessert, she had three chocolate éclairs, a finger of Christmas cake and a cappuccino. All shop-bought, and quite delicious. It was all over by five o'clock, and the kitchen was still spotless.

Then it was time to enjoy the evening. She went up to the attic, and carefully brought down the box of decorations. For two blissful hours, she fiddled with the tree and the lights until they were perfect, and hung up all the delicate glass baubles that were shaped like tear drops, and the fragile glass angels, and the little crystal sleighs and the fat tinsel that caught the light so beautifully. The sky was dark and velvety when she stood back to admire her handiwork. The tree stood majestically in the middle of the bay window. It was time to bring it to life. Sadie quickly vacuumed up the leftover bits and pieces of tinsel and fluff from the carpet, and then switched on the fairy lights. The bay window was filled with light, and outside the snow became heavier. It was perfect.

She switched on the television, and circled two soaps, three comedy specials and a movie premiere in the TV guide. For the first time in twenty years she would be able to watch something in peace and be able to hear what was being said, without the Smiths roaring at their own jokes, rowdy with drink. She wouldn't bother to light the fire this year, either. The house was warm enough. She lit three fat, ivory-colored church candles and set them in the grate and they looked just as good as the real thing. Finally, she laid out some nuts and chocolates in a silver dish on the coffee table, along with the rest of the wine and a big mug of tea.

She curled up on the sofa to watch several hours of programs and forgot entirely about Arnold and Patricia, and the chaos that the horrible Smith family turning up at Patricia's flat would have caused. The whole lot of them, standing round a tiny, glass table, waiting for Patricia to produce a lavish feast from her etched glass cupboards. They would be lucky to get a cheese sandwich in their hand, if Sadie's suspicions were correct.

·47·

Penny's Late Honeymoon

On the night that televisions all over the world counted down the seconds to the New Year and the New Millennium, Penny and Daniel were sitting beside the fire in their suite in the Lawson Lodge. There was a cabaret evening in full swing in the bar downstairs. Shouts and screams of delight floated up the stairs as Big Ben chimed, far away in London. Penny raised her glass and proposed a toast to new beginnings. Daniel touched his glass to Penny's, and said, "I love you, Penny Stanley, and thanks for everything. I don't know what I would have done without you, if you had . . . if the fire . . . well, I just don't know. I'll never tell you a lie, or hurt you in any way, ever again."

It wasn't enough, but Penny knew what he meant. They finished the champagne and Daniel put his arm round Penny's shoulders as they sat watching the fire burning merrily in the grand fireplace. Penny turned to Daniel and touched his face softly and kissed him tenderly on the lips. She moved his hands toward her breasts and held them there while they kissed for a long time. Daniel knew then that Penny had forgiven him for his madness and meanness, and he knew it was time to make her his wife, properly. He gently undressed her and led her across the room to the four-poster bed, piled high with fat pillows, and he lifted her onto the white quilt.

Penny waited silently for him to take off his own clothes, and she reached out her hand to him and their fingers entwined.

Then they went to bed, together, and made love so passionately that Richard

Allen himself would have blushed. That night was everything that Penny had daydreamed of for many years, and she decided that, truthfully, it was worth waiting for. The best thing about it was the feeling that they would never split up again. Penny just knew that whatever life threw at them, they would face it, and deal with it, together. Daniel was like a different person, now that he knew Penny was in his life forever. All his vague feelings of anxiety had just melted away. He knew, finally, that life was an unpredictable business, and no amount of worrying could change or alter its course, and that he could only go along with it and hope for the best.

They celebrated New Year's Day by sharing a bubble bath, and having Christmas cake and champagne for breakfast.

They spent the holiday walking in the countryside, having long lie-ins, making plans for the tea house and ordering delicious meals and cocktails. It was like a lovely late honeymoon, they both thought. And it was better late than never.

·48·

The Tea House Reopens

The regular customers in the tea house were amazed by what they saw when the shop reopened six months later. Of course, Daniel had not paid enough insurance to finance the rebuilding completely, but he did have his fortune in the bank. And they had great fun spending it. Outside, there was a new bay window, a new front door painted cobalt blue, and a new sign above the door with brass lamps over it. The sign read STANLEY'S TEA ROOMS, and it was very smart and dignified. Two neat bay trees stood sentinel in blue pots on the doorstep.

Inside, there was a coat of rich red paint on all the freshly plastered walls. There were huge mirrors in gold frames, little round tables with marble tops and wrought-iron chairs. There were hand-painted cups and saucers on the shelves behind the counter. A fat white sofa beside the window lent a touch of decadence. There were fresh lilies in a glass vase on the counter.

Daniel hired a chef to do all the cooking and gave him permission to choose the menu. Now, instead of scones and jam, there were French pastries oozing chocolate cream and Italian bread with exotic fillings. New tiles on the floor replaced the cracked linoleum. And the flat upstairs was converted into a magnificent dining room with a glass roof. Three waitresses, wearing jeans and T-shirts, with pencils behind their ears, carried meals to the tables on round silver trays. Penny and Daniel were thrilled with it all.

They bought a little flat beside the Lagan river. Richard Allen sold it to them and wished them well. When Penny went in to his office to collect the keys, she told Richard that she had rescued her marriage and that she wouldn't be seeing him anymore. Richard said that was great news but that he would miss her a lot. It was the truth.

Daniel and Penny came in to work at twelve o'clock each day, just to see how things were ticking over. Daniel's bank account was almost empty, and he had never been happier.

The editor of the *Belfast Telegraph* sent a reporter round to do a feature on the cafe, and several magazines wanted reviews for their social pages. Penny and Daniel were photographed standing behind the counter, holding up a cherry cheesecake on a glass cake stand, and smiling broadly.

Sadie was about to throw the paper in the bin, when she spied a small photograph of a happy-looking couple holding up a giant cheesecake on a glass cake stand. They were smiling tenderly at each other. The man had his arm firmly round the woman's waist. There was great tenderness in the way the woman looked back at him. Sadie read the article underneath. The people in the photograph were Penny and Daniel Stanley, the owners of a tea house on Mulberry Street.

"Well, well," said Sadie, and she read on. "So, they're back in business."

The Stanleys had just carried out extensive renovations to the property, which had been destroyed in a fire, and they had converted the upstairs flat into a conservatory-style dining room. The reporter seemed to think the establishment was well worth a visit.

She caught the bus at the end of the avenue and the trip seemed to take forever. When she finally stood outside the shop, her stomach was pleading to be filled. She went inside. Delicious smells, sweet and savory, were everywhere. Every table was occupied by ladies lunching. Sadie recognized Penny from her picture in the newspaper, with her new hairstyle and her lovely clothes.

Penny came rushing out from behind the counter to tell Sadie that she could be seated upstairs in their spacious new dining room. Sadie was delighted. Minutes later she was sipping caffè latte, and devouring a slice of strawberry cheesecake that melted on her tongue. She was still hungry so she ordered an Italian dish of toasted bread, cheese, tomatoes and red peppers.

Sadie thanked the pencil-thin waitress who brought her meal upstairs, and watched her as she stepped lightly down the stairs. She ignored her own generous hips, and her soft ankles, as she sprinkled salt and pepper on the little tower of gourmet heaven. The food was delicious. She read the menu as she ate. It was a story of ecstasy. The chef was Italian. He had selected all the dishes himself. There was carrot and chestnut soup with cream and croutons, homemade wheaten bread with stout and sesame seeds, chargrilled chicken strips with hot salsa and sour cream, spicy potato wedges with chopped leeks, roast-beef-and-chut-ney toasted sandwiches. There were twenty different kinds of coffee and forty varieties of pastry. Everything came drizzled with olive oil or dusted with icing sugar or cinnamon.

Sadie had plenty of time on her hands these days, with no one left in the bungalow to take care of. She applied for a position as a waitress in the tea house on Mulberry Street and got it.

Penny was very kind at the interview and said that Sadie had just the right personality for the job. Warm and welcoming and always smiling. Sadie celebrated her new life with a glass of champagne, a new perm and a slice of cherry cheesecake.

·49·

A Handwritten Note

When the day of Rose's departure arrived, Henry left Aurora a handwritten note. It was very tender and romantic, and it said that although his heart was breaking, he was leaving Aurora and her dreams, and following a dream of his own. Aurora thought it was very sweet, and she tied a blue ribbon around it, and kept it in a secret drawer in her writing bureau. She was not sad.

David Cropper was calling round all the time. Aurora had daydreams about him, reading poetry to her, in a Georgian overcoat.

Henry was leaving her the house. He had signed a legal document. And she loved her conservatory far more than she had ever loved Henry.

"Take me with you," said Henry to Rose, as they stood outside the tea house after their good-bye lunch.

"What?" said Rose. "You don't mean that. I'm very fond of you, of course, but—"

"I love you," said Henry. "I want to help you plant all those trees and flowers."

"But your wife, your friends, your shop . . ."

"None of that matters now. Please. Let me drive you to Connemara, and stay a few days, and we'll just see what happens. I know I am too old, and not nearly good enough for you, but my heart is young, and I love you, and I'm a great gardener."

Mrs. S. Fogarty, of Fogarty's General Store, Galway, was in great form. Her friend Bronagh Gilmartin came into the store at teatime for a tin of pear halves and found

Mrs. Fogarty dusting the shelves and singing merrily.

"What's up?" said Mrs. Gilmartin.

"My profits. That's what's up," said Mrs. Fogarty. "There was a couple in here not two hours ago, and they bought nearly the entire contents of the shop. They were on their way to Connemara, they said. They bought all the firelighters. I have none left, so I hope you weren't looking for any. They bought twenty bundles of peat bricks, and two bottles of whiskey, and enough tinned food to feed the famine. And the funniest thing of all—the gentleman, for that's what he was—he bought every packet of seeds on the stand!"

"Flower seeds? Holy smoke! All of them, you say?"

"Yes. Hundreds of packets. Look, it's empty. I'm glad I bought that cash register last year. I couldn't have counted it all up otherwise. The woman looked a bit younger than him, and she had a local accent. A bit of a hippy, by the look of her. But he was very distinguished, with a bow tie, and a hint of a Belfast accent. It's my guess they weren't married, at least not to each other. They looked too happy. But times is changing. We must remember that. Will you not be awful lonely? I said. Them wee cottages is miles away from anything, I said, for there's nothing out that way but stones and ghosts. I said at the time, Bronagh, as you well know, that those holiday homes were a complete waste of money. But, no, he said to me. We'll be just fine. Think you for asking, says he, but we have everything we need. So there you are now, Bronagh. What do you think of that?"

•50•

A Letter from Nicolas

August 1, 2000

Dear Mrs. Stanley,

I hope you can help me. I'm trying to get in touch with an artist called Brenda Brown. I don't know if she is a personal friend of yours, but she mentioned to me, in her letters, that she often ate in your restaurant. Her home got burned down and I do not know where she lives now. Even her mother doesn't seem to know where she is. She sent me a bunch of letters at Christmas but she has not written to me for some time.

I would be really grateful if you could ask her to contact me.

I do not usually reply to fan mail, but now that her letters have stopped, I miss them.

I would like to meet Brenda and thank her for the cool painting that she sent me. I'm coming over to Belfast soon, to make a film, and I'd like to arrange a meeting.

Thank you for your help.

Best wishes,

Nicolas Cage

PS. I'd be real grateful if you could give Brenda this snakeskin jacket. I wore it in a movie once, and she said that she liked it. Tell her it is to say thank you for the painting that she sent me. I've had the picture valued and my art dealer says it is real good. He says he would like to arrange to show Brenda's work in his gallery in Beverly Hills someday. If I can find her.

August 20, 2000
Dear Mr. Cage,

I hope you are well. I am sorry to tell you that I have not been able to find Brenda. She was in the shop a few months ago, but none of her friends or family members have seen her since. She seems to have disappeared completely. I will take good care of your jacket until she comes back. I hope you find her.

Best wishes,
Penny Stanley

August 29, 2000
To: Mr. Raymond Moriarty, Director
The Weather Center, RTE
Dublin
Dear Mr. Moriarty,

I enclose the recent rainfall readings for the area. I hope I have filled out the sheets correctly this time. I really love this job, and find the solitude exhilarating. I used to really hate rain, but now I find the whole subject absolutely fascinating. I am reading and walking and enjoying the scenery, so your fears that I would find the location too lonely were unfounded. I never want to leave. This little cottage is more than adequate for my needs and the turf fire is very cosy in the evenings. I am managing very well without electricity or a telephone, and I have mended the back door, which was broken. I am reading by candlelight in the evenings and have bought myself a bicycle, and a little dog for company. I hope you will find my work satisfactory and offer me the position on a permanent basis, when my period of probation is up. Thank you very much for all your help.

Yours sincerely,
Tatiana Cobalt-Clearwater

August 30, 2000
Dear Mum,

I hope you are well. I am having a fantastic time here. I feel so healthy and refreshed. My cheeks are pink all the time. The scenery is breathtaking, far nicer than any painting I could ever paint. In fact, I haven't even made a sketch since I got here and I don't miss it one bit. The cottage is very cosy and warm when the fire is lit, and don't worry, I am using a fireguard and I have bought three smoke alarms. My wee dog is the sweetest thing. I've called him Nick and he goes everywhere with me and he's really good. He sleeps in a little basket on the floor beside my bed.

I am really enjoying the work, and I feel like I'm doing something useful, for the first time in my life. I've met this nice fella called Sean, who lives a couple of miles away. He works for the government and he's carrying out research into coastal pollution, and he's explained to me all about the weather and the environment, and how everything we do affects the future, and it's fascinating. And how lucky we are in Ireland to have all the water we need. And he's quite dishy as well. We're going out for a meal on Saturday night. You never know, we might end up going out together. I think he likes me. He gave me his best anorak to keep me warm while I collect the rainwater data on my bicycle. Wasn't that lovely of him? I'm so glad I got over that thing I had for Nico-

las Cage. At least when I talk to Sean, he talks back to me.

Thanks for not telling anyone where I am, and thanks for dealing with the bank for me. I will send some money to you every month, and you can pay my bills for me when you're in town. I'm really grateful to you for everything.

Hope you and the girls from the dancing club are getting on well, and that you all enjoyed your trip to Nashville. I won't ask you if you bought a cowboy hat because I know rightly you did. Take care of yourself and hope to see you soon.

All my love,
Brenda

PS. Here is a wee watercolor of Connemara I bought for you in a craft shop. It's for your sitting room wall. I don't think I will paint again, myself. Although I have been making picture frames out of driftwood and things like that.

Mrs. Brown held the letter from Brenda up to her face. She closed her eyes and sighed with relief. Brenda had never sounded so happy. At long last, she seemed to have found her niche in life.

Mrs. Brown lifted the letter from Nicolas Cage from the hall table and the one from Clare Fitzgerald forwarded by the landlord, and she put them gently in the sitting room fire. In a few months, they would both have forgotten all about Brenda Brown, and that would be an end to the art career that had almost driven her youngest daughter off the rails. Let her enjoy the peace she's found, thought Mrs. Brown. She deserves it more than anyone.

•51•

All's Well That Ends Well

Penny and Daniel were delighted with how well the business was doing. Daniel handed over control of the finances to Penny, and said he would try not to worry about it anymore. Penny paid the staff well, took out more insurance and bought only the best quality ingredients for the restaurant. She bought some pretty blue gingham tablecloths, to give the tables a cosy French look.

Daniel sold the house on Magnolia Street and accepted that his mother was never coming back. They decided to keep her Welsh dresser to remember her by, and they put it in the cafe and displayed some pretty plates on it. He brought Penny to see his Aunt Kathleen's grave, and they left a bouquet of flowers on it, and arranged for a headstone to be placed there. Daniel told Penny everything about his mother and her disappearance, and the penny-pinching upbringing by his aunt. Penny held him close to her in the wind-blown cemetery and they cried together for the lost years.

Daniel found it hard to leave his thrifty ways behind him completely but he was trying hard not to save every last crumb. And as Penny reminded him, even with the increased overheads, they were still doing very nicely. Daniel was forty-eight by now, and Penny was thirty-six, and they knew that spending time together and getting to know each other again was far more important than making money. They went for another holiday in the Lawson Lodge and in December 2000, Penny discovered that she was pregnant.

* * *

Beatrice and Alice continued with the charity work, but they didn't boast about it anymore. They spent most of their spare time planning holidays and enjoying themselves, instead. Yes, it was important to do good things and live a pure life; but it was also important to enjoy life. They spoke of Leo sometimes, but it was William they still called their "dear father."

They wore Eliza's glass brooches to Sunday service each week, and they felt a kind of secret pride that they had such melodrama in their family history.

Sadie Sponge enjoyed her job at the tea house so much that she gave up eating family-sized bags of tortilla chips and began to lose weight. She was soon back down to 168 pounds, and thought she might even aim for 154 pounds. Maurice and Daisy were in love with their Greek island and sent her a postcard saying they were now going to language classes so that they could learn to be real Greeks instead of just ex-pats.

Maurice's arthritis was practically gone and Daisy had joined a chess club.

Patricia Caldwell had burst into tears, that fateful Christmas morning in 1999, when she opened Arnold's pile of gifts and discovered that he had given her a bread maker and a vacuum cleaner. Did he seriously think she was going to bake her own bread? And she already had a vacuum cleaner. Arnold pointed out that Patricia had said, many times, that she wanted to be his proper partner, not just his *bit on the side.* Well, now she could be his proper partner, and that involved a lot of cooking and homemaking. But that thought just seemed to depress her even more.

Even the black underwear and the set of massage oils were somehow annoying to Patty-Pat. They were really presents for Arnold himself, she wept. Weren't they? After all, wouldn't she be doing most of the massaging? How could he be so selfish? After she had generously allowed him to move in with her, and even keep his hideous mahogany desk in her lovely all-white apartment.

She was still crying when two carloads of Arnold's relatives landed on her doorstep at midday, expecting a big turkey dinner. They all trooped in, walking muddy slush onto her pristine white carpets, and announced they were starving. As if it was somehow her fault. Patricia was starving herself, as she had missed her Christmas Eve dinner in a fancy restaurant, thanks to Sadie Sponge turning up at the flat and taking nude photographs of her.

She had to give Arnold's greedy relations microwave dinners from the freezer, and they didn't mind telling her they were very disappointed, as Sadie had told them all that Patricia was a proper whiz in the kitchen. They were so disappointed, in fact, that they drank Arnold's entire crate of champagne from Walley Windows and Conservatories of Distinction, to console themselves. They got very drunk and made some derogatory remarks about Patricia's virtue.

Patricia had asked them all to leave, and Arnold had asked them to stay, and so they had stayed and eaten everything in the flat, like a plague of locusts. An entire Christmas cake, several boxes of nuts and chocolates, and all the cheese and biscuits. Arnold and

Patricia ended up having a blazing row in the bedroom, and missed the *EastEnders Christmas Special.*

EastEnders was Patricia's favorite program. And after that, their relationship was in the water and sinking fast. A few weeks later, Patricia broke down and rang Jason Maxwell and he came straight round in his Rolls-Royce, and Arnold was politely asked to leave.

He spent a few weeks sleeping in his office, phoning Patricia constantly. She refused to return his calls, telling him firmly that she had met someone else—a man who wasn't married, and who didn't buy her bread makers and vacuum cleaners for Christmas. Jason Maxwell knew how to treat a lady. Eventually, she changed her number altogether.

Arnold decided to move to the other side of the country and he set up a little double-glazing business in Enniskillen town. He decided to let Sadie keep the bungalow in Carryduff. He felt, in his heart of hearts, that she had earned it, and anyway he was very taken with the Fermanagh countryside. He bought a derelict pig shed beside the lake and turned it into a dream bachelor pad, with a lovely hexagon-shaped conservatory at the back, looking right onto the water. The local people were very friendly, and there was more rain there than there was in Belfast. The demand for new windows was high and Arnold was soon back to his old self. He had great fun flirting with the women of Fermanagh, and he became a familiar figure about the town of Enniskillen, with his blue Jaguar, his collection of designer suits and his award for Salesperson of the Year.

Aurora Blackstaff and David Cropper became an item and a regular fixture on the Belfast theater scene. The Brontë Bunch became an international model for literary societies, and Aurora lost count of its imitators. Sometimes, when they were sure that they wouldn't be interrupted, Aurora and David dressed up in their Victorian costumes and waltzed round and round the conservatory. Afterward, David would carry Aurora up the stairs to the master bedroom and ravish her with her petticoats still on.

* * *

Henry and Rose fell quietly in love in the wilds of Connemara. Henry bought a little cottage and a year's supply of turf, and they sat beside the fire each night reading gardening books and drinking red wine. They planted all the trees that they thought might survive the heavy rainfall and the strong winds coming in from the Atlantic. When Henry woke up in Rose's arms each morning, he thanked God for her long red hair and her freckles and her pale white skin. And for the tea house on Mulberry Street from where he had first glimpsed her. The first time Rose told him she loved him, too, he proposed to her, and she said yes.

Clare Fitzgerald and Peter Prendergast set the date for their wedding. They had wasted enough time, they said. She teased him sometimes, about his job. She thought he should have been able to find her a lot sooner, seeing that he was a detective, and he agreed that he probably could have, but that his male pride kept getting in the way.

"I thought you had gone off me—you

were a bit of a snob, as I remember," he said.

Clare wanted to hit him with her handbag but she couldn't find it.

Peter got a transfer to New York and moved into Clare's beautiful apartment. They got married in a simple ceremony, with just the two of them, and all the emotion that had been denied by fate for so long. Clare's assistant, Mike, and his boyfriend, who acted as witnesses, showered the newlyweds with pink and gold confetti, and Clare kept a handful of it in a glass box, on her bedside table.

Penny's father would have been very pleased with the tea house, if he had still been around to see it. The crowds were lining up to get into the place, and everyone said the atmosphere of happiness and love was the best thing about it. Penny had a special bulletproof, burglarproof glass case made for the shop. She displayed Nicolas Cage's snakeskin jacket in it, and Brenda's painting of him. Stanley's became a mecca for fans of his films. Penny was regularly offered a fortune for the jacket, but she refused to sell it. After all, it wasn't hers to sell. She was only looking after it for Brenda Brown.

Brenda Brown, or rather Tatiana Cobalt-Clearwater, was living in Connemara with her little dog, Nick, and she had never been happier. She was far away from Belfast and the Assembly, and the riots and the flags, and the police and the psychiatrists, and the credit card bills. But best of all, she was far away from art. By day, she cycled round the countryside, collecting rainwater statistics, with Nick barking at her heels. And by night, she listened to the crackle and hiss of the fire, and watched the patterns it made on the walls of the cottage. Sean called by from time to time, and they had great chats about the environment. They took part in a peaceful anti-pollution protest in Dublin, and held hands on the march. Sean said he thought Brenda would look beautiful with long hair, so she stopped shaving the back of her head.

She worried that she was losing her feminist backbone and might be falling in love with Sean, but then he installed a wind-powered electricity generator in the cottage, and she had to admit, men could sometimes be very useful indeed. She kissed him gently, under the new electric light, and thought that he was very handsome in his old denim dungarees. Sean didn't need a snakeskin jacket, or a vintage car, to make him attractive. He was lovely, just the way he was.

She asked him for a photograph of himself, and he gave her one, and she put it in a little frame she made out of pebbles and seashells. It was nice to have a face in a frame at last.

When Penny's baby was born, Daniel told every customer who came into the shop that his wife had had a healthy baby boy, and that she was going to call him Daniel, too. Danny, for short. He gave cups of tea and coffee away for free, for three whole days. They held a big party for all their friends, in the cafe, to celebrate the joyous occasion of Danny's christening, and even Millie Mortimer and Jack (and the weans) were invited. They showed up, looking slightly shamefaced, but left their toolbox at home. Penny filled the cafe with fresh flowers and balloons and streamers, and everybody wore brightly colored party hats and danced till dawn. Danny slept through it all, in the cafe that would one day be his. Passersby looked in the windows and wished they had been invited, too. The buffet was magnificent, and Daniel had even made a big sponge cake with a little sugarpaste model of himself, Penny and Danny on the top.

Stanley's Tea Rooms soon became the most fashionable cafe in the city and people came from all over the world to marvel at its marbled magnificence, and Nicolas Cage's snakeskin jacket in its shiny, glass case.

You too can enjoy a delicious slice of Cherry Cheesecake from *The Tea House on Mulberry Street.*

• Cherry Cheesecake •

(*Serves 8*)

FOR THE BASE:

4.5 oz ginger nut biscuits
2.5 oz butter
Vegetable oil for greasing cake tin

FOR THE FILLING:

2.5 fl. oz semi-skimmed milk
1 vanilla pod, seeds only
4 leaves / 1 sachet of gelatin
(soaked in cold water)
4 oz superfine sugar
1 lb, 2 oz low-fat Greek yogurt
Finely grated zest and juice of 2 limes

FOR THE TOPPING:
1 can of cherry slices
Sugar as needed
2 leaves / 1/2 sachet of gelatin (soaked in cold water)

OPTIONAL:
Raspberry coulis
Quarter pint cream whipped

1. To make the base, crush the ginger nut biscuits, melt the butter and stir into the biscuits, mix well. Brush a 9-inch cake tin with a removable base with some vegetable oil. Press the mixture firmly and evenly over the base of the tin and chill for 10 minutes.
2. To make the filling, heat the milk and vanilla pod seeds, add the gelatin and superfine sugar. Whisk in the Greek yogurt, add the zest and juice of the limes and whisk well.
3. Pour the filling over the set biscuit base and chill for 1 hour or until set.
4. To make the topping, blend the can of cherry slices, add sugar if needed. Heat 1 tbsp of water in a saucepan, stir in the soaked gelatin. Combine cher-

ries and gelatin. Pour the mixture over the filling and chill for 2–3 hours until set.

5. Remove the base of the cake tin and place the cheesecake on a plate. Serve with some raspberry coulis and whipped cream if desired.

Recipe supplied by Neven Maguire, RTE Television chef and author of the *Neven Cooks* series, published by Poolbeg Press Ltd.

ABOUT THE AUTHOR

Sharon Owens was born in Omagh in 1968. She moved to Belfast in 1988 to study illustration at the Art College. She married her husband, Dermot, in 1992, and they have one daughter, Alice.